SLIM TO NONE

—•—

A Lenny Moss Mystery

THE REVIEWERS PRAISE LENNY MOSS!

This Won't Hurt A Bit

Things get off to a macabre start in Timothy Sheard's offbeat procedural... when a student at a Philadelphia teaching hospital identifies the cadaver she is dissecting in anatomy class as a medical resident she once slept with. Although hospital administrators are relieved when a troublesome laundry worker is charged with the murder, outraged staff members go to their union representative, a scrappy custodian named Lenny Moss, and ask him to find the real killer.

Since there's no merit to the case against the laundry worker to begin with, Lenny is just wasting his time. But Sheard, a veteran nurse, makes sure that readers do not waste theirs. His intimate view of Lenny's world is a gentle eye-opener into the way a large institution looks from a workingman's perspective. "The doctors and the supervisors don't hardly notice us," a nurses' aide says of the orderlies, security guards, secretaries, seamstresses and other "invisible" service workers who keep a hospital humming. "But we see everything."

✱ Marilyn Stasio, *New York Times*

Some Cuts Never Heal

This well-plotted page-turner is guaranteed to scare the bejesus out of anyone anticipating a hospital stay anytime in the near future.

✱ *Publishers Weekly*

Sheard provides realistic details of hospital routine and budget-cutting politics...polished prose and elements of warmth and humor. Strongly recommended for most mystery collections.

✱ *Library Journal*

If your pulse quickens for ER on Thursday nights, you'll want a dose of Timothy Sheard's medicine ... The well-meaning, hard-working hospital folks will warm your heart, while the cold realities of modern medical care will raise your blood pressure and keep you turning the pages.

✱ *Rocky Mountain News*

If you're a devotee of TV's "ER," you'll devour "Some Cuts Never Heal" by Timothy Sheard. Sheard…vividly takes the pulse of James Madison University Hospital…This is a really good yarn, if that isn't too old-fashioned a phrase.
　✻ *Hartford Courant*

It's hard putting the book down. I raced through it but hated to see it end… The hospital scenes ring true. For mystery lovers, this one's a must!
　✻ *Challenge*

Our favorite union representative for the unionized workers at James Madison University Hospital is back… Sheard …has done a fine job of bringing alive those numerous men and women we never see—from dietary to laundry to maintenance who do the hospital's invisible work. I look forward to more Lenny Moss mysteries.
　✻ (The Lawyer, 5 Cats) *Kate's Mystery Books Newsletter*

Lenny Moss and his co-workers bend the rules just enough to figure out who-dunnit in this fast-paced, 80-chapter work of fiction.
　✻ *Sun Spots,* **Saskatchewan Union of Nurses Newsletter**

Sheard filled me with sympathy for the hardworking health care workers, each of which do their part in healing their patients. But what struck me most of all was how a handful of health care providers stood up to management, forcing them to allow the workers to go to the funeral of one of their own. Lenny Moss and his co-workers bend the rules just enough to figure out whodunnit in this fast-paced, 80-chapter work of fiction.
　✻ *New Labor Forum*

A Race Against Death

Looking for a murder mystery whose hero is a worker instead of a cop? Try this One! While most shop stewards do not get involved in murder mysteries, they solve tough problems at work every day. Now they can look up to a fictional role model—Super Steward Lenny Moss.
　✻ *Public Employee Press Media Beat: Book Review*

Timothy Sheard provides a delightful hospital investigative tale that grips readers from the moment that Dr. Singh and his team apply CPR, but fail.
　✻ *Mysteries Galore*

Also by Timothy Sheard:

This Won't Hurt A Bit

Some Cuts Never Heal

A Race Against Death

For my beloved sons,
Matthew and Christopher

And they put a whole world of hurt to you
To get another hour of work from you
Grinding the wheels of the machine
Your hand's in the coal and it's never clean.

from *Poor Man,* by The Times

Information about the Lenny Moss series and the author are available at: www.timsheard.com

To contact the author, email: info@timsheard.com

Cover art by Joshua Weiner

Project Management, Design, and Production by Michele Pridmore & Lisa Skopas

This novel is a work of fiction. Names, characters, places and incidents are the product of the author's imagination.

Printing: March 1, 2010, by Hard Ball Press

ISBN 0-9814518-3-7

Library of Congress Cataloging-in-Publication Data

Sheard, Timothy

Slim To None: A Lenny Moss Mystery / Timothy Sheard.

1. Philadelphia (Pa)—Fiction.   2. Hospitals—Fiction. 3. Lenny Moss.

SLIM TO NONE

A Lenny Moss Mystery

by
TIMOTHY SHEARD

PRESS

ONE

Carlton slung the bow over his shoulder and adjusted the quiver of arrows. As he pulled the night vision goggles down over his eyes, the murky blackness of the woods lifted, revealing trees and shrubs and a path leading up a steep hill. Fairmont Park lay before him as naked as a stripper in a red spotlight. He looked back to the street one last time, saw nothing moving, and strode into the dark.

He climbed the hill, the yawning night embracing him and his dark purpose. His leather moccasins fell silently on the earth, the day's cold rain having softened the leaves. He would bring down his prey without a sound, the razor-tipped arrow penetrating flesh. Splintering bone.

Death would come quickly.

He found a spot on a broad granite outcropping with a tangle of evergreen boughs to form a screen. Sitting cross-legged on the flat rock, he glanced at the luminous dial on his watch. Quarter past midnight. Time advanced as indifferently as the decay of the woods. Far above the leafy canopy, the moon shoved a cloud aside, illuminating the winding path. He watched the trail and waited for a target.

Carlton felt a deep satisfaction with his place in the greater scheme of things. Everyone knew that Fairmont Park was overrun with deer. The greedy critters stripped the bark from the young saplings, leaving dead skeletons to rot, and in the summer they spread *West Nile virus*. The animals made the park a hotbed of contagion. They were a major public health menace, but killing them was illegal. It was crazy!

They should bring back the wolf; *that* would cull the herd in no time. Be tough on the dog walkers, though, the wolf pack would tear those little poodles and terriers to pieces. Leave their carcasses scattered along the jogging trail. Still, there'd be a lot less yap, yap, yap.

The Indians had it right. Honor the sacred hunt.

Suddenly a shadow moving among the trees caught his eye. The figure lurched forward along the trail. It was large and hump-backed, not like any animal he'd ever seen. It was no deer, that much was certain. Carlton pulled an arrow from the sheath and slipped the notched end into the taut gut.

As the shadowy figure climbed the hill, Carlton saw that it was two figures, not one. A man, not overly tall, with another individual hanging limp over his

1

shoulder. Unconscious? Dead? At this distance Carlton couldn't tell, even with the night vision goggles.

Leaving the trail, the figure lurched toward a stand of tall trees, bent forward and dumped his burden. The victim lay on the damp earth as limp as a sack of grain.

Carlton stood to get a better look at the body. He saw long hair falling from the face and the outline of a bosom. He was glad she wasn't naked.

As the figure stood over the woman, Carlton lifted his bow, pulled back hard on the arrow and took aim. He held his breath. Felt the silence in the woods.

How the hell can I shoot somebody I don't even know? He realized it would be crazy to kill the guy. How many times had the cops arrested somebody for shooting a burglar going out the window? The tension in the bow echoed the powerful temptation to release the deadly arrow.

Shoot? Don't shoot? What the hell. . ?

He slowly lowered the bow. Waited. Watched as the perpetrator turned, found the trail and continued down the hill until out of sight.

Clambering down to the figure, he took out a small flashlight and shone it on the girl's face. She was a looker. Early to mid-twenties. Blonde hair, bleached, he could tell by her dark, hairy arms. Nice teeth. There were nasty bruises on the side of her face and a pool of fresh blood oozing through her blouse right over her heart. He didn't have to feel for a pulse to know she was dead.

He knew he should call the police, but they would ask what was he doing in the park in the middle of the night with a Mongolian bow, night vision goggles, and a hunk of rope. Then they'd find his van and realize he was poaching on the king's land.

Confused, scared and pissed off big time, Carlton made his way back toward the van, going over his options, wanting to do right but afraid of the consequences. He felt as helpless as a suspect in handcuffs. Seeing the street light ahead, he pulled off the goggles to wipe sweat from his face and cursed his bad luck. *Fucking dead girl. I got t' find a fucking dead girl.*

By the time he reached the street he knew only one choice made sense. There was just one path to take, case closed. Stowing his gear in the van, Carlton settled into the driver's seat, pulled out his cell phone and called Lenny Moss.

TWO

In his dreams Lenny Moss dimly heard a far away chirping. The sound pulled back the blanket of sleep, leaving him nakedly awake. He felt for his glasses, focused his eyes on the alarm clock. Quarter to one.

Struggling awake, he picked up the obstreperous phone, saw Carlton's name on the caller ID. *Christ. What kind of trouble is that bozo in this time?*

"Hullo?" Lenny croaked.

"Lenny! It's me, Carlton. I gotta problem!"

Seeing Patience lift her head from the pillow, Lenny cursed into the phone, annoyed that his friend had wakened his wife. He left the warmth of the bed and stepped into the hall.

"*Lenny!* You still there?"

"Yeah. What the hell are you doing calling me at one in the morning?"

"I'm sorry, man, I didn't know what else to do, my back's against the wall. If I call the cops there's gonna be a whole lotta shit comin' down on me, and I don't need the hassle. Not with all the deer skins hanging in my garage and the meat in my freezer."

"Carlton, what the hell are you talking about? Why would *you* call the cops?"

"That's what I'm tryin' t' tell you. I saw this dude dump a body tonight!"

"Say what? You mean in the ER?"

"No, man. I'm in the park hunting deer like I always do."

"Okay. . ."

"I'm in a blind, I got my bow and my night vision goggles and I'm minding my own business waiting for a deer, and up comes some dude carrying a girl. He dumps her on the ground and he splits."

"*Damn.* You sure the kid is dead?"

"Sure I'm sure, I'm a hunter, yo? It's a girl like in her twenties. I was scared to call the cops, you can understand that."

"No shit. Your hunting license doesn't cover Fairmont Park."

"So what I did was I got the hell out o' there and decided to call you. I figured you'd know what to do."

Lenny thought a moment. Weighed his options. If *he* called 911 from his cell, the police would want to know where he got his information about a dead girl in the park. The shop steward-co-worker relation didn't carry any sort of

3

attorney-client privilege; secrecy was his only protection. He wished he had a dollar for every time he advised a worker when the shit was hitting the fan, *"Nobody talks, everyone walks."*

Besides, when they traced his phone calls the cops would see that Carlton had phoned in the middle of the night and want to know why.

"Tell you what. Get your ass down to the Wawa on Germantown Ave, the one on the Mt. Airy border. Use the outside payphone to call 911. Okay?"

"Yeah, I got it."

"Then go home and don't tell anybody, not *anybody* about what you saw. I'll catch up with you at work later."

"Cool, I'm down with that. Later, dude."

Lenny didn't know which irritated him more, Carlton's hipster lingo or his penchant for getting into trouble. He claimed to be part Cherokee, part Louisiana Cajun, but Lenny didn't believe any of it. Carlton was white Catholic Northeast Philadelphia all the way.

Slipping quietly back into bed, he felt his wife wrap her arm around him.

"Is everything all right?" she said in a husky whisper.

"Go back to sleep, dear, it's just Carlton."

"Mmm. . ." Her voice trailed off as she drifted back to dreamland.

But Lenny was not so lucky. He was worried about the possible consequences to Carlton. If the cops found out about his hunting deer in the park . . . Not to mention his butchering the animals in his garage out in Manayunk and selling the meat to co-workers in the hospital. . .

Lenny closed his eyes and snuggled up to his wife, hoping to get a few more hours of sleep. *Don't worry,* he told himself. Carlton would make the anonymous call and that would be the end of it. Problem was, knowing it was Carlton, he understood things could never be that easy.

After hanging up on Lenny, Carlton drove along Park Lane, turned up Horter and made his was to Germantown Avenue. Heading north past Mt. Airy Ave to the Wawa at Allens Lane, he stopped the van across the street, thinking he better not park in their parking lot, somebody inside might remember the van. Probably they had security cameras, too. He crossed Germantown Ave, the cobblestones wet beneath his feet, and went to the pay phone at the front of the building.

"Don't be broke. Don't be fucked up," he mumbled as he approached the phone. The hand piece was connected to the box. That was a good sign.

He lifted the receiver and listened. A dial tone! *Grrreat!* He felt in his pockets for a couple of quarters, found them empty.

No change.

He slammed the phone down, swearing into the night air. Were there any coins in the van? No, he'd used the last of them to feed a meter couple of days ago. Meant to fill up the slots.

Then he remembered: *It was a 911 call!* You didn't *need* any quarters!

He picked the phone back up and punched in the numbers. A sleepy woman's voice asked him what was his emergency. Carlton had rehearsed exactly what he was going to say.

"There's a dead girl in Fairmont Park. She's fifty yards up the path from Park Lane between Upsal and Clivedon."

"Sir, did you say a dead girl? Would you repeat that again please sir, I'm not sure—"

Click. Carlton hung up the phone, knowing the police would replay the tape and get the directions to the site.

Delighted at having stuck to his plan, Carlton decided he was hungry. A cold drink and some beef jerky would hit the spot. He went into the Wawa, bought a yogurt drink juice and a packet of beef jerky, and carried them back to the van. On the ride home the dried beef was sweet and satisfying, the drink, cool and creamy. It was the perfect breakfast for a mountain man come in from the hunt.

He couldn't wait to get to work in six hours and tell Lenny all about the dead girl.

THREE

"Tell us about the patient, Shira."

As Dr. Samir Singh looked over the tall, malnourished man lying in the bed, the young resident, tall and lovely, fumbled with a raft of progress notes. Singh noted the washed out color of his patient's once chestnut color skin and the purple of his oxygen-starved lips.

"Mr. Jimmy Jones is a fifty-seven year old African American male admitted from the ER with fever, chills, abdominal tenderness and distention, and high pitched bowel sounds consistent with a partial bowel obstruction." The resident paused to catch her breath. "Mister Jones has a past history of pulmonary fibrosis. He is oxygen dependent at home, and he is currently on the waiting list for a lung transplant."

Dr. Singh turned to another resident. "What are common causes of pulmonary fibrosis?" he asked.

"Uh, exposure to asbestos. Smoking. Toxic chemicals. . ."

"Do not forget viral infections, which may trigger an auto-immune response," Singh added. "Does Mister Jones have signs of right-sided heart failure?" He pulled up the sheets from the bottom of the bed and squeezed the patient's ankles, leaving deep impressions, like footprints in wet sand. "Peripheral edema is one sign of heart failure. Remember, these patients require a high filling pressure. They should have a central venous pressure of twenty or more."

Soft spoken and always polite, Singh bent down over the patient and asked gently, "Are you feeling any better, Mister Jones?"

"I don't have no more chills. Is that 'cause of the antibiotics you gave me?"

"Yes, sir, I believe so." He pressed on the patient's abdomen. "Do you still have pain?"

Jimmy grimaced, stifling a cry of pain, and nodded his head.

Singh asked Nurse Gary Tuttle what was the patient's current temperature. Gary told him it was ninety-nine point eight. Singh told his team, "If the patient has acute appendicitis or ischemic bowel, he will need emergent surgery. When he recovers from the surgery he will go back on the transplant waiting list."

Asked if the abdominal x-ray showed any free air in the abdomen, Shira reported there was none.

"You going to cut me open, doc?" asked Jimmy.

"It's not my call, sir, that's up to your surgeon; I am in charge of the Intensive Care Unit. What did Doctor Farr tell you when he saw you this morning?"

"I ain't seen any doctor t'day 'cept for that young lady beside you."

"Doctor Farr did not make rounds in the ICU yet?"

"I ain't seen *any* of his people this morning."

Singh was puzzled that the surgery team hadn't come through the unit, but he did not want the patient to think there was any lapse on their part. "Doctor Farr probably had an emergency case. I'd give him a little more time." To the team he said, "Let's review the x-rays."

As he turned to go, Singh noted a copy of *Allegro,* the musician's union monthly newsletter, on the bedside table. "You play an instrument?" he asked, picking up the magazine.

"I play a little sax. Mostly I sing in a group. Leastwise, I used to, 'fore the cancer stole my wind."

"I see. My wife always said if a man who played a saxophone proposed to her she would say yes in a heartbeat. I only play a little piano, but it did the trick somehow." Looking at his patient's rapid, shallow breathing and pursed lips, Singh visualized the alveoli in the lungs thickened and stiff and unable to transfer oxygen from the lung to the suffocating blood.

Stole my wind. There was no more apt description of his patient's condition in the entire medical lexicon. He led his team to the conference room at the back of the ICU to look over the morning x-rays.

When the physicians left the bedside, Jimmy Jones asked Gary, who was hanging an IV antibiotic, "You play any instrument, son?"

"Just my stereo."

"That's too bad. And you, a married man." Jimmy looked at the nurse with sympathy. Gary was not bad looking. A little pudgy, true, but he had warm, blue eyes and a gentle manner. Best of all, he cared about people. Really cared.

Jimmy picked up his copy of the union newsletter and settled back in bed, saying, "It ain't never too late to learn. Keep your wife happy."

Lenny Moss ran the mop back and forth across the marble floor. He was a man of modest height and unremarkable appearance. In his blue custodian's work clothes and black, steel tipped shoes, he went largely unnoticed as he went about his work keeping his section of the hospital clean. A big nose in a wan face held up thick glasses framing dark eyes that could be mischievous one moment, deadly serious the next.

For a while he found the rhythm of the work relaxing. It put him in a zone where his mind could wander. But then his thoughts wandered to Carlton, breaking his reverie. Lenny usually ran into him at the time clock or at the cafeteria getting morning coffee, but here it was nine o'clock and he hadn't seen the troublemaker. Had Carlton even made it to work?

He saw his friend Moose Maddox roll up with the food cart, pull two breakfast trays out of the food cart and step toward a doorway. Moose was a tall, muscular man with milk chocolate skin, close-cropped hair and an easy smile. Moose looked for the patient names posted on the door, but found the slots empty.

Lenny called out, "They took the names down!"

"What a load a' crap. Taking down the names from the doors is killing me. It takes twice as long to deliver the trays!"

"It's the latest administrative brainstorm," said Lenny, walking over to his friend. "We're supposed to confirm the patient's identity every time we treat them. They don't want us going by a sign on a door that might be wrong."

"Don't make no sense no how. Some of the patients don't even know their own name." Shaking his head, Moose entered the room and addressed an old man in the first bed who was pressing his head tight against the side rail.

"Are you Fenty?" Moose asked.

"Mmnph," the man murmured.

Cursing softly, Moose bent down and lifted the man's hand to read the name tag on the wrist. The tag, smeared with blood, read: Fenty, Martin, along with an ID number. The identity confirmed, Moose set down the tray and went on to the next bed, glad that the second patient could talk.

When he came out of the room Moose said again, "Don't make no sense. They just about killin' me."

"Yeah, but look at all the new friends you're making," said Lenny with a twinkle in his eyes.

With big hands he once used in the ring, Moose grabbed two more trays and headed into the next room. "We goin' jogging Saturday morning. Right?"

"Aw, Moose, I heard it's gonna thunder and lightning." Moose came out of the room and glared at him. "They're talking hail and a killer frost," Lenny added.

"We're jogging," said Moose, grabbing hold of the cart, "and you're going the distance this time."

As Moose pushed the cart down the hall, Lenny yelled, "K-Y-W says there's an earthquake warning!"

Returning to his mopping, Lenny thought about the new initiatives and the new policies coming out the last few months. With all the confusion they created, were the patients any happier? Did they get out of the hospital any sooner? Lenny couldn't see any improvement, but he was just a simple custodian; what did he know?

Rubbing a stubborn stain with the mop, he saw Regis Devoe approaching, and he marveled yet again how Regis's landing the job in the morgue had turned the young man's life around. Lenny hadn't had to represent him in a disciplinary hearing in—could it really be *two years?* Who knew that assisting Dr. Fingers with the autopsies would give the angry young man something to dig his teeth into?

"Hey, Reege, how're things in zombie land?"

"What's up, Lenny? Ah, you know, same old same old." Lean, dark and broad shouldered, the young morgue attendant was quick to laugh and just as quick to anger.

"You gonna go with me to the gym in Chestnut Hill and introduce me to that new contact?" Lenny asked.

Regis's smile turned to a scowl. "Man, we gotta do something 'bout those damn gyms the hospital bought up. I heard they even take Medicare! For a fricking *mud bath?* That's *crazy!*"

"It's marketing, that's all it is. Enroll in the gym, get a free health assessment and some blood work and what d'ya know, you need a heart transplant and an ass lift."

"It's bullshit. James Madison is supposed to be nonprofit!"

"The oldest tax dodge in the book." Lenny leaned on his mop. "So you coming or not?"

"Damn straight I'm goin' with you to the gym. You need to meet this girl, she's a personal trainer, and is she *hot.* She'll tell you all the bullshit they got going there, for real. I mean—"

"*Wha-ooo . . . Wha-ooo . . .*"

Regis and Lenny turned toward the stairwell, wondering what was making the strange sound. The exit door was ajar. Perplexed, they cautiously approached the door and pushed it open. On the landing stood Carlton, his hands cupped around his lips.

"What the hell was that, the call of the flying squirrel?" Lenny asked,

"Tryin' t' get your attention, bro'. The dispatcher warned me, Joe West wants me down the security office STAT. He said he saw a couple a' cops talkin' to West!"

"Jesus H. Christ."

"How'd they find me so *fast?*"

"Maybe West just wants to nail your ass for selling all that deer meat around the hospital," said Lenny, not really believing his own words, but trying to assuage his friend's fears.

Carlton wasn't convinced. "Man, I'm not letting them throw my ass in jail. There's no way a free ranging man like me can survive in prison. No fucking way."

"Carlton, you don't even know that the cops have identified you."

"Why else would they be talkin' to West and calling for me?"

"Look," said Lenny. "We can't talk here. I need to find a place to stash you for a while. I'll meet you on my break and we can go over your story. Okay?"

"Yeah, okay, Lenny, you the man. Where do you want me to go?"

While Lenny considered his options, Regis stepped into the stairwell, saying, "I got just the place for you to chill out. C'mon, we'll take the stairs, it's safer." He began walking down the steps, with Carlton following behind.

As Lenny watched the two descend the stairs, he had a bad feeling that Carlton was going to end up facing criminal charges of some kind, and that he would ask Lenny to help defend him. Negotiating with a supervisor or an appeal board in order to save a co-worker's job was par for the course for a shop steward. But crossing swords with the Philadelphia police was way, way outside his job description.

FOUR

When break time came, Lenny hurried to talk to Carlton. All he had to do to find Regis Devoe's workplace was follow the smell. The foul, pungent odors of formaldehyde and bloody entrails filled the long, lonely stretch of hallway leading to the morgue. As he approached the door with the sign AUTOPSY ROOM in bold black letters, he reflected that morgues were always located in the basement. They were subterranean, like graves.

Inside, Lenny found Regis hosing out the gutters. A yellow barrel labeled TISSUE: HUMAN TYPE stood on a nearby table.

"Hey, thanks for helping me out with Carlton," said Lenny.

"Ain't no big thing, all the times you pulled my ass outta the fire." Regis shut off the water and coiled the hose. He pulled off a plastic apron and dropped it in the trash.

"Where's Carlton?" Lenny asked.

"He's chillin'," Regis said with a sly smile. "C'mon, I'll show you."

He led Lenny out of the autopsy room and down the corridor to the big fridge, with its heavy insulated steel door and padlock.

"You get many bodies escaping?" asked Lenny as Regis unlocked the door.

"We gotta keep out the organ snatchers, there's big bucks in fresh organs, ya know."

Lenny felt goose bumps along his arms as Regis opened the door and the cold, damp air washed over him. He remembered the day he was trapped inside that frigid chamber and unable to get out. "You sure I'll be able to get out okay?"

Regis flashed a devilish grin. "If you have a problem with the handle, knock three times, I'll listen for you in the next room."

"That's not very reassuring."

Lenny stepped in, heard the heavy door close behind him. He saw three stretchers with bodies wrapped in black, waterproof body bags. Carlton stood in the corner wearing a body bag like a cape wrapped around his shoulders and a paper cap over his head.

"What's with the hat, are you assisting doctor Fingers in an autopsy?" said Lenny.

13

"It's basic survival, yo. You got cold feet, put on a hat."

"Listen, we don't have a lot of time. I talked to Sandy in security. He told me the cops do want to talk to you about that dead girl in the park."

"*Fuck.* Did he say how they picked up my trail?"

"He didn't know about that part. Carlton, you don't have to run away, the cops have no reason to suspect you."

"I'm not feelin' it, bro'." Lenny was again irritated by Carlton's street language. Why did the crazy man have to claim to be part Cherokee Indian, part Irish, part *Mayan*. . . the list was always changing. "I was thinking I'd load up my van and take off for the mountains. Live off the land. Stay in the wild until this thing blows over."

"That's crazy and you know it."

"I can trap game and dry it. I'll make it through the winter all right."

Lenny tucked his hands in his armpits to warm them. "I don't understand how the cops got on to you so *fast*. You didn't park in the Wawa lot did you, they have security cameras?"

"'Course I parked in the street, my people were hunters. Cunning runs in my blood."

"So how did they know?"

Carlton's eyes became guarded.

"You think my goin' inside the Wawa and buying a smoothie and a beef jerky had something to do with it?"

"You went inside?"

Carlton nodded, still not looking Lenny in the eye.

"*Inside the Wawa?*"

"Yeah."

"Don't tell me you used a credit card."

"Lenny, I'm not stoopid."

"I'm not saying that. It's weird, though. They snap your face on the in-store camera, I get that, but how did they put a name to your face?" Lenny looked at Carlton's face. "You ever been arrested?"

"Nope."

"Get a photo ID for a state or a federal job?"

"Never." Carlton wrapped the bag tighter around him. "I did have to get my picture taken for my hunting license."

"That's probably how they found you. They must have used facial recognition software to match your hunting license photo to the video."

14

"Ain't that *always* the way? You try and obey the law like a good citizen and it only lands you in shit!" Carlton finally looked straight at Lenny. "What's gonna happen next?"

"We have to expect they'll execute a search warrant, if they're not in your place already. If they find the deer meat they might charge you with hunting on city property."

"I'll say I got it out in the country."

"Okay. Do you have any guns in the house?"

"Just an old double barrel shotgun."

"Just a shotgun. Is it *licensed?*"

"'Course it's licensed. But I ain't used it since I switched to the bow."

Lenny took a minute to put the pieces together. As many of them as he had, there were still a lot of unknowns.

"Okay, here's the plan. I hope the cops aren't dumb enough to think you had anything to do with the murder. You didn't know the dead girl, right?"

"Hand up t' god."

"Okay. We need a reason for you to be in the park at midnight."

"What about I was getting a piece of tail. Not the four-legged kind."

"Soliciting prostitution is a crime."

"Damn, that's cold!"

"I think the best we can do is, you were out driving your van and you saw a guy carrying what looked like an unconscious girl into the woods. You weren't sure, so you followed them to investigate, and when you realized she was dead, you went to the pay phone and called it in."

"Yeah. Yeah, that's good, but how come I didn't use my cell?"

"You had a dead battery. And you didn't give your name because you were afraid the police might try to connect you to whoever murdered the girl."

"Solid."

"Can you remember all that?"

Carlton tapped the side of his head. "It's stamped in the brain."

"Okay. Now call your supervisor and tell him you're sick and get Employee Health to sign you out. You can hold a mouthful of hot water before they take your temperature; that should do it. When you get home, ditch the deer meat, and if the cops find you, stick to the story."

Lenny punched the handle and opened the door. When he stepped out into the room, he realized for the first time that he was chilled to the bone, while

Carlton wasn't shivering at all. It must have something to do with all his years sitting in the woods at night. He watched Carlton slip down the corridor and out of sight.

With a shake of his head, Lenny climbed the stairs to his ward on the seventh floor, knowing the exercise would warm him. The walk up from the basement would also provide time to try and convince himself that Carlton's luck hadn't finally run out.

FIVE

Shaking and feverish, Jimmy Jones pulled the thin hospital blanket up to his chin, telling Gary Tuttle, "Man, it feels like I'll never get warm again."

Gary gave him an acetaminophen suppository, saying he would feel better as soon as the medication took hold.

"I hope so, I ain't never been cold like this, even when traveling with the band and singing in Minneapolis in January. Talk about *cold.* Did you know they got all kinds a' underground connections for the buildings so's folks don't have to come up above ground hardly ever?"

"When did you stop performing?" asked Gary.

'That's goin' on four years, since my lungs got bad. I'm on all kinds a' pills and inhalers and oxygen. They helped me for a while, but the last couple a' months, seems like things just up and went from bad to worse."

While he listened, Gary kept a close eye on Jimmy's blood pressure on the cardiac monitor. It read 90/50—too low and still dropping. Gary lowered the head of the bed and raised the legs to support his pressure, then he caught the resident's eye.

"Shira, Mister Jones's blood pressure is falling."

The young resident came to the bedside and gently laid her fingers on the patient's wrist. The skin was cool and moist, the pulse, thready. She pressed softly on his swollen abdomen, eliciting a groan of pain.

"He is septic. I think maybe he perforated his colon. Hang a liter of normal saline and start a Levophed drip; I will call for an x-ray of the abdomen." As she stepped to the phone to call radiology, she remembered what Dr. Singh had said about maintaining a high filling pressure and called out to Gary, "Be sure to check his CVP! It must be kept high! At least twenty!"

Spiking the bag of intravenous fluid, Gary asked Shira when was Dr. Farr coming and taking the patient to surgery?

"That is up to the surgeon. We will have to see what Doctor Farr decides to do."

"Hey, Boop," Lenny greeted his housekeeping partner, Betty, as she pushed her cart down the hall. "How're you doing?"

"Dear heart, the Lord saw fit to wake me up this morning; I am grateful for his blessing." Short and bow-legged, with curly gray hair and a dark, weathered

17

face, Betty wasn't afraid of blood, death or the devil, so strong was her faith. She pulled a roll of toilet paper and a box of tissues from her cart to take into a patient room. "Say, did you hear about that poor young nurse what was killed last night in the park?"

"Yeah, I heard. I didn't know she was a nurse."

Betty placed her hands on her hips and smiled broadly. "What do ya know, for once I have the news before you do! The poor young thing worked right here at James Madison!"

"Really? *Damn.* Where did she work?"

"They say she worked nights in Recovery. Lord, what devilry is upon us, dumping a young woman's body in the park like so much garbage. We live in evil times, my dear, you mark my words."

"I can't argue about the times," said Lenny, tired of hearing his partner's religious pronouncements but touched by her compassion for the patients and workers. "Whatever she was doing, she didn't deserve to die."

"Amen to that. I'll say a prayer for her in church tonight, yes I will." She pushed off with her cart humming a gospel song.

As Lenny went through the ward picking up trash liners and dumping them in the big rolling cart, he reflected on the odd coincidence that Carlton had stumbled on the body of a dead nurse who just *happened* to work in the hospital. Carlton had always been honest with Lenny; it wasn't like him to hide things. But still it was a curious overlapping of events.

Lenny was glad he wasn't involved in the murder case, he had more than enough grief with his duties as shop steward. Especially since James Madison bought up the local gyms and staffed them with non-union people, with no benefits and no representation. Bringing them into the union was going to be a tough nut to crack.

Still, he couldn't help thinking about what the police would do next. They would question Carlton, he was a witness at the scene, and then they would look for a connection between him and the dead nurse. Since there wasn't any, aside from them both working at James Madison, they would probably let it go at that. *Probably.*

Lenny recalled other cases he had investigated where the cops charged the first blue collar suspect they came upon. One time they even arrested Regis Devoe while leaving the upscale suspect who really did commit the murder untouched and free to kill again. The real possibility that the police would repeat their past mistakes and charge Carlton with the murder pissed him off. He threw a garbage bag into the big cart, splitting it open, and cursed the police under his breath. He wanted this time to be different, but knew history was a nightmare that returned night after night.

He looked at his watch. It was nearly eleven in the morning; time enough for Carlton to get home and throw out the incriminating venison steaks. Lenny sent him a text message telling him to call, then he finished collecting the trash from the patient rooms. By the time he delivered the big rolling cart to the basement, Carlton still hadn't answered the text. The silence made Lenny even more concerned that his friend was in the hands of the police. They were no doubt searching his home, finding the Mongolian bow, the night vision goggles and the deer meat.

He just hoped Carlton didn't evoke the name of Robin Hood when the cops interrogated him.

Responding to the resident's page, Doctor Singh entered the ICU and went right to Jimmy Jones's bed. "Read me the blood gas, please," he told the nurse.

Gary read the latest blood gas results, which showed the patient was becoming increasingly acidotic. The nurse told him how much he was adjusting the dose of Levophed to support the patient's blood pressure.

"Did you bolus him with saline?"

"I hung a liter; it's infusing wide open," said Gary.

The resident reported to Singh that the flat plate of the abdomen showed increased free air in the peritoneum.

"He's septic from his bowel. Gary, hang a unit of albumin, it will buy us a little time." To Shira he said, "The patient needs his abdomen explored. Page Doctor Farr STAT. I want the surgeon in the ICU, *now.*"

Turning back to the patient, he saw that Jimmy Jones was breathing with an open mouth, like a fish out of water. Singh told Gary to mix two amps of Bicarb in a liter of dextrose and run it at two hundred fifty cc's an hour once the liter of saline was finished.

Singh stood over the patient and said, "Sir, your bowel appears to be leaking. I don't believe you will live much longer if Doctor Farr doesn't take you to the OR and repairs your colon."

Weak and out of breath, Jimmy reached a hand up and squeezed Singh's hand twice, indicating he understood, then his hand fell back into the bed.

Going to the nursing station, Singh opened the chart and began to record the patient's vital signs and lab values. As he considered just what to put in his progress note, he heard the automatic doors swish open and saw Farr, who towered over his team members, march in accompanied by a phalanx of house staff, students and a Physician Assistant. They descended on Jimmy Jones, surrounding the bed, pulling up the sheet and baring his belly and chest.

After a cursory examination, Farr went to the desk where Singh was sitting with the chart. "What is my patient's status?"

Singh repeated his findings, including the distended, tender abdomen, and pointing out that the patient had a profound acidosis.

"I agree with your management, although I would add a unit of blood, it will give him more oxygen carrying capacity and more volume as well."

As the surgeon turned to walk toward the patient, Singh asked, "How soon will you be taking him to the OR?"

Farr gave a double take. "I have no intention of opening up this patient, he is too unstable. Taking an infected patient in shock to the OR is a recipe for disaster."

"If you do not open his belly and repair his leaking colon, he will certainly die," Singh said in a hard-edged voice, holding his anger in check with difficulty.

Staring into Singh's face, Farr spit out the words, "Do not elect to tell me how to assess my patient, doctor. You are an intensivist, not a surgeon. Stick to what you know and leave the difficult decisions to others."

"Very well, if that's the way you wish to handle the current situation." Singh opened the patient's chart and turned to the progress notes. "But you should know I am writing in the chart that the patient will not survive without an emergency exploratory lap, and that Doctor Jean Farr refuses to take the patient to the OR for a life-saving procedure."

Farr gave Singh a look of loathing. For several seconds they stared at each other, like two mortal enemies in a duel. Finally Farr picked up the phone and punched in some numbers.

"Cynthia? Doctor Farr. Prepare Room seven for an exploratory laparotomy and possible resection. The patient will be down shortly. His name? Jimmy Jones. Yes, Jimmy Jones."

He hung up the phone, turned to his team. "Get a stretcher and take him down. Cielo and I will scrub in."

The surgical intern scurried off to locate a stretcher while a resident called for an anesthesiologist. The Physician's Assistant picked up the portable monitor and carried it to the bed. At the center of the storm Jimmy struggled to draw in enough oxygen to stay alive.

Watching the surgical team hustle about the unit, Singh wondered what would possess a physician to withhold a lifesaving procedure in the face of overwhelming evidence that inaction would kill him.

SIX

Carlton stood on his tiptoes at the dead end of Osborn Street looking over the cement wall and across the train tracks at his house on Cresson. The house was nestled in a copse of trees that had dropped half their leaves. The garage, an old shed, stood empty and forlorn off to the side. His van was parked around the corner. In forty-five minutes of watching he saw no signs of the police. Nothing stirred in his house. No one came out of the garage. No sign of life.

If I wait, the cops'll come. It's now or never.

He made his way on foot through the cut, crossing Ridge Avenue, entered his muddy, rutted street, and walked past an old abandoned factory. It was a narrow, forlorn lane that looked more like the entrance to some Appalachian holler than a street in a modern northern city. Reaching his house, he gave a quick look in the back door window. The kitchen was empty. He crept around the north side, concealed by fir trees he'd planted for a wind brake. Nobody in the dining room. The living room was empty, too.

Beginning to relax, he unlocked the front door and slipped inside. A silent walk through the first floor found nothing out of place. He figured if the cops had searched the place they would have left a mess.

He went down to the basement and opened the freezer. There was a good thirty pounds of dear meat, bundled in packages of five pounds each. He grabbed a heavy plastic bag and loaded it with meat, then lugged it back up the steps, the frozen packs banging against the wooden handrail.

As Carlton stepped into the kitchen he was startled to find a stranger sitting at the Formica table holding a double-barreled shotgun in his lap. The stranger was tall and dark skinned, with a weary face. He was wearing a gray suit and polished brown shoes.

Carlton froze, thinking, *this is my day to die.*

"Carlton Rogers," the man said quietly. He pointed the gun at Carlton's belly. It was the quiet in his voice more than the shotgun that made him scary.

"You gonna kill me?"

"Only if you act stupid."

"What d'ya want?"

"Now don't play dumb with the police, Carlton, you know exactly what I want." The detective stood, letting the shotgun point at the floor. "I'm

Philadelphia police detective sergeant Joseph Williams, and I want you to tell me how you came to make that 911 call last night."

"How's that?"

The shotgun came up to point at his belly again. "You've got a nice old fashioned weapon here. It's reassuring to know it will never jam. Of course, the downside is you only get two shots."

"If you tuck extra shells between your fingers you can reload in ten seconds," said Carlton.

Detective Williams reached inside his jacket, pulled out a paper and slapped it on the kitchen table. "Here's the search warrant. You can read it on the way to the station." On cue a gang of uniformed officers poured in from the front and rear doors and began tearing up the house.

Leading Carlton to an unmarked police car, Detective Williams opened the rear door for Carlton, saying, "You can also tell me about this friend of yours you like to call in the middle of the night, Lenny Moss."

Dr. Singh and Shira were in the conference room behind the nursing station when the surgeons brought Jimmy Jones from the OR, hooked up to the monitor, and then hurried away. Singh went to the bedside and opened the chart to read the brief operative note, which described the repair of the perforated colon. There was no mention of any tumors. That was hopeful, malignancy was always a worry when the bowel is ruptured. If Jimmy recovered from the surgery and he developed no more complications with his bowel . . .

"How high are the pressors?" Singh asked.

"Twenty mikes of Levo," said Gary.

"He's dry," said Singh. "The idiots in the OR never give enough fluids. Give him two liters of saline and get Respiratory to run a blood gas."

He noted that Jimmy was not triggering the ventilator machine. He hoped that was just the lingering effects of the anesthesia and not a result of brain damage suffered on the table.

Singh told Gary, "Try to wean him slowly from the pressors. If he can maintain a systolic pressure of ninety or better on his own, I think he'll stabilize." He noted the small amount of urine in the Foley bag. "If his urine drops below thirty cc's for one hour, tell Shira, she's on call tonight." Gary promised to make that clear when he handed the patient over to the night nurse.

Singh told the resident to re-order the antibiotics with a STAT dose. He understood that the perforated bowel had sent a flood of bacteria into the abdominal cavity. Even though the surgeons had washed out the area, the bacteria had had plenty of time to infect the organs there. Another epic battle was joined, the patient's immune system supported by troops of antibiotics, while the legions of pathogens, several species strong, were releasing their toxins into the body in a determined effort to kill the host.

Singh's usual optimism was tempered by the knowledge that Jimmy's body was weakened by his long-standing pulmonary disease and steroid use, which suppressed his immune system. Watching Gary and Shira labor over the patient, the usually unflappable physician, with years of Buddhist training, cursed Farr for delaying the surgery.

SEVEN

With a turn of the key the big V8 let out a brutish roar, triggering chirps from the security alarms in the cars on either side. Every time he heard the old small block Chevy engine turn over he thought of his dad, a union organizer back in the day who left him the car when he died. No money, but a lot of good memories. And the car.

"Man," said Regis. "What kind a' exhaust system have you got on this old thing?"

"The rusty kind," Lenny said with a laugh. He pulled out of the hospital parking lot onto Germantown Avenue, the big tires chewing up the uneven pavement as they headed for the gym. He drove through Mt. Airy and up the long gentle slope into Chestnut Hill, the upscale neighborhood with the high-income patients that James Madison Hospital coveted, while it served the poorer Germantown residents.

"Hey," said Regis. "I hear that girl what got herself killed worked at the hospital."

"Yeah, she was a nurse worked nights in Recovery."

"The graveyard shift. How come you didn't tell me about it when I was hidin' Carlton for you?"

"I didn't have time, Reege, I had to come up with something quick and get him out of the hospital." Lenny filled his friend in on what he knew so far: the phone call from Carlton in the middle of the night; his instructions to Carlton to call 911 anonymously; Carlton going into the Wawa to buy something to eat; and the plan they agreed to at work to ditch the deer meat and tell the police he just *happened* to see somebody carrying a suspicious bundle into the park.

"You don't think Carlton had anything t' do with the girl gettin' killed, do you?"

"No, I think it's just a coincidence she was found in Fairmont Park and Carlton hunts deer in the park."

"Yeah, and it's a coincidence the dead girl worked at James Madison, just like Carlton."

"Hey, "I've got to give Carlton the benefit of the doubt," said Lenny. "That doesn't mean I think he's telling me the whole truth. They never tell you the whole truth the first time around, believe me."

Regis said, "He could've run into her when he was doin' overtime. Bein' on the float team, he cleaned every fricking floor in the whole damn hospital one time or another."

Lenny agreed. As he slowed the car looking for a parking spot on the avenue he said, "Tell me more about this girl we're going to meet at the gym I'm going to see. How did you hook up with her?"

"It was like I said. I went in to check the place out, like we talked about. Laticia's a personal trainer. I got to chatting her up; told her where I worked in the morgue and all. She was interested in the autopsy stuff. I think she wants to go to school for something."

"And you asked her about the working conditions are at the gym. That's good work, Reege."

"Yeah, well, she said one of the reasons she took the job was so she could use the facilities, but the job didn't have any benefits, so she can't go to a doctor or a dentist or nothin'."

"And that let you talk about the need to unionize the workers there to give them a contract with benefits. Smooth move."

"She said the people work there come and go. The manager's a real control freak. He's a Schwarzeneggar wanna be who couldn't make the cut in competition, so he went into the body building business."

"His brain is probably fried on steroids. What's the guy's name?"

"Brunner. Albert Brunner. The staff all call him 'Ahl-bert.' Not to his face."

"Well, let's see if we can talk to the young lady without *Ahlbert* finding out."

Lenny parked the car in the parking lot across the street. Approaching the New Body Spa and Fitness Center, they saw poster-sized pictures in the windows of beautifully toned men and women. The posters hid the sweaty, misshapen bodies working out inside from pedestrians and drivers on the avenue. A banner in the window warned that a person's chances of losing weight and keeping it off without a personal trainer and a program were *SLIM TO NONE*, a slogan they played repeatedly on radio advertisements. Lenny was already sick and tired of the jingle.

Inside, a shapely platinum blonde in leotards and tank top with a gleaming smile and a perky voice greeted them from behind a counter. "Hello, guys! How can I help you start building your new body today?"

"Is this like the Twilight Zone?" asked Lenny. "The episode where the old couple only has enough money for one of them to get a new body, and after he gets it he gives it back 'cause he doesn't want his elderly wife to feel bad?"

"Uh, no sir, there is no magic in our system, we use strict scientific principles to help you reshape and retain a slim, healthy body." The girl noted Lenny's custodian uniform and hospital ID tag. She knew his health plan covered the spa facilities if he had any medical condition that justified exercise.

When Regis explained that he already purchased a ten-day trial membership and that he brought his friend for the one day free lesson and workout, the perky blonde handed Lenny a clipboard. "Just fill out this simple little form and sign it, and I'll find you your own personal trainer."

"Um, I had a really good lesson from Laticia," said Regis. "I don't guess she's working today."

"This is your lucky day, Laticia *is* here, and I'm sure if you will be patient that I can arrange a personal session with her. It will just be a little wait while she finishes with her client. Why doesn't your friend fill out the form so I can personalize a list of services that are best for him? Okay?" She spoke the last word with a big smile as bright as toothpaste commercial.

Lenny ignored the questionnaire and looked at the brochures. The first had a chart that showed your ideal weight, overweight and underweight for your age, sex and height. Lenny saw that he was in the upper limit of normal weight.

Above the chart their pet slogan was repeated in bold letters: *What are the chances that you can lose weight and keep it off all by yourself? Slim to none!* The brochure went on to extol the long-lasting effects of a program tailored by a personal trainer.

Regis leaned in close to Lenny. "I still don't get how come you don't go to law school. You'd make a hot shit lawyer."

"I'd have to finish college first, I dropped out when my old man died. It would mean a year of courses. Maybe more, then three years of law school."

"So do it, man. You'd be great doing legal stuff for the union."

"Ah, I like what I'm doing right now. The suits in the union hall are kind of disconnected from us. They don't have the fire in their belly like we do down in the trenches."

"Then you go and stoke the fire! Fan the flames! Throw some cherry bombs in the union office; tell 'em to get out there organizing the gyms."

"Yeah, well, I've got my hands full helping Patience raise her two kids. Maybe when they're out of the house."

Turning to watch people working out, Lenny didn't understand why yet another worker thought he would make a good attorney. Even his wife Patience had broached the subject. Granted, there were superficial similarities between a shop steward and a lawyer. Both interviewed people in trouble. Both had to know the relevant regulations and past practices. Case law was the legal term. And they had to be fast on their feet in negotiations.

But Lenny cherished his place in the hospital: the camaraderie with the other workers, the respect he commanded from the supervisors, some of whom even helped him with problems. Give it all up for a legal-beagle job? No thanks, it just didn't feel right. Slugging it out in the trenches—that felt right.

His thoughts were interrupted when Laticia approached. She was a tall, slim black woman with well defined muscles and the legs of a professional dancer.

"Hi, Regis. Back for more punishment, I see. Who's your friend?"

"This is Lenny. He works with me in the hospital. I've been telling him about the place. I think he's gonna join."

Laticia held out a hand. Her grip was strong and her smile, sublime.

"I have a friend in the hospital who's been bugging me to try some free weights," said Lenny, "but I don't have the time to come in regularly and work at it."

"Weights don't have to take up a lot of time. We're just up the street from your hospital, and we open at five am. You could come before work."

"That might work."

Laticia mounted some weights on a barbell and instructed Lenny to lie on his back on the bench. She showed him where to grasp the bar. "We'll start easy. Don't lift anything you feel you can't handle. I'll be right here in case you think you can't hold the weight."

As Lenny began the first set of repetitions, he looked up at her face, which was upside down as she spotted him. "Regis tells me the workers here don't have any health benefits."

"That's right, no benefits. I have a little girl I can't afford to take to the doctor. I have to use the Emergency Room, and then the collection people call me night and day. It's really the pits."

"What do you know about unions?"

'I know they can mean the difference between a paycheck and being out in the street."

"There is *some* job security with a union. It's not a guarantee, but it's more than you have now."

Laticia looked around the gym, making sure no one was listening to them. "I think a union would be a good thing, but the manager for this place is a real dictator. If he got wind I was talking to you about this stuff I'd be out on the sidewalk in a heartbeat."

Finishing the first set of repetitions, Lenny said, "Why don't we meet some place private after work one day?"

Laticia looked around again. She leaned over him and said in a whisper, "I'd like to, really I would, it's just, my boss is so . . ."

"Scary." Lenny lifted the barbell off the holder and repeated the repetitions, finding it a good deal heavier the second time. He watched Laticia's face as he worked.

"He's *very* scary. Albert runs the gym like it's his own personal empire."

"I know the type, we've got a guy like that running the security department back at the hospital."

As Lenny struggled to lift the weights on the tenth rep, she grasped the bar and helped him ease it onto the brackets above his head. "Okay," she said. "I guess if we find someplace out of the way it should be safe."

Lenny suggested they meet for brunch at the Trolley Car Diner on Germantown Ave. Laticia agreed, saying she was free Saturday in the late morning. Lenny thanked her and went to find Regis. When his friend was finished with his workout, they passed the front counter on the way out. The perky girl at the desk told them the gym offered a free health assessment that includes blood pressure and blood sugar level. "It's completely free. I can draw your blood right now, did you fill out the health assessment form?"

"Uh, I need to get home to the kids," said Lenny. "I'll come back another day and fill it out."

"Great! And just for coming in, I want to give you a free sample of our rejuvenating lotion. It restores skin and reduces age spots!" She slapped a tube of lotion into Lenny's hand with a practiced smack.

"I'm not old enough to have age spots, but I married a mature woman, I'm sure it'll do wonders for her skin." Regis jabbed Lenny in the side, telling him it was a good thing Patience couldn't hear the sarcasm.

After dropping Regis off, Lenny called Carlton's cell phone again, but it went to voice mail. He tried to convince himself that the guy's battery really was low or he was off in the woods somewhere, but deep down he knew the cops had him and were going over his story again and again and again.

Lenny hoped Carlton didn't go making up more of his crazy stories; that he stuck to the plan and would walk away without any charges, because *if* Carlton was charged with the murder, the shit was going to come down on Lenny, too. The workers at James Madison would be coming up to him expecting him to perform some sort of magic trick that would set Carlton free, and sure as hell felt nothing like a miracle worker.

EIGHT

In the Chestnut Hill branch of the New Body Spa and Fitness Center, Albert Brunner stared hard at the video screen. A thickly built man with a block-shaped head, deep-set eyes, veins like ropes in his arms, and a slim waist, Brunner favored tight-fitting pants and short sleeve shirts that clung to his barrel chest.

Seated in his office, he had views on the security monitors of the entire gym, including the front desk and parking lot. He watched as Laticia attached weights to a barbell and spotted the client, who was flat on his back on the bench. Seeing her talking to the two hospital workers, he zoomed in on their uniforms and saw the familiar James Madison ID badges on their shirts.

Brunner couldn't hear what they were discussing, the video system had no sound, but since his contact at the hospital told him that a particularly zealous union member would be coming to try and organize his gym, he was confident that the ugly fellow on the weight bench was Lenny Moss, James Madison's number one trouble maker. Judging by the paltry number of weights on his barbell, the man was a lightweight.

He sat back in his chair and considered what a stroke of luck it was that the annoying union man had come to his club. It meant that Moss was planning one of those foolish drives to "organize" the employees in some corrupt, money-grubbing organization. His people were already *organized.* The Chestnut Hill spa ran like a well-oiled machine. His employees either loved or feared him. Either way, they were loyal.

Any attempt to spread union poison was just the opportunity he needed to increase his standing with James Madison's president. Brunner had already nearly doubled his enrollment in the Chestnut Hill gym—clear proof of his managerial superiority. Now he would crush these puny "union" people and throw them into the street like garbage. His triumph would elevate him even higher. President Lefferts would *have* to put him in charge of all the gyms. After that, Brunner would take the business national and build a franchise to rival the titans of the industry.

As he saw Moss and his friend make their way out of the building, Brunner used an online search engine to read about Lenny Moss. There were countless news articles about his exploits solving crimes and making the Philadelphia police look like chumps. It seemed there was more to the ugly little man than his appearance suggested. Brunner knew well the value of concealing genius behind a bland exterior. But this gadfly would be no match for Albert Brunner. He would swat the little man like a fly and crush him beneath his foot.

But first things first. Brunner needed to give Laticia a strict lesson about personal loyalty to your boss. He would instill absolute loyalty in the trainer who dared speak to Moss. Nobody fraternized with the enemy in *his* organization. He pressed the button for the intercom and announced over the gym loudspeaker, "Laticia Gordon, see me in my office when you are finished with your present client."

Watching Laticia freeze in the middle of her demonstration, Brunner felt a rush of pleasure as her face sank and her shoulders drooped at the sound of his voice. Love and fear, the twin legs of a loyal employee, especially the female employees. And he would have them both.

Joe West strode through the door with the sign, "EMERGENCY RESPONSE COMMAND CENTER, his new title for Hospital Security. He changed the name to mirror the Homeland Security. Once inside his office he saw his phone had two new messages waiting to be heard.

The first message told him that the Philadelphia Police were questioning an employee of the hospital, Carlton Rogers, regarding the death of Briana Nearing. This news brought a hint of a smile to the corners of West's mouth. Carlton was one of the many irritating little people who flagrantly disregarded hospital rules. His arrest would mean West had one less termination to execute.

The second message warned him of a danger to the hospital. Lenny Moss was talking to employees at one of the new exercise gyms. West was ready for the news; he'd been expecting it, Moss was a compulsive do-gooder who couldn't resist sticking his ugly face in other peoples business.

Threats to the hospital came in many forms, not just terrorist bombs or lunatics rampaging through the ER shooting off automatic weapons. Moss was one of the gravest threats the institution ever faced. He encouraged employees to challenge authority. He argued with supervisors, filed grievances, called impromptu meetings and even led vigilante groups on marches into the administrative offices.

West was confident he could crush this particular problem, especially with his ally in the gym. He would take a special pleasure in crushing the offending individual. It would finally be the end of that annoying gadfly, Lenny Moss.

Dr. Singh asked Gary how much Levophed Jimmy Jones required to support his blood pressure. The nurse reported he had reduced the dose to 10 mikes. "Very good. We are heading in the right direction. With a little luck his immune system will rally and the infection will be beaten."

Singh asked the nurse if he knew that Jimmy had been on the waiting list for a lung transplant.

"Everyone's heard about it," said Gary. "There's a fund raiser planned for him a week from Saturday. Is there a chance he'll be able to go to the event, it's going to be held at the medical school?"

"That is highly unlikely. Transplant surgeons don't take candidates who have active infections. Mister Jones will have to be completely clear of infection for a prolonged period before he can undergo a procedure such as that."

Sing instructed Gary to tell the night nurse she must continue titrating the pressors down as long as the blood pressure was stable. "Be sure they send off two sets of blood cultures if he spikes a fever," he added. To the resident he said, "Shira, I want you to page me tonight if Jimmy's condition deteriorates, regardless of the time."

"But Doctor Singh, Doctor Billingham is the Attending on call for the unit tonight."

"I know, and Billingham's a good doctor. You should call him and bring him down to assist you, but I still want to be notified. If Mister Jones develops a bleed or shows signs of a leak at the anastomosis I want to be sure the surgeons take him back and explore him."

Singh gave one last look at the patient, who was sedated and breathing comfortably. His color was better and his extremities were no longer cool. The doctor left the ICU vowing that if the situation turned bad, he would be damn sure Farr didn't duck his responsibilities again.

After the customers and employees were gone for the night, Albert Brunner gave himself a workout with the free weights. He reveled in the effort required to lift the barbell packed with weights, feeling his body strain and expand. No ancient knight or Greek warrior ever possessed such strength.

Finished with the workout, Brunner stripped off his clothes and stepped into the shower. He ran the water hot; as hot as the boiler could provide. He relished the sting of the steamy spray on his body. In his mind the clouds of steam billowing about him cast him into an ancient age of conquering heroes.

An age in which he ruled absolutely, and with absolute success. He ran a soapy wash rag over his body, relishing the rippling muscles.

So the union was going to try and lead his employees astray, as the hospital had warned him they would when they purchased the facility. Brunner knew how to crush that effort before it began. It would be easy, like pulling out a weed and grinding it beneath his shoe, and Lenny Moss would be the first to feel the force of his will.

NINE

Lenny was cooking spaghetti. He crushed a clove of garlic with the flat of a butcher knife, diced it and added it to the tomato sauce bubbling on the stove. Since the kids loved garlic he was tempted to add two more cloves, but Patience's stomach would get upset, so he let it go.

Takia opened the oven door a crack and inhaled deeply. "Mmm-mm. Lenny, you make cornbread better than mommy do."

Tossing the greens in a big ceramic bowl, Patience said, "Say 'better than mommy *does*,' not mommy *do*. I won't have that street talk in my house." She handed her daughter a stack of plates and told her to set the table.

"Yes ma'am."

Malcolm came in carrying two fists full of action figures.

"When do we eat? I'm *starving*."

"Right after you put your toys away."

"Can't I have them at the table?"

"No!" Patience took the cornbread out of the oven and set it on a cooling rack on the dining room table.

"Who's gonna guard the food?"

"Lenny and I can keep it safe from robbers, now go wash up."

Lenny dipped a wooden spoon into the sauce, blew on it and held it out for Patience to taste. "What do you think? Needs more salt?"

"No, it' fine. Add a little more hot sauce."

Lenny shook the bottle over the saucepan, then he drained the noodles and plopped them in a bowl.

"I hope Carlton isn't in too much trouble this time," said Patience, taking a bottle of salad dressing from the fridge.

"Carlton is *always* in trouble. He's not answering my phone calls or my texting. It looks like the cops picked him up." He poured the tomato sauce over the noodles and brought them to the dining room, where the children had already started on the cornbread.

Takia lifted a few noodles on her fork and leaned over her plate. "These stupid noodles drip on my shirt!" Lenny advised her to use a spoon to help twirl it around her fork.

"Like this," said Lenny, winding a big helping of spaghetti around his fork and raising it high above his mouth like a sword swallower.

When Malcolm tried the trick he dribbled sauce from the swinging noodles all over his shirt and the table. Patience glared at Lenny, who pretended not to notice. "More cornbread, dear?" he said.

Malcolm was trying the spaghetti twirl again when there was a loud rapping at the door. Patience looked at her husband. "Are you expecting someone?" she said.

"Not me. It's probably those Pentecostals." Lenny got up from his chair, ambled over to the front door and opened it. One look and he knew his appetite was lost. Philadelphia police detective Joe Williams was standing on the front steps looking pissed off, as usual.

"I need a word with you," said Williams.

"I'm right in the middle of dinner. Can't it wait? Like, till next year?"

"You know it can't wait. You can talk here or you can come down town. You want to spend the night in a cell?"

Lenny sighed, stepped aside and let the detective in. "You can have some spaghetti, just be careful you don't dribble on your shirt."

Patience took the children upstairs with a tray to finish their dinner, then she sat in the kitchen finishing her own meal while Lenny sat with the detective in the dining room.

"What's on your mind?" Lenny asked once the detective had declined the food.

"It's about your buddy Carlton. Tell me about his connection with the dead girl in the park."

"There is none, as far as I know. Did he *say* he was involved?" Lenny knew the detective would never tell him what Carlton said in the interrogation. Play the two witnesses against each other: that was par for the course for the Philly PD. He just hoped his foolish friend stuck to their plan and didn't go off on some ludicrous tall tale.

Williams continued. "We know your boy was in Fairmont Park last night. I want to know what he told you when he called at . . ." The detective pulled out a small notebook. "Twelve fifty-one AM."

"Okay, he called me. I was fast asleep. I didn't follow most of what he said. His voice was hard to hear, like he was in an area with poor reception, or maybe his battery was weak."

"Try to remember exactly what he said." When Lenny hesitated, Williams looked hard at Lenny and added, *"Try very hard."*

Lenny weighed the advantages and disadvantages of clamming up. If he refused to talk, it would cast more suspicion on Carlton, plus, it could mean his going to the precinct and sitting in a chair all night without any sleep. His best bet was to stick to their story and hope the cop bought it.

"He told me he saw a guy carrying a large bundle into the woods. It was dark, he couldn't make it out clearly, so he followed the person along a trail. The person dumped the bundle and took off. He determined it was a dead young woman so he called me for advice."

"Why call you?"

With a rueful laugh, Lenny said, "Everybody calls me. I'm the shoulder to cry on for every lost soul in the hospital."

"I know all about your reputation. All right, the man needs help, he calls his shop steward. What did you advise him?"

"I told him to call 911. Then I went back to bed."

The detective stared at Lenny a long minute. Lenny had searched faces enough times to know the detective was estimating how much truth was in the story. The story was true as far as it went; it just left out a few minor details.

"That's *it?*" said Williams.

"Yes that's it."

"How come he called from a pay phone and didn't use his cell?"

Lenny put on a puzzled look. "Gee, I dunno. Like I said, his voice *was* weak and broken up. Could be his battery was running out." Lenny said this with his most innocent look; a look developed from years of bluffing supervisors and negotiating with appeal boards.

"Your story still doesn't explain what was he doing in the park in the middle of the night."

"That he didn't tell me; it was a very short conversation."

"You're full of crap, Moss, as usual. You know he hunts deer in the park, we found a shit load of meat in his freezer. Meat he was trying to get rid of when I caught up with him."

"Like I said, Carlton didn't share with me the nature of his midnight sojourn. All he said was he found a body and what should he do about it."

Believing he wouldn't get any more useful information for the moment, Detective Williams gave Lenny his business card and got up to leave. At the door he paused, saying, "Don't think your innocent act fools me one bit. You're not half as simple as you let on."

As Williams strode out the front door and down to the street where his unmarked police car announced his presence, Lenny called after him, "Thanks for the compliment! I think."

In the dining room Patience said, "I knew that crazy man's hunting in the park would get him in trouble. Do you think they'll charge him for it?"

"Hunting is the least of his troubles. I think there's a good chance they'll arrest him for the murder."

Patience put her arms around him and squeezed. "What about you? How much trouble are you in?"

Although Lenny wanted to bluff his way through, he knew he couldn't get away with it, she knew him too well. "I gave Carlton advice. I'm no lawyer, but I guess they could charge me as an accessory of some sort." He tried to put on a carefree smile but couldn't hide his anxiety from the woman who saw through all his stratagems. He held her tight, relishing the warmth of her slender body and the comfort she brought him.

From his seat at the top of the stairs Malcolm heard the entire interview with the detective. He held two of his action heroes, Flamethrower and Mothman, imagining they were joining the fight to save Lenny's friend. Looking at the figures clutched in his fists, the child decided his collection was badly incomplete.

The world needed a Lenny Moss action figure.

TEN

————•————

Putting on a water resistant isolation gown, surgical cap and mask with a face shield, Lenny mumbled to himself, "There's nothing like shit raining down on your head to make a morning complete." Taking up his mop, he sang, "When it rains it rains, pennies from heaven." He'd been called from his regular area on Seven-South to a social worker's office, where a broken soil pipe had leaked waste products through the ceiling and onto her desk.

The social worker, a short, pudgy young woman with orange-red hair and the tattoo of an angel on her arm, stood outside the office, hands on her hips and eyes blazing. "Am I going to get *hepatitis?* Or *HIV?* I can't work in my office after this, it will never be clean! I stepped in that filthy water, I've been exposed to contagion. *Who's going to pay for new shoes?*"

Lenny looked down, saw that the woman was wearing hospital slippers, and continued mopping the floor. "Replacing damaged personal property isn't my department, I'm just the custodian."

"Well, how can I be sure my office is completely disinfected?" she went on.

"I'm soaking everything with a ten per cent bleach solution. That kills everything, even spores."

"But there's shit all up in the ceiling! Are you going to clean up *there?*" Her face was contorted with anger.

Lenny looked up and saw the wet, brown tiles. "I'll pull down the tiles and wipe down the pipes. Engineering will install new tiles." He picked up a teddy bear with a face smeared with stool. "What d'ya want me to do with Papa Bear?"

"Throw him out! Throw everything out!" She backed away as if just the sight of the bear would infect her. "I'm going to Employee Health, they can sign me out to go home. Nobody's making *me* go back in that office after I've been exposed to all that contagion!"

Contagion? What did she know about exposure to germs? Lenny was tempted to tell the young woman that he'd been stuck with needles left in the trash and unable to trace them back to a patient, leaving him worrying the source patient might have had AIDS or hepatitis. Or that he'd been ordered to climb into big trash containers and scrub out blood and stool. He'd washed shit off the ceiling and walls in a bathroom with an exploding toilet: the list went on and on.

39

It was a great relief when the social worker left him to do his job in peace. Finally he could focus on the work and not worry he'd end up saying something to her he would enjoy, but regret.

After taking morning report, Gary Tuttle checked Jimmy Jones's temperature, looking for signs of infection. It was up to one hundred point four: borderline fever. The white count was very low at two point four, a bad sign. It probably meant the bacteria were knocking out his immune system. Gary knew that once the immunity was gone, no amount of antibiotics would help him.

When Gary showed the findings to the doctors, Singh confirmed Gary's fears. "He is severely septic. You see his lactic acid level? And his platelets are dropping as well. The next twenty-four hours will be troublesome." He studied the latest lab results. "Shira, let's broaden his antibiotic coverage. Add an aminogylcocide."

"Is Gentamycin all right?" asked the resident.

"That will be fine. Be sure to get levels after the third dose, we don't want to shut down his kidneys." Singh bent down and spoke into Jimmy Jones's ear. "Mister Jones, can you hear me, it is Doctor Singh."

Jimmy opened his eyes, focused on the physician's face just a foot from his own. A smile formed on his face. Singh was a comfort. A solid footing in a world falling apart. He nodded his head.

"Good!" Singh slid two fingers into the patient's open palms. "Squeeze my hands for me, show me how strong you are!"

Jimmy made a weak effort to wrap his fingers around Singh's hand.

"Excellent! You are very sick, my friend, but we are giving you medication that will turn things around. Just let the breathing machine help you. All right?"

Jimmy nodded again, then he closed his eyes, as if the effort to communicate had been exhausting.

Singh went on to the next patient. He was listening to the night resident's report when he spied Farr leading his team toward him and looking as if he could spit bullets.

Reaching Singh, Farr stopped abruptly. His team spread out on either side in a flanking maneuver. Singh wondered idly if they were going to scrimmage.

"*Doctor* Singh," Farr began, approaching Singh and towering over him. "I have issued a written complaint to the chief of surgery regarding your inappropriate comments in the patient's chart."

"What comments would that be?" Singh's face held a look of boyish innocence.

"Your comments that my reluctance to perform surgery on an unstable patient would result in the patient's death. That was inexcusable, and Doctor Slocum agrees."

"I don't recall writing anything like that." Singh continued his show of innocence. Seeing that Farr didn't believe him, he added, "See for yourself. Read the chart."

A surgery resident hurried to the chart rack and returned with Jimmy Jones's chart. He placed it on the bedside table and opened it to the progress notes. Farr read Singh's notes, his lips moving as he read. When he finished the note he realized that there was no mention of his refusal to perform the required operation.

"You didn't write it."

"There was no need, sir, you went ahead and did the right thing, and, as you can see, the patient's condition is, while critical, somewhat improved. We have been able to lower his pressors a bit, and he is less acidotic."

"He wouldn't *be* critical if I hadn't been forced to open up his belly!"

"Yes, on that I believe we are in agreement," said Singh, closing the chart and removing it from the bedside table. "Had you *not* taken the patient to the operating room, he would not be in critical condition, he would be dead." Singh carried the chart back to the station and placed it in the rack.

Farr turned back to the bedside and listened while his resident gave a cursory report of the patient's condition. While listening to the resident, he saw the Daily News lying on the bedside cabinet. On the cover, a photo of a smiling Briana Nearing, the nurse murdered in the park the day before. The surgeon stopped listening to the report and stared at the picture. He turned abruptly and stalked out of the ICU without a word. His resident stopped in mid-sentence, dumbfounded, then the team broke ranks and hurried to catch up with their chief.

Watching the scene, Gary Tuttle thought that Dr. Farr was so angry with Dr. Singh he couldn't listen to the full report on his patient. The nurse picked up the newspaper with the photo of the dead nurse on the front. As he opened a drawer to tuck it out of the way, he stopped to study the photo. Was it the image of the murder victim that upset Farr, and if so, why would he care so much about the nurse's death that he left the unit in the middle of report?

Gary closed the drawer, putting the photo out of sight, but not out of mind.

After throwing the soiled items from the social worker's desk into a red trash bag, Lenny cleaned the furniture with the bleach solution, wiped it dry, then covered everything with a plastic sheet. As he taped down the corners, Tyrell from engineering came in with a stepladder.

"Yo, Lenny, you wanna help me move the desk out the way?"

"Sure Ty, let's do it."

They shoved the desk into the corner, Tyrell set up his ladder, and he soon had his head inside the ceiling. "The soil pipe's gotta be replaced. I'm gonna have to cut it and bring in new pipe."

"I figured. That's why I covered everything with plastic. I'm gonna take a break while you work on the pipe. I'll catch you later."

Lenny went back to Seven-South and poured a cup of coffee from the pot Betty made in the tiny kitchen across from the nursing station. He was looking forward to sitting in the housekeeping closet on an overturned bucket and enjoy ten minutes of peace and quite when Celeste, the ward clerk, called to him. "Hey, Lenny! You got a phone call!"

"Damn it, now what?" Lenny said, crossing to the station. His face sank as he heard the report.

"Bad news?" asked Celeste.

"I have to go, Human Resources has Carlton in his office. They're suspending him."

"Damn. That boy can't stay out of trouble."

As he hurried to Human Resources, Lenny reflected that he wasn't really surprised by the call. When your day starts with shit raining on his head, you know it can only get worse.

ELEVEN

Lenny walked up to the secretary in the Human Resources Office, saying, "Hey, Dolores. How's it going?" She shook her head and made a sour face. "I know what you mean," Lenny said. "But I can't stop to talk right now, Mister Freely is expecting me."

He found the HR Director seated in his big leather armchair, dressed in his usual pastels and a polka dot bow tie. The security chief Joe West stood ramrod straight beside his desk, a pair of handcuffs dangling at his hip and a sour look on his face. Lenny wondered, as he did so often, why West's crisp navy blue blazer didn't have the royal crest of Vlad the Impaler.

Lenny went to stand beside Carlton, who was seated on a straight-backed chair in the middle of the room. It was a cheap trick, making him feel like a prisoner being interrogated. West was all about power and making the victim feel helpless.

"Mister Moss, good of you to come on short notice," said Freely. "We are suspending Mister Rogers immediately with the intention to terminate."

"On what grounds?"

"He left work yesterday without permission. It's a black and white violation of the hospital work rules."

"That's bull!" said Carlton. "I told my supervisor I had a family emergency. He knew I was leaving!"

"Facing a police interrogation is not by any stretch of the imagination a family emergency," said Freely. "A wife in labor, a father suffering a heart attack, *those* are family emergencies."

"But he *did* notify his supervisor he was going," said Lenny, "and his supervisor didn't order him to stay."

Freely looked at West, who maintained a deadpan look.

"Claiming a family emergency was making a false statement. Lying to a supervisor is itself grounds for dismissal."

"It's not false," said Lenny. "Carlton constitutes a family of one. He had an emergency and he went home to take care of it."

Freely shook his head in disbelief. "In addition to leaving without just cause, he was forty-eight minutes late punching in this morning, and he did not phone in as required to notify the hospital that he would be delayed."

"That's 'cause the cops took my phone and had me locked up in a room all night! How'm I supposed to call in to work without a phone?"

"The police could have easily made the call for you had you bothered to ask them," said West.

"I did ask! They just gave me the run around."

Freely turned to West, who stated that he had spoken to the detective assigned to the case, and the officer had assured him that Carlton had made no effort to contact the hospital and inform them he would be late to work.

"I am inclined to believe a Philadelphia police officer over and above the word of an employee who has been disciplined multiple times," said Freely.

Lenny came back citing a prior case where a worker had been stuck in an airplane that was hours late arriving at Philadelphia and the passengers were not allowed to use their cell phones. The worker called when the plane landed, but by then it was the start of her shift.

"In that case," said Freely, "the employee had a note from the airline that the flight had indeed been delayed and that she was incommunicado. In the current case there is no such confirmation. The suspension stands."

Lenny rolled the word *incommunicado* over in his mind, wondering why Freely had to use such highfalutin words. He glanced at Carlton, wishing the man had followed his instructions and gone to Employee Health, they would have signed him out just from the high level of anxiety he was showing.

"I'll file a grievance this afternoon," said Lenny.

"As is your right," said Freely.

Lenny walked with the condemned man to his locker with Joe West following them. Carlton emptied the contents of his locker and stuffed them into a trash bag, with Joe West observing every item that came out. On the way to the loading dock, Lenny said to Carlton as soon as they were out of West's earshot, "Carlton, why the fuck did you tell your supervisor you had a family emergency? I told you to get Employee Health to sign you out! You could've told them you had chest pain. Anything!"

"C'mon, bro', I had t' get to my house before the cops did. I couldn't take all that time to wait on line for them to see me, you know how slow they are down there, all them students getting physicals and all."

"But now you don't have any cover for going AWOL!"

Carlton scuffed his shoe on the dock and kept silent. They stood a moment on the edge of the dock, Joe West watching from inside Central Receiving. Two workers began loading cans of medical waste onto a truck to be taken to the incinerator.

"The cops searched my place, anyway. I didn't get a chance to stash the meat."

44

"Forget the meat, did they charge you with anything?"

"Nope. They just asked a lotta questions and left me to sit up all night in a room."

"That could be good news. What did they ask you about?"

"It was just like you said, what was I doing in the park? They found the deer steaks from my freezer. And the hides in the garage. And the bow. They took my Mongolian bow, Lenny. They can't do that, can they?"

"Use your head, Carlton, it's a murder investigation."

"But the girl was shot with a gun!"

"You know that for a fact?"

"Hey, I seen plenty of bullet wounds in my day, I know when a gun is used. She was shot. Not a big bore weapon, either. And not at close range, there was no burn marks on her shirt."

"What else?" said Lenny, noting the detail in Carlton's description of the wound.

"They said they knew I was hunting deer in the park, they was gonna charge me for it. I told them no way, I always went down the country to hunt. I showed them my hunting license and everything." He spat onto the pavement below them. "Think they'll buy it?"

"Would *you?*" Seeing that his response had wounded Carlton, Lenny said, "Hey, as long as they don't have any witnesses to you hunting in Fairmont, I don't think they can bring a case against you."

"They asked why I called in the 911 from a pay phone. I told 'em like we said, my battery was low."

"I told them the same thing, so we have that covered."

"What if they seen the battery was good when they took my phone away?"

"So you charged it this morning. No big deal."

"Right. I charged it. Good." Carlton spat again. Lenny held back reminding him he could be cited for a public health violation, the man had enough to worry about as it was.

"Man, you think they're gonna finger me for killin' that nurse?"

"I don't think so. You didn't know her. Right?"

"Swear t' god."

"That means you don't have any motivation. You don't own a gun that could have killed her. I'm no lawyer, but it doesn't look likely, at least to me."

"I got a bad feeling about this bro'. The way they kept me so long, it looked like they wasn't gonna let me go. I guess they need t' find some bullshit evidence before they take me down."

Carlton's mention of finding evidence triggered Lenny's warning system. "Is there some kind of evidence they *could* find on you?"

"You know how they do, planting evidence, bribing witnesses, giving them suspended sentences for making shit up. I think that's what's gonna happen t' me."

"But the search of your home, that's going to come up with nothing. Right?"

"Yeah, 'cept for the deer meat." Carlton glanced at West watching from the hospital. He knew Lenny had to get back to work or he'd be in trouble. "Know what I'm gonna do? I'm heading for the deep woods. Gonna live off the land. Stay low until you can bring in the bastard that killed the nurse."

"Carlton, that's crazy. If you run, you'll look guilty."

"I look it already, don't try to say it ain't so. I mean come on, I'm a hillbilly hunter with deerskins in his shack. They'll say I'm psycho. They'll say I'm crazy enough to kill that girl."

"But how will I be able to reach you if you go to ground?"

Carlton jumped down from the dock, looked up at his friend with a sly grin, the first smile Lenny had seen since the affair began. "Look for the signs, bro'. Look for the signs." With that he strode quickly away, not looking back, his shoulders hunched, his arms close to his body as if to keep warm.

Lenny watched until Carlton disappeared around the corner of the building. *Look for the signs.* What was the crazy fucker talking about?

TWELVE

Soft pretzel and coffee in hand, Lenny entered the sewing room in the basement, where he found Moose seated beside his wife Birdie at her machine repairing torn sheets. She fed the fabric into the big machine, a leftover piece of equipment from one of the knitting mills that once operated in South Philadelphia.

"Them nurses always use a sheet to lift a patient out 'a bed," said Birdie. "It's no wonder they get torn up so bad."

"Baby, they *got* to use a sheet," said Moose. "Them Hoyer lifts are dangerous. Last month one of 'em tipped over and the patient broke his hip."

"Tell me about it. I had to defend the aide at a grievance hearing."

"There goes another lawsuit," said Moose, shaking his head. "Seems like half the city's suing James Madison over one screw up or another." He drained his coffee and threw the cup in the trash.

Lenny dipped his pretzel in his coffee. "Okay, how are we doing with the food for Jimmy's fund raiser? It's a week from Saturday, don't forget."

"We got plenty o' folks donating food," said Birdie. "An' Carlton's gonna bring a stack of his venison steaks for the grill."

"Which means," said Moose, stabbing Lenny in the chest with a finger. "You got to find who killed that nurse, or our boy'll end up in jail for sure and we won't have no deer meat for the fund raiser."

"Christ, like I don't have enough on my plate already?"

"You *know* the cops are gonna try t' pin it on Carlton," said Moose.

"They sure will!" said Birdie. "That crazy man was made to order. All his hunting and stuff, like he's some kinda wild man of the forest."

"Let's be optimistic," said Lenny. "They haven't charged Carlton with anything, all they've done is question him, which is reasonable, he was at the scene of the crime."

"They'll have the arrest warrant by sundown," said Moose. "Trust me."

"Well if he is arrested, we'll buy frozen beef patties to replace the deer meat," said Lenny. "Now can we stick to the plans for Jimmy Jones?"

"That's such a shame," said Betty. "Jimmy worked in Admitting all those years and his insurance won't cover all the costs of a lung transplant."

"The co-pay is ten thousand plus," said Lenny. "That's why we have to make this a big night."

"Stanley's gonna bring a sound system with his band," said Moose. "They gonna be the opening act, then Jimmy's group'll come on."

"He has such a beautiful voice. So warm and tender," said Betty. "It's such a shame he got so sick he can't sing no more."

"We have to be prepared for the worse than that," said Lenny. "Tuttle tells me Jimmy's condition is critical. We may have to make the party a wake instead of a fund raiser for a transplant."

"In that case we'll give the money to the family for the funeral," said Birdie. "I know he don't have no savings, all the sick time he's taken over the years."

"Lord, lord, why do the good folks always die young?" asked Betty. "There's so much suffering in the world, and here poor Jimmy takes a turn just when he was getting ready to get his self a new pair of lungs."

"I'm not saying we should give up," said Lenny. "Just be prepared. To me it looks like—"

Rap, rap, rap.

A knock on the door interrupted Lenny. It was Abrahm, from housekeeping, who stepped hesitantly into the room.

"I'm sorry, Len'ye," the Russian said. "There is problem in locker room. Young man is vury sick. He take drugs, I think. You better come see."

Grumbling, Lenny left the sewing room and followed Abrahm to the Housekeeping locker room, asking himself why was shit always raining on his head? They found Luther Moore in the bathroom throwing up. Lenny was glad he was keeping all the vomit in the toilet.

"Len'ne, our boy take some bad drugs. I am much worried about him."

"Luther, what's going on? What did you take?"

"Ohhh, man, Lenny, I'm so fucked up. I scored a couple uppers when I got t' work. I was up all night playin' cards and drinking and I ain't got no more sick time in my bank, ya know?"

"So you bought some amphetamines. Okay. Have you ever taken them before?"

"Sure, I took em plenty of times, and they never made me feel like this. I'm seein' double. Your face is even uglier than it used to be."

"Thanks, Luther."

"Everything's like blue and fuzzy, and my head is pounding like guns goin' off in my skull. I feel like I'm fixin' t' die!"

Lenny looked over the young man as he puked in the toilet again. The vomit was streaked with bright red blood. The blood worried him.

"Look. You have to go to the ER and let the doc check you out."

"No way, man, you crazy? Joe West'll fire my ass soon as he learns what I did."

"Not necessarily. Patient information is confidential. We should be able to keep it out of the hands of Human Relations."

"I don't trust 'em down the ER, man."

"You have to see a doctor, Luther, this is serious shit. Those dealers put all kinds of poisons in their drugs to boost them. Cyanide. Strychnine. You could end up dead."

"For real?"

"Yes, for real! I've dealt with this a shit load of times. C'mon, I'll go down with you."

"I don't know, I can't lose this job, man. I'll be homeless."

Seeing the fear in Luther's eyes, Lenny had no doubt that Luther was more afraid of losing his income and hence his drug connection than of losing his apartment. He didn't tell Luther that he could very well lose his job. It all depended on whether he could talk the ER physician into keeping the visit on the QT. Sometimes the doctor was cool; sometimes he had it in for the workers.

Lenny was frustrated and angry, and sad that Luther could throw a good life down the toilet for drugs. The double vision and the bloody vomit were bad signs. He hoped that this time the young man would choose life, even if it meant losing his job at James Madison. But he knew what choices addicts always made.

THIRTEEN

His arm around the sick worker, Lenny led Luther through the automatic doors into the Emergency Room, where he spotted Doctor Daniel Holden at the nursing station. Holden let out a loud groan when he saw Lenny guiding the stumbling Luther to a stretcher.

"Don't tell me you brought me another OD," said Holden, a tall, handsome physician with a long ponytail and pink scrubs. Lenny always admired a straight man that wore pink scrubs.

Holding on to Luther's arm to keep the man from falling on his face, Lenny said, "Don't shoot the messenger, Dan, I just work here."

"Who's selling all these bad drugs?" the doctor asked, approaching the stricken worker. "We have enough work with the strokes and heart attacks; we don't need the extra volume."

"I try to stay out of the drug stuff, that's security's problem," said Lenny, helping Holden lay Luther down on a stretcher. "Not that they give a shit."

"I hear security is in on the sales. That's the rumor, anyway."

"I've heard it too. How else could a dealer sell to so many workers?"

Dr. Holden shone a pen light into the stricken man's eyes. Luther tried to grab the doctor's hand and push it away.

"He was vomiting up blood back in the locker room. He's got a headache and blurry vision and he says I look ugly," Lenny explained.

"Well, at least he's not hallucinating, that's one positive sign." Holden liked Lenny. One time a young, muscle-bound paramedic bringing in a patient picked a fight with the ER housekeeper, a slightly built, quiet Vietnamese man who never got in trouble. The diminutive housekeeper kicked the EMT's ass across the ER, for which he faced immediate termination. Lenny successfully defended him, and Dr. Holden appreciated keeping a solid employee in his unit, telling Lenny, "You never know when a man like that might come in handy dealing with a violent patient."

After a quick neurologic examination, Holden said there was no sign of meningitis or stroke.

"Can you see a stroke in a guy so young?" Lenny asked.

"Unfortunately it's all too common among drug-taking men. Does he shoot up?" Holden examined Leroy's arms.

"No way I use no needle," Luther protested. "I just snort a little coke now and again, on weekends, mostly."

"And last night?"

"I did a couple lines, yeah, but that was all."

The doctor handed Luther a plastic cup. "I need a urine sample."

"No fuckin' way!"

Holden grasped Luther's shoulder and gave it a strong squeeze. "My friend, somebody in the hospital's been selling bad drugs. We had one guy in a coma for three days from the strychnine he ingested. I thought he wasn't gonna make it. I *have* to know if there were any toxic substances in what you took."

"I don't know, doc. Joe West'll have my ass in a sling, he finds out what I took."

"Nobody sees your medical records unless they have a medical need to know," said Holden.

"For real?"

"Scout's honor." The doctor made a curt Boy Scout salute.

Putting on his most serious face, Lenny said, "You need to do this, Luther. Whatever the test shows, it stays locked up in your file. If you don't get a tox screen, you could be really fucked up. For life."

Luther dropped his legs over the examining table, sat up and took the cup from the doctor's hand. With Lenny holding his arm for support, he set his feet on the floor and unzipped his fly. Lenny reached for the curtain to pull it closed, thinking, *The shit I do for people.*

But he had a bigger issue to deal with than Leroy's possible loss of employment. If a dealer was in the hospital selling bad drugs to the workers, somebody had to do something about it, and chasing down drug dealers was the one fight Lenny had no interest in taking on. As dangerous as Joe West was, he was a Keystone Cop compared to drug dealers.

Somebody had to deal with them. The question was, *who would take it on?*

Albert Brunner looked over the month's accounts. The numbers were good. *Very good.* Gross income was up fourteen per cent, and that was in a lean month for the city's economy. Even more impressive, expenses were flat. Brunner took a special satisfaction in holding down costs. He personally negotiated with all the vendors who supplied him, threatening to switch to another company if they did not meet his terms, and squeezing extras from them until they were practically in tears.

A leggy young female sales rep for athletic wear came into the spa and asked to speak with the manager. Brunner called her into his office and looked her up and down, satisfied with the view. She had long legs with good muscle tone, and blonde hair curling over her shoulders. Deciding she had been a cheerleader in school, he pictured her hair falling over her face as she went through her routine. Then he imagined her peeling off her clothes as she continued jumping and kicking and bending over, shaking her ass.

"Ahlbert Brunner," he said, taking her hand and squeezing it gently. "I am the manager of this facility." He pulled out a chair for her to sit.

"Megan Fairfield," she said, showing him a dazzling smile. "Can I show you some photos of our workout clothes? They are very stylish. And all with breathable fabrics."

Megan opened a catalogue and leafed through it, extolling the virtues of each item. Brunner hardly looked at them; his eyes were focused on the cleavage showing through her artfully unbuttoned blouse. He always enjoyed stroking a breast in a woman with well developed pecs, they never sagged.

"I must warn you, Megan, I am a very hard bargainer." He took her hand, placed it on his upper arm, and flexed. "You feel the strength in my biceps? That is the strength that I bring to everything I do! You will have to lower your prices to the bare bone if you want to do business with me."

"I'm sure we can work something out, *if* the order is large enough," she said, offering a provocative look. She removed her hand from his arm and turned her head back toward the spa. "You seem to have a room full of customers."

"I have *doubled* our number of clients in only one year! Nobody does that. Next week I will be promoted to area manager for the entire chain of James Madison spas. Then I will be ordering clothing for the whole city! One day I will take the operation to the *whole nation*. I will be in every state of the union!"

"Wow. So I guess I better get in on the ground floor so I can ride your coat tails to the top."

"Yes! Yes, you will ride to the top with me, my dear. To the top of the world!"

After a little banter, he told the young woman that he was not prepared to close a sale at the moment, but he promised her a large order when the hospital made his promotion official. As she rose and turned to go, Albert grasped her arm and spun her around to face him. Holding her in his iron grip and looking down into her face, he decided that he would ravish her before he signed her contract. He would call her to the spa at closing time, and when the gym was empty and just the two of them remained, he would tie her to one of the weight benches and thoroughly enjoy every inch and every orifice of her lithe, supple body.

"Believe me when I tell to you, I will give you much business and much pleasure." He released the young woman and watched her make her way out of the gym. Then he watched her on the video monitor as she walked to the parking lot, unlocked her car and settled into the driver's seat. As she pulled out of the lot, Albert decided that he would definitely do business with her.

FOURTEEN

Gary gently snaked the suction catheter down Jimmy's breathing tube and into his trachea, triggering a violent spasm of coughing. He applied the suction and withdrew the catheter, drawing thick, yellow-green mucous into the tubing. The nurse realized that the antibiotic was not working, the secretions were copious and purulent. He hoped they would kick in soon.

Looking up from the bedside, Gary saw a black woman dressed in a brown sweatshirt and black sweat pants watching. She had short, black hair slicked straight back, accentuating a handsome face. The Visitor card in her hand told him she was not a hospital employee.

"Can I help you?" he asked, pulling off his gloves and taking a squirt of alcohol gel from a wall dispenser to sanitize his hands.

"Hi. Is it okay if I visit awhile? I mean, I'm his sister, so if I'm not in the way—"

"Of course! Come, let me get you a chair, you can sit at the bedside."

Gary placed a chair beside the bed and let the woman settle close to Jimmy.

"I'm Gary. I'm one of the nurses."

"How do you do? My name is Gloria. They call me Glory; that's the name Jimmy gave me when we were kids. He even wrote a song with that name."

"Glory. That's nice."

Gloria looked at her brother for a moment while Gary wrote down the latest vital signs.

"Can he hear me? Can I talk to him?"

"Sure. We're giving Jimmy sedation to make him comfortable, so he's not going to answer you." When Gloria looked anxious about the sedation, Gary explained that the breathing tube was uncomfortable seated in the airway, so they routinely sedated the patients to help them tolerate the tube and to better breathe in sync with the machine.

"Jimmy?" she said, leaning in toward her brother and taking his hand. "Jimmy, it's me, Glory. How ya doing, baby brother? You hanging in there? You keeping the faith?'

Jimmy half opened his eyes at the familiar sound of his sister's voice. His breathing became labored and he set off the alarm on the ventilator. The clanging of the alarm frightened Gloria, who let go of Jimmy's hand and started to rise from her chair.

"I didn't touch anything. Honest, I didn't!" she said.

Gary drew up five cc's from the IV bag of sedation and injected it into the intravenous line, giving Jimmy an extra dose of the medication. In another minute he was breathing comfortably in sync with the ventilator.

"Patients get agitated sometimes when they hear someone they know. They want to communicate but they can't with the tube in their throat. It's very upsetting." Gary encouraged Gloria to take her seat again and just sit with Jimmy.

She settled into the chair. After a few moments, instead of speaking to her brother she hummed an old spiritual. The music was calming. Jimmy no longer bucked the breathing machine, and even his heart rate slowed to below one hundred.

Gary was pleased to see his patient finally made comfortable, whether by the drugs or by the soft music of his sister's voice. If only the singing would clear up those nasty, thick secretions.

After his suspension from the hospital, Carlton drove out of the hospital parking lot and made his way along Germantown Ave to Walnut Lane. When he turned down Walnut he saw the unmarked police car following him. Pissed off but not wanting to get pulled over, he drove carefully down through Fairmont Park into Manayunk and made his way home. When he slowed on Ridge and made the hard turn into Cresson, he smiled to see the cops struggling to make the one hundred eighty-degree turn onto his narrow street.

Carlton drove slowly past the abandoned warehouse, the narrow lane pitted and only half paved. He pulled up beside his house, noting that the police car had parked not far up the road.

Making sure that the cops hadn't left their car and walked down to his property, *the lazy shits,* he unlocked his bicycle from it's place beside the back door and slipped it into the back of the van. Then he went inside and gathered the materials he would need for the next stage: hunting knife, sleeping bag, tarp, rain gear and plenty of rope. He tossed in a bundle of waterproof matches in case there was a lot of rain.

He planned to cook game over an open fire or boil water in a sack with hot stones from the fire. He would dry game in the smoke and store it in plastic bags hanging high up in a tree. He would travel light, leaving no footprint, always moving on. Sleep in a tree tied to the trunk or find a cave and hunker down for the winter like an old bear.

He carried his duffel bag to the van. Satisfied, he got in and drove back out past the police, not giving in to the temptation to give them the finger. His escape would speak for itself.

The cops watching Carlton's street made no effort to conceal their identity. One of them, a fat tub of lard, was biting into a big sandwich. He looked annoyed that they would have to be on the move once more.

Carlton was sure that once lost the cops, he could get to French Creek, leave his van, and disappear into the wood. The police would never find him. Not those city slickers. Not with dogs and helicopters and State Troopers. It would be as if he went up in smoke and disappeared.

FIFTEEN

While his partner followed Carlton's van as it exited Cresson Street and headed down Ridge Avenue, the detective in the passenger seat took another bite out of his sandwich. "I don't care what those South Philly cock suckers say, D'Alessandro's makes the best fuckin' cheese steak in the city."

He fished out his chirping cell phone. Listened. Hung up and stuffed it back in his pocket. "How 'bout that?" he said, his mouth full of onions and greasy beef. "The DA finally got off the pot. He gave the order to arrest the son of a bitch."

"It's about time, my butt is sore sitting in this car all day. Hit the siren, I'll pull him over."

"Jesus Christ, can I at least finish my *lunch?* I missed breakfast!"

"Fine, finish the sandwich. But don't leave your scraps in the seat this time, will you, it's starting to smell."

The second cop ignored his partner's request as he took another bite. He wiped a streak of grease from his chin and licked his greasy fingers. "Mmm, mmm. Ain't nothin' like a cheese steak hoagie with lots of onions and hot peppers."

Carlton watched in his rear view mirror as the undercover cop in the unmarked car talked on his phone. When the cop hung up with a smug grin on his face, Carlton was sure he got the word to make the arrest. It was now or never. Do or die.

Riding down hill past the bus depot, Carlton drove down Ridge at a leisurely pace. At the double entrance to Route One and Wissahickon Drive he suddenly nailed the gas pedal and broke for the entrance. The van leaned heavily as it raced down the entrance. Bearing to the right, Carlton aimed his van for the drive, not Route One, but on the uphill stretch he suddenly turned off again, heading back to Ridge Avenue.

In the mirror Carlton saw the unmarked police car far behind him but closing the gap. Racing up Ridge toward his home, Carlton made the acute turn into the Wissahickon train station on the opposite side of the avenue. He drove deep into the lot and pulled into a parking spot facing Ridge. From his vantage point he watched the unmarked car pull into Cresson Street. A moment later the car came back out and raced up Ridge, lights flashing, siren blowing.

Once the sound of the police car had faded, Carlton drove back down Ridge and took the exit for Route One, avoiding the highway. Avoiding the major highways, he drove through Norristown and kept going west, skirting Valley Forge Park. He kept on through Phoenixville, fighting not to look at the police car parked on the side of the road as he passed, the driver not seeming to notice him. They must have got a description of his car by now.

Carlton watched in the rearview mirror, afraid the cop would pull out in pursuit. He was so intent on watching the police car, he nearly rear-ended the car in front of him slowing to make a left hand turn. Carlton cursed and swerved to the right. A quick glance in the mirror: the cop hadn't pulled out. Still, he could have called in the sighting. They might be sending unmarked cars to follow him.

The rest of the drive he watched every car behind him to see if any of them looked suspicious. All of them did, but nobody flashed their red light and pulled him over.

Joe West felt the vibration in his cell phone and pulled it from his hip. He read the message with deep satisfaction. *Carlton Rogers arrest warrant issued. Arrest imminent.*

This would soon turn into a double dose of good news. First, once Carlton was arraigned, West would be rid of the annoying wilderness man, so admired around the hospital. Second and even better, as soon as the District Attorney charged Moss with aiding and abetting a fugitive, West would be able to terminate the pest once and for all.

He called Freely in Human Resources and told him to convert the Carlton Rogers suspension to a termination. "Send out the certified letter, I want it in the mail today." Freely was happy to oblige. "And prepare a termination order for Lenny Moss, he's next on the list to be charged."

"Oh?" said Freely. "That will raise a lot of eyebrows. Are you confident that he will be indicted?"

"I have it on good authority that Moss spoke with Rogers on the phone the night that the girl was killed. He's a compulsive do-gooder, he's certain to have helped the suspect elude the police."

"I want to be on firm ground here, Mister West. Lenny Moss has a lot of respect at James Madison, even among some of the attending physicians."

"Count on it. I'll call you as soon as the DA files the charges." West was certain that Moss would soon be in jail. And with him out of the way the union drive at the spas would dry up and blow away. Nobody else had the drive that Moss had. Nobody else cared like he did. This time his compassion was going to be his undoing.

By the time Carlton reached French Creek it was mid-afternoon. He parked the van in the visitor's lot, grabbed his duffel bag and stood a moment in the parking lot. A ranger was talking to a young couple, pointing at a map and then toward the road heading south. The ranger didn't seem to pay any attention to Carlton. Maybe the park officers didn't get the bulletins from the State Police.

Concealing his bike behind a stand of trees inside the park, he started down a trail, walking into quiet solitude, his bag slung over his shoulder, his heart light. There was no one on the trail to notice his passing. A flock of birds passed overhead winging their way south. Carlton felt as if he were nearly as free as the birds. He had the whole park in which to roam, plus wilderness areas on either side. He would tread lightly on the earth. Leave no imprint. Become one with the creatures of the forest.

He skirted the southern shore of Hopewell Lake, walking at a steady pace, breathing deeply, letting the moist smells of the lake and the forest clear his head and flush out the foul city air. The shortening days and falling temperatures were forcing the birds south. Insects were burrowing into the ground to leave their eggs. Squirrels were hoarding their nuts for the long winter ahead.

It would not be easy, surviving in the woods. There were animals to hunt, nuts and edible plants to gather. He had the knowledge. And the courage. Carlton was confident he could survive the winter. Hell, with just one deer skinned and smoked, the meat cured and bagged and stashed high in a tree, he would have food for a month.

Carlton came upon an old oak tree, its gray trunk wrinkled and wide. It must be a hundred years old. Maybe two. Thick branches hung low over the trail. Reaching out his hand, he ran his fingers over the rough bark. He could sense the energy of the earth gathered in the tree's roots and pulsing up through the bark and out into the branches and leaves. He gripped the branch with both hands, gathering his energy from the old tree's stores.

Beyond the great tree came a burbling sound. The headwaters of French Creek where it drained the waters of the lake. He walked down a slope to the creek. It was usually a shallow stream at its origin, but recent rains had swelled it.

He pulled his cell phone from his belt and held it up to the light. Although he couldn't see the radio waves it was sending out, he knew the phone had a

GPS signal that the police were tracking. They were following his movements already, he was sure.

He reached into his backpack and pulled out a hand carved wooden boat. He dropped the cell phone into a Ziploc bag and placed it in the hold of the ship. It fit snugly. He stepped down to the creek, slipped the boat into the water and watched as it floated merrily down stream.

Carlton turned and walked in the opposite direction, singing like he was a bird in a tree calling for his mate. The Indians once used trickery to throw their pursuers off their trail. They would walk backward in their own foot prints, leap onto an overhanging branch and then jump from tree to tree until they were far from the trail. Carlton was pleased to employ a trick the ancient warriors would have approved.

SIXTEEN

Malcolm and Takia were lying on the living room rug on their stomachs watching cartoons, their chins resting on their hands. Malcolm had a bowl of breakfast cereal without milk. Every once in a while he dipped his mouth into the bowl and sucked up the colorful dry pieces of wheat, barley and sugar.

Patience was in the kitchen washing dishes. Lenny was putting a meatloaf in the oven when his cell phone warbled. It was Regis.

"Lenny, turn on the evening news, quick! Channel six. They're talking about Carlton!"

Lenny hurried into the living room, picked up the remote and switched the channel.

"Hey!" Takia cried. "We be watching somethin'!" She saw her mother glaring at her, hands on hips.

"You mean, you *were* watching."

"Whatever." Takia got up and went upstairs to the second TV in her parent's bedroom. Malcolm rolled over and sat with his back against the sofa. He figured if Lenny wanted to watch something bad enough to turn off cartoons it had to be important.

The news showed a blonde newscaster, thin, buxom, with full lips and puffed hair, standing in front of a van. *Carlton's van.* A dour uniformed police officer stood mute beside her. State and Philadelphia police cars were parked haphazardly about the lot.

"I'm standing here at the entrance to French Creek Park. You can see behind me a van. That van. . ." She pointed at the vehicle, "belongs to Carlton Rogers, the Philadelphia resident charged with the brutal murder of Briana Nearing, a nurse who worked with Rogers at James Madison Hospital."

The camera panned to the trailhead leading into the park.

"Police believe that Mister Rogers, a known hunter and survivalist, has gone into hiding in the park. At over seven thousand acres of woodland, hills and valleys, plus the adjoining Hopewell Furnace wilderness area, the police will have their work cut out for them finding this elusive suspect."

The camera went back to the newscaster, who turned to the police officer standing beside her.

"I have Detective Joseph P. Williams of the Philadelphia police department with me. Detective Williams, what finally led you to bring murder charges against the suspect?"

"We know that Mister Rogers was in Fairmont Park the night of the murder. He admitted as much in our first interview with him. What we did not realize during that interview was that the suspect had a personal relationship with the victim. We also found physical evidence in his abode that confirms he was intimately connected to the murder victim."

"Intimate relationship," said the reporter, glancing briefly at the camera. "That certainly sounds pregnant with possibilities. Can you be more specific?"

"I'm not at liberty to describe the specific evidence that we uncovered. There are other pieces of forensic evidence that likewise link him to the victim."

"Do you believe that the suspect's flight is a sign of his guilt?"

"Again, I'm not at liberty to draw inferences from flight about his guilt or innocence. I'm going to let the facts of the case speak for themselves."

The newswoman turned back to the camera, saying, "This is Candy Calloway for FIX News, reporting from French Creek. I'm now handing you over to my colleague, Larson Flood, at the home of the suspect. Take it away, Larson."

The image switched to an exterior shot of Carlton's house.

"Larson Flood here. I'm walking down the driveway of Carlton Rogers, a co-worker of the beautiful young nurse who was gruesomely murdered and dumped in Fairmont Park like so much garbage. Rogers was originally questioned as a witness to the shooting but is now wanted by the police . . . *for murder.*" Lenny grimaced at the cheesy melodrama the newsman employed in pausing before saying the words 'for murder.'

Flood continued. "The suspect is a known hunter and outdoorsman. Neighbors tell me he often has deer carcasses hanging from the rafters of that garage. We have heard unsubstantiated reports that Rogers hunted for deer not in the western national forests, but in *Fairmont Park.* The police recovered night vision goggles, which supports these wild accounts of illicit hunting within the city."

The camera followed the reporter as he walked down the driveway and around to the back of the house. The video panned the exterior of the house, then turned to show the freestanding garage. Flood pointed to the garage. "That is where the hunter skinned and dismembered his kill."

Dismembered? This fucker doesn't know shit about the butcher's trade, Lenny thought as he watched the camera following the reporter to the back of the house. He leaned closer to the television when he saw the chain that normally held Carlton's bicycle hanging empty.

"We have learned from an anonymous source in the District Attorney's office that Carlton had a prior relationship with the victim which he denied in his police interview, and that that relation was *troubled*. Our source was unwilling to give specifics, but no doubt more about their past entwinement will be forthcoming as the investigation continues. For now, Carlton Rogers is a hunted man who has fled to the deep woods northwest of Philadelphia. He is considered armed and extremely dangerous." A photo of Carlton appeared on the screen. "If you catch sight of this fugitive, do not try to apprehend him. Call 911 and allow the police to take on the dangerous task of bringing him to justice." As the camera drew back, placing the reporter in context, he ended with, "This is Larson Flood for FIX News on the trail of murder."

Lenny hit the mute button as Regis yelled into the phone. *"Lenny! What the hell we gonna do?"*

"I was afraid of this. They're making Carlton the scapegoat."

"It's just a matter of time 'fore the cops catch up with Carlton. They just as likely shoot him like a dog as bring him back to Philly. You got to find out who killed that nurse!"

Lenny felt Patience's eyes staring at him. He asked himself why did people think he was some kind of wizard-detective who could say "Abracadabra" and everything turned out right? He was just a custodian with a chip on his shoulder, not a miracle worker.

"Lenny! You still there?"

"Yeah, I'm here. Unfortunately, so is my wife." He glanced at Patience, who now had her hands on her hips and was staring daggers at him. "I'd like to help Carlton, of course, but I'm up to my nuts in shit already. I've got drug sales in the hospital, the union drive at the hospital's health clubs, the Jimmy Jones fundraiser. I can't do it *all.*"

"What're you talkin' about? You've got the whole hospital behind you!"

Lenny didn't say that it felt more like the whole hospital was pressing down on him, breaking his back. "Look. We're supposed to meet that trainer from the spa at eleven tomorrow at the diner. I'm going jogging with Moose early. We'll hook up for coffee and make some plans."

"Eleven, cool. I'll see you then."

As Lenny put some potatoes in a pot and set them to boil, he felt the weight of his commitments like never before. The campaign to organize the gym workers, the overdoses from the drug sales in the hospital, the appeal for Carlton's job, the fundraiser for Jimmy that might turn out to be a wake, and now the impending arrest. He didn't know how he was going to carry it all. And the pressure was giving him a monster headache.

Stacking the dry plates on the counter, he heard the television in the living room play the jingle for the New Body Spa and Fitness Center: *"What are your chances of keeping the weight off? Slim to none! Slim to none!"*

"Turn that off!" he yelled. Malcolm happily switched the channel to the cartoon network. Lenny felt a wave of relief as a dumb cartoon jingle played. At least it wasn't tied to all the crap at work. What a bitch that life was nothing like a cartoon, where the innocent ones always prevailed and nobody got hurt.

He looked at Malcolm lounging on the rug, one leg up on the sofa, a bowl of dry cereal beside him ready for snacking, hardly aware of the prejudice brooding in the world outside his home. He wished he could protect him from the many injustices awaiting a young African-American man, but knew he could not. His greatest fear was that when Malcolm and Takia came of age and encountered a lot of the racist shit the world would throw at them, they would be broken by it, and Lenny would be unable to heal their wounds.

After dinner and homework and some more television, Patience took the remote control from Malcolm and told him, "Time for your bath."

"S'not fair!" said the boy, but the look in his mother's eyes told him not to push it.

He submitted to the bath, and then hated to get out when the bubbles were all dissolved and the water grew cold. Malcolm lined up his boats on the edge of the tub and got out. Patience took a towel and began to dry Malcolm's hair.

"*Mom.* I can do it myself, I'm nine years old."

"You'll always be my little boy," she said, releasing the towel and leaving the bathroom. "You have to treat your hair right or you'll get a bald spot like Lenny."

"I heard that!" Lenny called from the hallway. He stuck his head in the bathroom. "Hey, you *are* growing bald! Just like me!"

"I am not!"

Patience tossed a pair of pajamas into the bathroom.

"How come I can't wear a T-shirt and jockeys like Lenny?"

"When you have muscles like him, then you can wear a T-shirt to bed."

Malcolm came out of the bathroom and flexed his muscles. Patience ignored him as she went in and hung up her son's towel. She looked at Lenny. Saw that he was bone tired.

"Why don't you jump in the bath? I'll heat up the water for you."

"That's okay."

"You're worn out, it's all over your face. The hot water will do you good. It'll relax you." She turned on the hot water and swirled it around the tub.

Hearing the suggestion, Malcolm stuck his head in the door and said, "You can play with my boats!"

"Gee, thanks." Lenny began undressing as Patience shooed Malcolm out of the bathroom. He turned off the tap, tested the water temperature with his toe, and eased himself into the water. He had to admit, his wife was right, the warmth was soothing. The weight of the day started to lighten and all the shit he'd had to deal with began to melt away.

He looked at the boats lined up along the edge of the tub, smiling at Malcolm's joy in a boy's simple fantasies. *Why can't we float away on our dreams?* He picked up the tugboat, Malcolm's favorite, and admired the detail in the casting, which even included the old car tires lashed to the sides.

Lenny let his mind wander. He imagined Carlton in the deep woods shooting deer, gathering wild vegetables and nuts, cooking on an open fire. One thing puzzled him: why Carlton would take his bicycle with him. The crazy mother had often talked about the Viet Cong carrying ammunition and heavy weapons down the Ho Chi Minh trail on bicycles. Maybe Carlton was pushing his bike through the forest loaded with gear.

Then it hit him. Carlton's wasn't a *dirt* bike, it was a *street* bike. He wasn't hiding in French Creek living like a wild mountain man, preparing for winter, he was back in Philadelphia. In Fairmont Park!

Chuckling over his friend's subterfuge, Lenny dropped the tugboat in the water and gave it a push. The little boat sailed between his legs toward his feet, which stuck out of the water like a pair of buoys.

"Rrmmm, rrmmm," he said as the tug made it's way toward a safe harbor, happy that he had a handle on Carlton his crazy schemes.

SEVENTEEN

Lenny jogged along the trail in Fairmont Park, sweat running down his face and neck. The morning sun, hazy in November mist, cast a gray light across the jogging path. Moose beside him said, "I'll catch you on the way back," and sped off around a bend, flying as if his feet had wings.

Okay, so I'm no superhero, he told himself. At least he was in better shape since Moose nagged him into running in the park with him. Now he was jogging five miles—a big advance from the days when he ran out of steam after a mile or two.

As he came down a gentle slope past a pair of dog walkers with matching white poodles, he noticed a bird in a nest nestled in the crook of a tree. The next was just a few feet above his head, which was weird, birds build nests high up and out of reach, and *they build their nests in the spring, not October!*

Stepping up to the tree, Lenny saw right away that the bird was dead. Probably stuffed, too. As he stood looking up at the bird he felt a tap on his shoulder from behind and instantly realized only one crazy person would put a stuffed bird in the crook of a tree in Fairmont Park in the Fall where Lenny would be sure to see it when he went on his weekend jog with Moose.

"What's on your mind, Carlton?" said Lenny, not turning around.

"*Damn!* How'd you know it was me?"

Lenny turned, not sure if he was angry or glad to see his friend. "You took your bike to the wilderness. It's a street bike, not a mountain bike. You rode back on it at night and hid out in the park, and you planted that dumb ass bird to get my attention."

Carlton let a big, shit-eating grin fill his face. "Yo, my brother, I *know* my ass is gonna be fine s' long as I got you on my side!"

"Yeah, well, your ass and mine are both gonna be in a sling if we don't get off the trail, the park is crawling with undercover cops."

They stepped through a thick stand of evergreens and continued over boulders and bushes until out of sight from the trail.

Shielded by a great oak tree, Carlton said, "Lenny, man, I need t' know what you got so far."

"On the murder?"

"*Yeah, on the murder!* What d'ya think?"

"I got nothing."

69

"What the fuck? You're supposed to be helping me!"

"I'm going to try and help you, Carlton. But first I have to know why the cops are saying they have evidence against you. *What evidence?*"

"It's bullshit, man, swear t' god!"

"They must have *something* if they put out an arrest warrant."

"Nothin' I tell you. Man, they plant shit all the time, you know that."

Lenny studied his friend's face, looking for signs of evasion. Carlton looked him square in the eyes when he swore there was no evidence against him. If he was a liar he was an awfully good one.

"You didn't know the girl in the park. Correct?"

"O' course not. She worked nights, I worked days. I mean, I might've walked past her mopping the floor in Recovery once or twice, but that's it, end of story."

Lenny kept silent, watching. Listening. Wondering. "And you just *happened* to be there hunting deer that night?"

"Like I always do!" Carlton heard a rustling sound. He looked behind him. Saw a squirrel jump onto a tree and scamper up to a high branch. "You gonna work on the case. Right?"

"Regis and Moose and me will work on it. But I still think you're better off giving yourself up. How will you survive on the run?"

"I'll be all right. There's game in the park. Berries and nuts and wild herbs. I'll be cool. You just find the killer before the cops get me in their sights and blow me away."

"All right. But I'll need a way to contact you. How can I find you again?"

"Look for me in your back pocket!" he said, turning and plunging deeper into the woods, leaving Lenny to ponder another of Carlton's cryptic messages.

Returning to the trail, Lenny jogged back toward the parking lot where he had started. Hearing Moose coming up behind him, Lenny looked back to see the big man running hard, arms pumping, sweat bristling on his dark face. When he reached Lenny he slowed and jogged in place.

"I talked with Carton," said Lenny.

"No, shit. Heh, heh. I gotta give that boy credit, he's got balls, all them cops looking for him."

He told Moose how Carlton had pedaled back to the city in order to throw the cops off his trail, and that he swore it was a coincidence that he was in the park the night of the murder.

"That boy always finds his self in the middle of trouble," said Moose.

"Tell me about it, all the times I defended him at the hospital."

As they came in sight of the parking area, they saw several police cars parked in the open space between the cars. Lenny looked at Moose, a tightening sense of fear coming over him. A police van roared into the lot. The doors opened before it came to a stop and a swat team spilled out onto the macadam. The heavily armored men ran single file into the park, automatic weapons held against their chests.

Detective Joe Williams walked up to Lenny, a don't-fuck-with-me look on his face. "We tracked you through your cell, Moss. It's got a GPS signal."

"What, a guy can't enjoy a run in the park?"

"Running is fine. Going off the trail, not fine."

"Okay, I confess," said Lenny, holding his hands up in the air. "I needed to take a dump, Mother Nature was calling me. I figured, the dogs do it, the deer do it, why not me? I dug a little hole with my shoe, dumped my load, wiped my ass with some leaves, and pulled up my drawers."

The detective looked at Lenny's earnest face. "Moss, you are so full of shit you couldn't bury it all in this park." Williams pointed down the trail. "First, we're going to pick up your pal. Then, we're coming for you as for aiding and abetting a fugitive."

"Bull shit! You can't prove I had anything to *do* with Carlton!"

"When we catch your buddy in the park I'll have all the proof I need."

"Oh yeah? Then you call me when you have the cuffs on him. In the meantime, I'm outta here."

Seeing that Williams was making no effort to detain him, Lenny walked with Moose to his car. Unlocking the door, he said, "Ya know, three square meals a day and no nagging wife sound like paradise to me." He settled into the seat and reached across to open the passenger door for Moose. They sat and watched more police arrive and run into the park.

"Think they'll catch him?" Moose asked as they drove up Lincoln Drive.

"No way, he's long gone. Carlton knows all about the GPS unit in cell phones. Otherwise they would have used it to track *his* phone. He's on his bike and long gone by now."

"That's good for him, not so good for you," said Moose.

"How do you mean?"

"They don't need no GPS to track you on your cell phone. Wherever there's trouble, that's where you'll find Lenny Moss."

EIGHTEEN

After dropping Moose off at home, Lenny drove to the Trolley Car Diner on Germantown Ave and met Regis Devoe. He ordered coffee and breakfast: pancakes with eggs on top, a side of potatoes and toast.

"Lumber Jack Special? Damn, you're hungry," said Regis, who ordered a bagel with bacon and cheese.

"I need to carbo-load, I just ran fifty miles with Moose."

"You supposed t' do that before you work out."

Ignoring the remark, Lenny told Regis about his encounter with Carlton in the park, including Carlton's denials about knowing the murdered nurse and having no particular reason to be there on that specific night.

"You believe him?"

"I believe him, yes, but . . ." Lenny stirred his coffee. "The thing is, not every worker tells the truth, even to me."

"O' course they lie to you, they're afraid the truth will land them in deep shit. Which it do." Regis paused. Looked Lenny in the eye. "I was always straight with you."

Lenny nodded. "If we're going to help Carlton, we have to find out everything there is to know about the victim. I mean, *everything*."

"When I get back to work I'll start asking questions."

"Moose is going to dig around, too. I want to know what Briana was into. If she did drugs. If she slept around. Was she a loner? Was she a nut case? I mean—"

He stopped when his eyes caught sight of Laticia standing a few feet from their table. The personal trainer had come in quietly and stood waiting to be acknowledged.

Lenny stood and pulled out a chair for her. "Hi! Thank you for coming out, did you have trouble finding the place?"

"No, it was easy, right on Germantown Ave." She settled into a chair, keeping her hands in her lap like a shy penitent.

"Can I get you something to eat? Some coffee? A bagel?"

"May I please have tea?"

"Of course!" Lenny flagged down the waitress and ordered the tea. He took a bite of his pancakes and washed it down with coffee.

"Listen, it's really great that you came out. I know it can be a little scary talking about joining a union. The hospital's made it clear they want to keep the spas unorganized."

"I almost didn't come. I have a little girl; I had to find a sitter."

"I'm sorry, I didn't know," said Lenny. "We would have come to your place."

"No, it's okay. She has a playmate. We swap babysitting."

The tea came. Lenny noticed Laticia took no sugar, just a little milk. She probably didn't give her daughter sugary cereals, unlike his habit of buying whatever the kids asked for.

He looked at her hands; saw neither wedding ring nor light band of skin where a woman would wear a wedding band, and assumed she was a single mother.

"How'd you get into the personal trainer business?"

"Oh, well, after my daughter was born, you know, I had to earn a living and support a child, and I've always worked out and played sports. I was in competition. The training thing seemed like a natural thing to do."

"It pays the bills."

"Yes. It pays the bills. Well, most of them. If I have to take my little girl to the doctor, it is very hard to pay the bill. And the medicine is so expensive!"

Regis explained how joining the union would give her the same benefits they had in the hospital: health insurance, sick time, and a pension. "Most of all, you'll have somebody to stick up for you and talk to your boss if they don't treat you right."

"Treat me right? Mister Brunner is a very hard man. He is cruel, even. If I talk about the union at work and he finds out . . ."

"The best way is to talk to your co-workers off site," said Lenny. "Like we're doing now. You have friends at the gym, don't you?"

"A few."

"Any of them have children?" asked Regis

"Yes, some of the girls do."

"So bring your girl over to their place and talk about how you all need to have health benefits for the kids."

"Yes, I can do that. But . . ." She held her teacup in her hands without drinking it. "I can not afford to lose my job. It would be very hard on us."

"That's all the more reason to vote in the union. Once you're a member you'll have job security," said Regis.

"You'll have *some* security," said Lenny. "There's no guarantee working for these people, but you'll be miles ahead of where you are now once you vote the union in."

"And health benefits," Regis added, handing her a few union brochures and signature cards. Laticia took them and promised to share it with her co-workers. Discreetly.

Lenny took down her phone number and gave Laticia his. "I'll text you in a week to see how it's going. If you can get one or two co-workers to come over to your place, I can meet you there. Okay? Are you all right with this?"

Laticia nodded her head. She stood, leaving the tea nearly untouched, and slipped out of the restaurant. She moved with grace, but her head was not held high. It was bowed, as though in fear. Or despair.

After Laticia left them, Lenny said, "Say, Reege, there's one thing more you could do that would help Carlton a lot."

"What's that?"

"You have friends work in the Medical Examiner's office. Any chance you can get a copy of the dead girl's autopsy?"

"I know a guy I bet could get me a copy."

"That'd be great. Carlton said she was shot, but we need to know all the details."

As Lenny paid the bill, he couldn't stop himself from worrying that the more he dug into Briana Nearing's murder, the closer he'd be to a jail cell of his own. It was easy for Patience and the others to urge him on with the investigation; *they* weren't facing possible charges of obstruction of justice or aiding a fugitive. Not to mention co-conspirator to murder.

As much as he felt bound to help Carlton, Lenny was troubled that his family might lose him to prison, and there was no way *he* was going to run away to the woods and make like Tarzan.

NINETEEN

Lenny turned the ten o'clock news on the television in the bedroom while Patience slipped into a nightgown. The news opened with images of a SWAT Team leaving Fairmont Park. A somber Larson Flood looked into the camera and said, "Earlier today, a team of Philadelphia police restricted joggers and dog walkers from Fairmont Park as they searched the rugged terrain for a suspected killer."

The image switched to a pair of police vans with cops standing around the entrance to the park. Flood's voice continued. "This morning a Philadelphia police SWAT team staged a massive dragnet in Fairmont Park. They were looking for Carlton Rogers, a suspect in the brutal murder of Nurse Briana Nearing, who worked with the suspect in James Madison University Hospital. Rogers is a hunter and survivalist; a man proficient with weapons of all types, from the hunting knife to the crossbow, the sniper's rifle and the animal trap."

The camera panned to a pair of German shepherds barking and pulling on their leashes ahead of more police entering the park. "The police scoured the entire length of the park, including the surrounding neighborhoods of Germantown, Mt. Airy and even Chestnut Hill. '"

"*Even* Chestnut Hill?" Patience exclaimed. "What do they mean, there are no criminals in that hoity-toity part of town? Ex-*cuse* me." She turned from the television. "Do you think they'll catch him?"

"Not in the park they won't, he was already gone."

"How can you be sure?"

"Because I know Carlton. He's not dumb enough to stay in an enclosed area like Fairmont. He knows they'll have dogs on his scent and eventually find him. He got on his bike and is already miles away."

"I understand he's out of the park, but *where* did he go?"

"I don't know, I'm not a mind reader! I just hope it's far away from me, I'm in enough trouble with Joe West as it is."

When the news went to commercial, a slim, pretty young woman in a leotard exclaimed she had lost fifty pounds at the New Body Spa and Fitness Center. "And I'm keeping it off with my own personal trainer, because my chances of staying in shape all by myself would be, *Slim to none! Slim to none!*"

A choral group sang the theme song *Slim To None* as the young woman did a cartwheel. Lenny turned off the set in disgust.

"I am so sick of those stupid commercials."

"They are annoying," said Patience. Would you do my back?" She lowered her nightgown, bowed her head and relaxed as Lenny gently rubbed lotion into her smooth, dark skin.

"You smell nice," he said, kissing the nape of her neck.

"It's the free cream from the gym. I love it. The redness and irritation in my hands is gone completely. Can you get me some more?"

"I'll see what I can do. They'll probably want me to sign up for a year's subscription."

"They're hungry for new customers, they'll give you lots of freebies," she said, settling into bed and picking up a magazine. "Poor old Carlton. He always lands in the middle of trouble." She adjusted the reading light over her head while Lenny picked up a book. As he found his place and started to read, she began to softly hum to herself. Lenny could usually ignore her little musical quirks, but this time he found it irritating.

Lenny put down the book and groaned, saying, "Not *that* tune! *Not the theme song for Slim to None!*"

Carlton slipped silently down the stairwell to the hospital subbasement. His feet, shod in soft moccasins, made no sound as he reached the landing. He opened the door, saw the empty hallway, and made his way along the corridor. He found a large cardboard box propped against the wall of the corridor, empty and flattened, waiting to be sent out with the recycling. He carried the box to one the cages where the hospital stored materials long term.

From his pocket he withdrew a large key ring with over thirty keys. He selected the key for the storage cage, unlocked it and entered. The area was damp and moldy. He reached up to the single bare bulb, unscrewed it, shook it vigorously, then put it back. The shaking had destroyed the filament, leaving the room in shadow.

Carlton opened the empty box and taped one end shut. The other end he left unsealed. He positioned it behind a stack of boxes, out of sight from the front of the cage. The box was large enough for him to sleep in. He would bring a hospital blanket and pillow on another trip. Food would be a problem, it would attract the rats, but he'd dealt with bigger threats than rats.

He stood for a few minutes listening. There was utter silence. That was a good sign. During the day workers came for supplies, but at night nobody entered the area. It was the perfect place to sleep. And to plan his next move.

He slipped out of the cage, locked it, and went out to hunt.

TWENTY

While strips of bacon sizzled in a skillet, Lenny dropped two eggs into a bowl, added some salt and a dash of hot sauce, poured in a little condensed milk and beat the mixture until it was frothy. Then he dropped four slices of bread into the egg batter. Malcolm sat forward in his chair watching, his mouth watering.

Lenny removed the bacon strips from the pan and dropped them on paper towels to drain. He gently lowered the slices of bread into the bacon fat, being careful not to splatter any grease. "You want melty cheese in your sandwich?" he asked, as the fat bubbled and spat beneath the bread.

"*Yeah!*"

"Okay." After a minute he flipped the slices of bread, revealing deeply browned surfaces bubbling with bacon fat. Lenny scooped some soft cheese from a jar and spread it over two of the browned slices. He dropped a few bacon strips over the cheese. When the cheese began to run into the fat, he removed the bread to plates and made a pair of thick sandwiches, the cheese oozing out the sides.

As Lenny placed a sandwich in front of Malcolm, the boy said, "What about the syrup?"

"You want syrup on top of all that?"

"*A course I want syrup, it's French toast!*"

"Okay." He got out the syrup and poured a generous amount on both their sandwiches.

Lenny poured syrup over the sandwich. As Malcolm picked up his fork and knife and cut off a big chunk of sandwich, Patience and Takia came into the kitchen. Patience took out a box of whole wheat cereal for herself and Cheerios for her daughter, while Takia brought the skim milk from the fridge.

Settling down at the kitchen table, Patience was about to pour the skim milk over her cereal when she saw Malcolm's sandwich, now partly eaten, the cheese dribbling out from between the slices of bread, the bacon sticking out the sides, and the maple syrup glistening in the bright kitchen light.

"*What in god's name are you feeding my son?*"

Lenny looked perplexed. "It's French toast."

"*French toast?* Nobody from France eats crap like that!" Malcolm popped another piece in his mouth and rolled his eyes around and around. "You're clogging up his arteries and he's only nine years old!"

"I'll get him a script for Lipitor," said Lenny. "A lot of kids are on it these days."

He popped a piece of sandwich into his mouth and winked at Malcolm, who chewed happily.

Before Patience could reply the phone rang. She read the caller ID and handed Lenny the phone.

"Hey, Reege," Lenny said, his mouth full of French toast.

"What's the plan for today?"

"*Today?* Today I'm making breakfast for the kids and then I'm taking them to the park. And I'm turning my cell phone off."

"You can't do that, man, what if the cops grab Carlton?"

"Then he'll get a lawyer and we'll work on the investigation."

"Damn, I was thinking we'd visit a couple of nurses worked with Bri. I got their addresses and everything."

"This is my day off, you know what I mean? *Off.* Why don't you take Salena and the baby to the park, it's a nice day out there."

"She wants me t' go with her visitin' her moms."

"I feel your pain, but I still can't help you." He listened to the silence for a minute, tempted to give in, but saw Patience staring daggers at him and held back. "Okay, look, if you want to do something, call that friend of yours in the Medical Examiner's and see can you get the autopsy."

"Yeah, okay, I'll roll on down there. I'll bring it to work on Monday."

"Good. Monday. In the meantime, don't call, I won't be here."

As he hung up the phone, Patience leaned over and kissed him softly on the mouth.

"What was that for?" he said, glad her displeasure with his cooking had blown over.

"Nothing." Patience reached for his empty plate.

"Wait, there's still some syrup left!" Lenny grabbed a fresh piece of bread and soaked up the last of the syrup, while Malcolm looked on with approval.

Dressed in a scrub suit and cap and a surgical mask, Carlton pushed a dust mop into the Recovery Room and began sweeping the floor. One nurse was in the tiny day room having coffee, the other had her head buried in a fashion magazine. There was only one patient on a stretcher, sleeping soundly.

Reaching the medication cabinet, Carlton pulled the narcotic ledger out and slipped it into a trash liner. He made his way along the floor until reaching the back of the Recovery. There he stashed the broom and carried the trash bag into a men's bathroom across the hall. Seated on the commode, he ran his finger down the list of patients, comparing the drugs administered and the nurse's signature. He was glad that the nurses had to print as well as sign their names, it made his task much easier.

Carlton compared the drugs Briana administered with other nurses' work. The information confirmed that Briana never administered narcotics. Carlton wanted to know if Briana had been using drugs. Now he was sure she had been clean.

He slipped the book back into the bag and returned it to the medication cabinet, the nurse on duty still studying the latest dresses and shoes in her magazine. Then he left, an unnoticed minion cleaning floors.

He couldn't wait to tell Lenny what he'd found.

Albert Brunner looked over the statistics one last time. The numbers were impressive. He had grown the business, nearly doubling the spa's income in a little over a year. On Tuesday, when he went before the Board, he was certain that they would appoint him manager for the entire chain of spas. How could they not? He proved he was the best man for the job. The *only* man for the job.

Still, a seed of doubt nagged at him. His English was not crisp and fluid as it was in the American-born managers. He didn't attend the high-class business schools. No MBA from Wharton for him, he had earned his degree online, and even that had been an arduous process.

His biggest fear was that the board would pick a relative of one of the senior doctors or administrators. Some young snot in a silk suit he couldn't even fill out, with one of those impressive resumes and honors degrees. Somebody born to wealth and assured of success.

Brunner tried to brush the negative thoughts away. He had climbed so high, accomplished so much in his ten years in America. Surely there would be no stopping him.

He went out into the gym, now empty, stripped off his shirt and began his workout. The sweat and the strain would clear his head. In a few days he would command an entire army of employees who submitted to his commands. Who feared the sound of his voice on the phone. Who understood that there were the few who must lead and the many who must follow. Who must carry out their orders without question. Even if it is to the death.

TWENTY-ONE

B efore starting his shift in the kitchen, Moose packed a plate with biscuits and bacon, filled a thermos with coffee, and hurried to the Recovery Room. The night shift was still on duty, the nurses finishing their notes, the aides emptying the Foley bags and entering the volume in the twenty-four hour flow sheets.

Moose stood in front of the nursing station, pulled off the lid, and said, "I thought you'd be hungry, so I brought a little breakfast."

The nurses and aides cooed with delight. "Put it in the back," said Agnes, a senior nurse with streaks of gray in her hair and crows feet around her eyes. She followed Moose back to the tiny lounge. As Moose poured her a cup of coffee, she asked him what was the occasion for the special treatment.

"Can't I just want to share the love?" he asked.

Stuffing some bacon into a biscuit and rolling her eyes, Agnes said, "Come on, Moose, everybody knows you and Lenny are working on Briana's murder. You came for information."

"You're right, I did. You feel like talking?"

"If it helps you find the son of a bitch murdered our Bri, hell yes. What do you want to know?"

"Anything and everything. What was she like?"

"Well, you should know first off our girl was on probation for drugs."

"Okay. For how long?"

"Oh, she was put on restricted duty about five, six months ago."

"Restricted. What's that mean?"

"It means we were supposed to not assign her to patients who were on opiate drips. You know, continuous infusions of morphine or Fentanyl. It's too easy to remove some of the IV fluid and replace it with saline."

"And Bri—she was doing okay with the probation?"

"Oh, yes. She seemed to be doing great. She was short-tempered sometimes, but that's natural for somebody trying to get off drugs. I mean, it didn't make her any less popular with the doctors, if you know what I mean."

Agnes pointed to a photo on the bulletin board. It showed staff members at a Christmas party. Briana was wearing a low cut dress that showed off her figure. "All the docs wanted to get with her, but the word was she saved herself for one of the Attendings."

He studied the photograph on the bulletin board. Briana had the kind of figure most men hungered for: full breasts, narrow waist, full hips and long legs. Her face was as lovely as her body was alluring.

"She was a looker."

"Yeah, but she wasn't looking so good the last couple of months. She was losing weight, and she was irritable some of the time, like I said."

"So who was the lucky doctor?"

"I never heard, but you can believe it was somebody who could buy her expensive things. Briana wasn't going to waste her time with a lowly resident with big debts to pay off."

Moose considered the possibility that a jealous boyfriend had killed Briana. He knew some of the surgeons had big egos and even bigger tempers. It could be one of them lost it when she traded up to a higher class sugar daddy, but it didn't look like the Recovery Room nurses could help him find out who.

Before he left, Moose asked the nurse if he could make a copy of the photograph. Agnes unpinned the photograph and handed it to him, saying, "If it helps find out who took her life, you can have it."

Lenny brought his bucket to the sink and was about to fill it with water when he saw a piece of yellow paper folded in the bottom of the bucket.

"What the hell" he mumbled, plucking the paper from the bucket and unfolding it. Scrawled in a shaky hand were the words, *Girl was clean.* In lieu of a signature there was a sketch of a dog, one foreleg raised, pointing.

Carlton was in the hospital now. It was just like that fool to identify his message with a hunting dog instead of a name. "I'll be in your back pocket," he said when they met in the park. Lenny realized he should have taken the crazy man at his word, because now he was right here, in the belly of the beast.

Lenny was getting enough heat from West already. The Gestapo commander would go ballistic if he got wind of a wanted man running around the hospital. West would accuse Lenny of harboring a fugitive the one time he was an innocent bystander. And just what did the crazy man mean by *Girl was clean*?

He didn't have time to puzzle over the note, Celeste the ward clerk was calling him to the desk. Human Resources was on the phone. They were firing Luther Harris, the worker he had convinced to go to the ER for a drug overdose.

Looked like it was gonna be raining shit every fucking day.

TWENTY-TWO

When Lenny entered the office of Human Resource, he saw Simon Freely, the Director, seated at his desk. Joe West stood ramrod stiff beside the accused, Luther Harris. Luther was seated in a straight-backed chair in the middle of the room, looking like he was facing his execution.

"I'm surprised you don't have him bound and gagged," said Lenny. "With a blindfold over his eyes."

West said, "You're a day late and a dollar short, Moss. Mister Harris was on duty Friday under the influence of illegal drugs." West dropped a copy of Luther's lab reports on the desk. "It's cut and dried. You come to work high, you're terminated."

Mr. Freely added that it wasn't the first time Luther had been cited for drug use. He'd been on probation the year before. Only the fact that he finished the year without another violation made it possible for him to continue working at James Madison.

Luther was seething with anger, but more at Lenny than at the chief of security or the Human Resources Director.

"My body is my private property!" cried Luther. "You got no business knowing my personal business!"

"Privacy does not obtain if the blood samples are taken while you are on duty," said Freely. "Ask your steward here, he will tell you the contract is quite clear on this point. Had you come to the Emergency Department on your day off, that would be a different matter entirely."

"You should 'a told me that, Lenny! You should 'a let me be!"

Lenny kept silent. He didn't want to debate his tactics with Luther in front of the security chief or Freely. As West collected Luther's hospital ID and ordered him to clean out his locker; Freely explained he could come to the security office at the end of the week and pick up his terminal paycheck.

As Lenny walked with Luther to his locker in Housekeeping, Luther demanded to know how West heard about his drug use. Lenny explained that West had snitches everywhere, one of them must have got a favor for giving up the information. He tried to mollify the young man, promising he would file a grievance that day, but Luther wasn't appeased. He slammed his locker, then kicked it for good measure.

As Luther reached the loading dock accompanied by a security guard, Lenny tried to hold out hope for the fractured young man. A trash truck was picking up the medical waste from the red dumpster to take it to the incinerator. Luther stood on the edge of the bay watching.

"You shit on me, Lenny, I'm gonna shit on you." Staring daggers at Lenny, he added, "You know what my pops always said. Don't get mad, get even." He jumped down from the loading dock and strode off toward Germantown Ave without looking back.

Lenny didn't bother repeating his promise to file the grievance, it was clear that Luther wouldn't listen. Or care.

Albert Brunner stood behind a full-figured redhead in her forty's as she pulled down on the bar attached to the fixed weights. Each time she extended her arms, the weights clanked as they fell back to their resting position. Just an inch taller than the woman, he was close enough to smell her hair and her sweat. There was nothing sexier than a woman bathed in sweat. He enjoyed licking the salty moisture from a woman's body. This one, although not a ripe young female, still had good muscle tone. He had given her extensive instructions on strengthening her pectoralis group in order to keep her breasts from sagging. The work was paying off; he intended to reap the benefits of his instruction in the near future.

Seeing two hospital workers come in for their exercise, Brunner made a point of stationing himself within hearing distance of them in order to pick up any talk of politics or union matters. There was none, just the usual banter about their petty jobs and their pointless dreams.

Brunner kept a watchful eye for Lenny Moss, certain that the pest would return to the gym soon. All the information about him online added up to a stubborn, arrogant busybody who abused his workplace to garner fame and publicity from his supposed exploits. Moss exhibited the worst form of anti-authority prejudice. When he returned to the Chestnut Hill spa in a vain attempt to spread his trade union poison, Brunner would be ready to snuff him out like a candle pinched between two hard fingers.

The scared little minions in James Madison tolerated Moss's mouth. No surprise, those managers were timid mice, like the prissy fool in Human Resources, Freely. If only all the leaders were like Joe West. There was a man of hardened steel. There was somebody who knew how to deal with troublemakers.

Brunner was as ready for Lenny Moss as he was certain that Moss would not even see his punishment coming.

Catching up on his work, Lenny mopped a section of the floor, setting yellow caution signs out to direct passersby around the floor. A gaggle of doctors and students came through. The Attending physician was discoursing on an ethical conundrum and not noticing the yellow sign.

"Hey," said Lenny. "Watch you don't trip and fall, I don't have liability insurance."

Seeing the sign, the physician led his crew around to the dry side of the hallway without a break in his exposition. Lenny admired the man's powers of concentration. Lenny moved his bucket down the hall and began mopping another section, enjoying the rhythm of the work; the physical push and pull. He wished he had time to work the buffer and really put a shine on the floor, but there was too much to do. Too many tasks he hadn't had time to—

"Lenny, my main man, how's it hangin'?"

Lenny didn't have to turn around to know it was Tony O coming up behind him. The hospital's resident loan shark, a messenger who managed to spend most of his day carrying nothing more than debts, came up to Lenny and held out his hand. His big fist squeezed Lenny's hand to the point of pain. Lenny had strong hands, but they were as fragile as Malcolm's compared to Tony.

"Hi, Tony. How's business?"

"Not what it should be, one of my customers skipped out on me."

"That's a shame. You can't find him?"

"Nah. Gone beyond my reach. Listen up, I just stopped by to tell ya, I got no hard feelings about your boy, Carlton."

"How's that?"

"Ah, of course!" Tony smacked the side of his head. "Your boy wouldn't tell you he was into me for five large. That's a lotta bread for him, he usually didn't come t' me for more than a hundred."

Lenny wondered why Carlton would need so much money from Tony O, but he knew not to ask. Tony had sources even Lenny couldn't reach, and he played his cards close to his chest. If the loan shark knew what the money was for, he wasn't going to give Lenny the information unless Lenny had something to offer in return.

"Anyways, seein' as your boy's on the lam, I know he won't be good for it, so when you see him tell him he don't have t' watch his back on account o' me, I'm writing off the loan."

"Gee, that's really decent, Tony, I'm glad to hear it. Carlton has enough on his mind."

Tony slapped Lenny hard on the back, nearly knocking him off his feet. "You know what Tony O always says: any friend of Lenny Moss is a friend o' mine!"

"I'm not sure I have too many friends left in this place, Tony, but it's kind of you to say so."

Tony laughed long and hard as he walked away. Lenny could hear the laughter even when Tony had crossed the double doors into Seven-North.

Lenny resumed his mopping. Suddenly he froze in place, a wicked smile forming on his face. He recalled that Tony had said, *When you see him.* That could only mean that Tony *knew* Carlton was in the hospital. No surprise, Tony had snitches in every department, even security. Especially security. They were the ones who allowed him free range throughout the hospital to ply his trade. But forgiving a loan for Carlton was a surprise. What did it mean?

What was Tony getting in return?

TWENTY-THREE

Lenny entered the sewing room, coffee in one hand, soft pretzel in the other, relieved to see his friends sitting there. He always felt a relief coming into Birdie's basement sanctuary. The bosses never entered, it was some sort of unwritten understanding. The sewing room was his refuge and clubhouse rolled into one.

After unfolding a battered metal chair and greeting Birdie, Betty, Moose and Regis, he asked how they were doing with the fund raiser for Jimmy Jones. Birdie told him the decorations and the cake were lined up. Betty said, "I sold sixty tickets already, and we still got nearly a week 'til Saturday."

"Nobody sells like you do, Boop. That's great."

"I just pray poor Jimmy gets his self better and they give him the new lungs," she said.

"I hear he's not doin' good," said Moose.

"No, he's not. Tuttle tells me he has pneumonia, and with his lungs in bad shape to begin with, an infection on top of all that damage . . ."

"Such a beautiful man," said Birdie. "With such a beautiful voice. He could've been big, like the Four Tops, even."

"He knows he's tops with us," said Betty. "That's a comfort and a blessing."

Moose pointed out they would be short of meat if Carlton was still wanted by the police. "He was supposed to bring twenty pounds o' venison." Lenny suggested they make it up with extra beef and turkey patties.

"How's about I make some o' my big mushroom burgers?" Moose said.

"*Mushroom burgers?* That's gross," said Regis. "I want red meat in my burger."

"That's the problem with black folks diet," said Birdie. "All that beef and pork and fried foods, it's tearing up our bodies."

"Hey, I eat bacon and cheese, too," said Lenny, "and I'm proud of it."

"That's nothing to be proud of," said Birdie, wagging a finger at Lenny. "You got to teach those children good habits!"

"So Patience keeps telling me."

Seeing that the plans for Jimmy's fundraiser were more or less on track, Lenny asked had anybody heard any more about Briana Nearing. Moose told him he learned from one of the nurses in Recovery that Briana was working on probation for drug use. "She was doing okay, s' far as the nurse could tell."

"Her urine tests must have been clean or they'd have pulled her from duty," Regis said.

"Druggies have ways to get around the testing," said Lenny. "I'll talk to somebody in the program." He dipped his soft pretzel in mustard and asked Regis if he was able to get a copy of the autopsy report.

"I got it right here," said Regis, pulling an envelope from his bag and handing it to Lenny. "They don't got the drug tests back, though. That takes the city a week."

Lenny spread the photographs out on Birdie's sewing table as the others gathered around him. "Damn, she was beat up." He looked over the pictures as Regis read the report out loud. It described the general appearance of the body and the wounds to the face and chest.

As Regis continued reading, Moose studied the photos of the body. "Blunt trauma to the occipital and parietal bones." Regis pointed to the areas at the back and the sides of the head. "Bullet entry at the fifth intercostal space shattered the left fifth rib, perforated the left ventricle, and lodged in the posterior chest wall." He pointed to the bullet wound in the dead girl's chest. "The cause of death was cardiac rupture with resulting vascular collapse."

"So she was beat up and shot," said Lenny. "No surprise there."

"Yeah, but this is. It says a male fetus, approximate twelve weeks gestation, was in the uterus." He looked up at Lenny. "That means she would've had a son. If she lived."

"Christ." Lenny stared at the photos with deepening sorrow. "What sort of monster snuffs out a beautiful young mother and her unborn child?"

"The children always get hurt," said Birdie. "Always."

Moose picked up one of the photos of the corpse. "Somethin' ain't right," he said. He took out the photo from the Christmas party that Agnes had given him in the Recovery Room and placed it beside the autopsy image. "Here's what she looked like when she was clean last year. Or least ways she was healthy."

They all studied the full-figured young woman in a low-cut dress, her full lips scarlet and smiling, one hand holding a drink, the other hand on the shoulder of a hunky doctor.

"The girl looks happy," said Birdie. "What a shame to end up the way she did."

"Drugs always take you down," said Moose. "But that's not what I'm talkin' about. Look-a here."

"What is it, Moose?" asked Lenny, turning his attention from one photo to the other.

90

"Check out her figure from the Christmas party."

Lenny studied the picture. "She's lost some weight, unless she was padding her bra in the earlier picture."

"That ain't no padding," said Moose, picking up the same revealing photo.

"Crack addicts lose a lot of weight," said Regis. "I seen it in an autopsy."

"Yeah, they do, but her bein' pregnant, she should be puttin' on weight, not losing it," said Moose.

Lenny placed the photos and the report back in the envelope. "I'm going to show the photos to a doctor who knows about drug abuse. I'll go over on my lunch break." Sealing the envelope with the metal closure, he added, "Oh, you all should know Carlton's in the hospital."

"You're shittin' me!" said Regis, laughing and slapping his leg.

"The crazy bastard left me a note in my wash bucket. The note said, *Girl was clean*. I knew it was him, it had a drawing of a hunting dog pointing.

Moose was equally delighted. "Heh, heh. That man better keep his ass out of Joe West's face. I hear West has a shoot to kill order out on Carlton."

"That's a load of crap," said Lenny. "Just because he's an ex-cop doesn't mean he's going to go blasting away inside the hospital."

"Don't forgot how come West left the force," said Moose.

When Regis gave Lenny a puzzled look, Lenny said, "He shot an unarmed suspect. A young black kid, who survived, luckily. It turns out the kid was a cousin of the mayor, otherwise they would have just covered it up."

"I don't remember him bein' charged with anything," said Regis.

"He wasn't charged, he was allowed to resign and he got the job here."

"Hey," said Regis, following Lenny to the door. "We're still givin' out union cards at the gym after work today, right?"

Lenny sighed. He felt the weight of his commitments pressing down on his shoulders. Too many promises. Too many obligations. But he'd given his word.

"Yeah, we can go. I'll meet you at my car after we punch out."

Regis went off to the morgue, Moose and Lenny walked to the stairwell. When Lenny stopped at the elevators, Moose said, "Ain't you takin' the stairs? You can't stay lean an' mean riding them cars."

"Not today, Moose, I'm beat to shit. Next time."

"Okay. Just don't make a habit of it."

Lenny stepped into the elevator. Riding to the seventh floor he reminded himself what a good friend he had in Moose. He considered asking Moose to join him and Regis at the gym to give out union cards, but the spa had a very small workforce, two would be more than enough to talk to the workers coming out. He wanted to keep things quiet and under control. Two on the sidewalk would be inconspicuous. Three was almost a crowd that would catch attention, and he wanted to keep things nice and peaceful.

Joe West slapped a photo of Carlton Rogers on the desk, saying to the security guard who was watching the video monitors, "Scan this face and search for it with the new facial recognition software on all the security recordings." The program, newly received from a friend in Homeland Security, compared the facial patterns in a photo to every individual frame of a video recording. With eighteen security cameras continuously recording images at twenty-four frames a second, the computerized system captured millions of frames a day. West knew the analysis would be a slow process, unless they were lucky and Carlton showed up in one of the early tapes.

As West watched the program counter tick off the number of frames it had reviewed, the guard said, "Sir, do you really think that this fugitive would be dumb enough to try and return to James Madison?"

"Sure he would. Perps like him need to return to familiar ground. He'll come back all right. And I'll be ready for him." With one hand resting on the butt of his gun, he let the fingers of his other hand stroke the stainless steel handcuffs dangling from his belt as he watched the numbers click over and over, a hungry shark listening for the flutter of a hapless swimmer asking to be eaten.

TWENTY-FOUR

Lenny waved to Marge at the Employee Health reception desk. "How ya doin' today?" he asked.

"My husband's driving me to drink," she said, sadly shaking her head. Marge was a white-haired nurse with swollen ankles and puffy eyes waiting to finish her thirty years and retire. "He keeps telling me I need to lose forty pounds on account of my sugar is up."

"That's love for you."

"*Love? Hah!* He's just doin' it because I wake him up two, three times a night when I get out of bed to go pee."

"You could sleep in separate beds."

"I don't know. We've been sleeping butt to butt for so long, my ass would catch cold without him beside me."

"Yeah, I see what you mean. Listen, is Alex in?"

"Sure. Go on in, he's just catching up on his charting."

Lenny went back, knocked twice on the open door and stepped into Dr. Alex Primeaux's small office in Employee Health. He saw the diplomas on the wall and the stack of medical journals on the desk threatening to fall over. As he had so many times before, Lenny suppressed a smile over the secret he and Alex shared about the doctor's past; a secret they had long ago agreed to keep to themselves.

"What can ah do for you this time?" Alex said in his Carolina drawl.

"I've got kind of a delicate situation."

"Not like all the other situations ah guess."

Ignoring the crack, Lenny said, "You know about Briana Nearing, the nurse who was murdered in the park."

"O' course ah do, everybody's talkin' about it. Terrible thing. I'm not surprised you're investigating, I read in the paper the police suspect somebody from the hospital."

"They charged a guy from housekeeping, Carlton Rogers. I know that he didn't do it, but the only way to get the police to drop the charges is to find the one who really killed her."

"And you want to know about the dead girl."

"That's it. Know the victim, you're half way to knowing the killer. Don't you agree?"

"In theory, sure. The police have already been to me for a copy of her medical records. But they had a legal basis for examining them. You don't."

"The laws were written to protect the guilty; you know that, Alex."

Alex grasped the edge of his desk and leaned back. "Politics is not my forte, Lenny. You know that, too."

Lenny considered what it would take to get Alex to open up. From countless interviews with reluctant witnesses he knew you had to find the right trigger that will loosen a stuck tongue. He took out the photos from Briana's autopsy and laid them out in front of Primeaux. "I understand your wanting to stay out of trouble, but you know sometimes you just have to bend the rules when the situation calls for it." The physician's face sank as he stared wordlessly at the gruesome images.

"I know you want to see that justice is served," Lenny went on. "So how's about we go to that old trick detectives use when they're talking to a reluctant witness. I'll make a statement, and as long as I'm not too far from the truth, you say nothing. If I say something that's flat out wrong, you can contradict me. Okay?"

With a sigh, Alex gestured for Lenny to continue.

"Okay. First, I heard from her co-workers that Bree had been a drug user and was working under restriction."

He looked at Alex, who kept a poker face, saying nothing. He liked the doctor's integrity.

"Second, she reported to you for random drug testing. That's standard operating procedure for Employee Health. I know, I've defended plenty of workers in the rehab program."

Primeaux sat back, hands folded in his lap, his face in neutral.

"Her tests were all negative. They had to be or she would have been taken off duty and suspended, which she wasn't." He glanced at Primeaux, pleased his friend was cooperating, even if it was in a totally passive manner.

"She was about twelve weeks pregnant, which would have made her needing to stay off drugs even more important to you, her doctor. To her, too, I would hope."

"Hold on a second. Are you sure about the pregnancy?"

"The Medical Examiner found it when he did the autopsy."

"You have the ME report?"

Now it was Lenny's turn to not answer a question. He opened an envelope and placed the report on the desk. Chuckling, Primeaux spread the photographs out, telling himself he shouldn't be surprised at anything Lenny did.

"We never tested Briana for pregnancy. She didn't request it, and she was showing no overt signs." "I can understand her wanting to keep the pregnancy secret," said Lenny, "but there's one thing that's puzzling." He pointed to one of the autopsy photos and told Alex how Briana seemed to have lost some of her figure. "Shouldn't she be putting on weight with the pregnancy?"

Puzzled, Primeaux pulled up the dead woman's health record on his computer. "My, my, her weight was down eleven pounds at her last visit. Normally, a pregnancy *increases* the weight. Drug addiction can cause an imbalance in glucose storage and fat deposition." He looked at the photos one last time. "Ah really believed she was clean, all her urine tests were fine. . . "

"Could she have been sick?" Lenny asked.

"Possible. Some forms of pituitary disease can interrupt estrogen production. Certain cancer drugs block them, but I don't believe she was receiving chemotherapy."

"I didn't see any sign of cancer in the autopsy report," said Lenny.

"Then she was probably taking drugs of some kind. I'd have thought her being pregnant would make her want to stay clean, but you know how addicts are." Alex started to fold the photos into a pile when he stopped, picked one up and examined it closely. "She underwent a severe beating. What does that tell you?"

"It tells me that the killer is either a sick sadistic bastard who gets off on hurting women, or somebody was very, very pissed at her."

The doctor handed the photos back to Lenny. "Anything more I can do to help you, just call. Any time."

Lenny thanked Dr. Primeaux and returned to his ward. He hadn't cleared up the reason for the weight loss, but at least he had some ideas to follow up. His friend had confirmed that the dead woman had been reporting for drug testing and coming out clean. That was encouraging, so long as Briana Nearing hadn't been faking her tests.

Lenny had defended enough co-workers to know that not every plea of innocence was honest. If he was going to find out whether or not Briana really had been clean, he needed the opinion of someone a lot closer to the user than Alex Primeaux. She could have told secrets to a girlfriend, but Lenny knew that addicts lost their friends when they gave all their loyalties to the drug.

After leaving Employee Health, Lenny went on to the Intensive Care Unit, where he found Gary Tuttle at the bedside of Jimmy Jones. Jimmy was still on the ventilator; Lenny thought that was a bad sign.

"How's Jimmy doing?" he asked the nurse.

"Hi, Lenny. He's not good, he has a pneumonia. It looks like the infection is spreading to his kidneys, his urine output is down. We're giving him medication to try and kick start the kidneys."

"Damn. Damn it to hell."

"Are you going ahead with the fund raiser?"

"Yeah, everyone wants to do it, even if it turns out to be a wake." He looked at Jimmy again, saw the eyes closed, the chest rising and falling rapidly, the tangle of intravenous lines feeding him drugs. It was a sorrowful sight. The shit was raining down on all of them.

"Ya know, Tuttle, this is a tough place to work. How long have you been working in the unit?"

"It's been two years," said Gary.

"Good for you. Listen, have you got a minute? I've got something personal I need to ask you." Lenny followed the nurse to a quiet spot beside the laundry closet. "How easy would it be for a nurse working in the Recovery Room to use a patient's urine to cheat on a drug test?" Lenny explained his concerns about Briana having gone off the program and started using.

"It would be very easy," said Gary. "For a nurse, anyway."

"That's what I was thinking. How would she do it?"

"Let me show you." Taking Lenny back to the sterile supply closet, Gary showed Lenny a kit containing a urinary catheter and drainage bag. The kit was clear plastic, so Lenny could see the contents.

"First, you would withdraw a large volume of urine from the Foley catheter. There's a sampling port you can use—see?"

Lenny saw where a nurse could stick the catheter with a needle and syringe and collect a urine sample.

"You would need to use a Toomey syringe." Gary showed Lenny the 100-cc syringe. "Then you go to the bathroom and pass your urine. After that, you insert a red rubber catheter into your bladder, connect the syringe, and instill the urine."

"Is there any way to tell from the test that the sample is fake?"

"Hmm. Like test the urine for DNA? I doubt that the lab would do that here, they're only looking for a specific list of drugs."

Satisfied that Briana could have been filling her bladder with a patient's urine, Lenny asked himself, if she was still using, who was her source and how much did she owe her dealer? Walking up the stairs to the seventh floor, he recalled Tony O's casual comment that one of his clients had "moved beyond his reach." It seemed like an innocent remark at the time, but Tony O always had a reason for everything he did. Could the loan shark have been telling Lenny that Briana owed him money?

What did Tony know about her death, and how much would he be willing to share with Lenny?

TWENTY-FIVE

Joe West stood in front of the video screen as the security guard ran the tape forward fast. The young officer carefully watched the counter spin forward until it reached the point on the tape he was aiming for. He hit the stop, then ran the tape at normal speed.

The video was from the camera in the sub-basement. It showed a long corridor that led to the cages where Central Stores kept large quantities of items. A worker pushed a flat dolly towards the camera. He was going to the elevator, bringing supplies from deep storage to the main Stores room one floor above. As he neared the camera, another man in a custodian's uniform, a cap on his head pulled low, came up beside the dolly. The second man's face was hidden by the boxes, so that only the cap was visible.

"He's hiding from the camera," said West.

"Yes, but look," said the young guard. As the dolly passed beneath the camera, a gap in the stack of boxes revealed a brief glimpse of the interloper. The guard froze the frame.

"The software picked out his face," he said. "Check it out."

The guard brought up a photo of Carlton and placed it next to the image from the basement. They were obviously the same man.

"He's made a base in one of the cages," said West.

"Should I bring in the employee who works down there?"

"Don't be an idiot, that would alert our fugitive that we know where he's hiding. No, we'll take him while he sleeps in the early morning hours. I'll assemble the team."

West printed out the photo of Carlton in the sub-basement. It was grainy, the cameras only providing a low-resolution image, but it was enough. He knew the police would want to take over and make the arrest, but West was confident in his abilities. Besides, he had full police powers within the hospital and its immediate grounds. Given the public announcement that Rogers was armed and dangerous, West even had the right to shoot a suspect on sight.

West hoped that when he confronted Rogers, the fugitive gave him a reason to discharge his weapon, it had been years since he shot anyone. Too long. And besides, a dead murder suspect was so much easier to pronounce guilty than a live one protesting his innocence.

Lenny was walking with Regis toward his car in the employee parking lot when Sandy rode up on one of the little electric carts. The old security guard, who had helped Lenny in several murder investigations, came to a stop beside him.

"I got news for you, Lenny, and it's a trip, lemme tell you."

"It better be good news, I've had nothing but bad news coming down on me all week."

"Your boy Carlton? He's hiding out . . . in the hospital!" The old guard let out a hearty laugh, his jowls shaking with delight. "Ain't that a hoot? Joe West is having kittens trying to track him down."

"Yeah, we know about it," said Regis. "That crazy Carlton had the cops looking for him out at French Creek. Maybe the boy's part Indian like he always said."

"I shouldn't be surprised," said Sandy. "Carlton loves to stick it to the administration." He dabbed his eyes with an old handkerchief. "How long have you boys known?"

"He left me a note in my wash bucket this morning, but I already knew he was back in Philly, he took his bicycle with him when he left the city. It's only fifty miles to the city."

Sandy pointed out there are a lot of places to hide in the hospital. "He's got the medical school, the research labs, all the store rooms."

"Not to mention he was a floater on the housekeeping night shift. They gave him keys to every department in the joint that he could've copied. He's got a million options."

"Joe West is really feeling the agita," said Sandy, smiling with delight. He tucked his handkerchief away. "Where are you two trouble-makers off to?"

"We're talking to workers at the gym in Chestnut Hill about joining the union," said Regis.

"Yeah, I know it, I heard their jingle on the radio. *Slim to none. Slim to—*"

"*Stop, I hate that jingle!*" said Lenny. "Don't ever sing that in front of me. *Pu-lease.*"

Sandy gunned the cart and took off, still singing the irritating tune. Lenny and Regis got into his car and turned onto Germantown Ave heading for Chestnut Hill.

At the *New Body Spa and Fitness Center,* Lenny & Regis positioned themselves on the sidewalk on either side of the entrance. When a young woman with an employee badge approached the entrance, Lenny handed her a flyer. "Hi, I'm Lenny. I'm a steward with the Hospital Service Workers Union. Would you look over this information sheet?"

The woman, anxious about being seen, didn't take the brochure from Lenny's hand, but said in a whisper, "They have security cameras."

"I understand," said Lenny. "What car did you drive?"

"Car? Uh, a red Fit."

"Did you park it in the lot out back?" The worker cautiously nodded her head. "Great. I'll leave a brochure on the windshield, you can pick it up when you get off."

The young woman hurried into the building, head bowed.

Moments later, Albert Brunner, came out of the gym and walked toward Lenny. An intimidating presence, with broad shoulders, a thick neck and bulging biceps, Brunner barreled toward Lenny like a fourteen wheeler and stopped closer than a stranger had any right to.

"You are interfering with the operations of my biz-i-ness," he said in a heavily accented voice. "You will leave from the vicinity at once."

Lenny turned to Regis, not sure what to make of the stocky guy. Figuring he was a security guard, Lenny said, "I'm not interfering with anything, pal. This is a public sidewalk. You don't own the street."

"The street is mine!" said Albert, "You will leave from here at once or you will be in the deepest trouble."

Regis joined Lenny. "What, is the hospital hiring Polish bouncers for their gyms now?"

"I am the manager of the establishment." Without warning, Albert knocked the papers out of Lenny's hand, then he kicked the papers down the street, scattering them in the breeze.

"You asshole!" Lenny cried. He jabbed Albert with his open palm, intending to push Albert away, but found himself pressing on a rock hard chest that did not budge an inch. With a malicious grin, Albert drove a sledge hammer fist into Lenny's face, sending him stumbling backward until he fell on his butt. As Lenny scrambled to his feet, Regis came charging at Albert with fists cocked and let loose a punch. Albert easily blocked it, then he drove his fist into the side of Regis's head, sending the young man to the ground.

"I have called for the police. You will vacate the area at once or they will arrest you for making the riot."

Albert spat on the sidewalk, turned and walked back into the gym. As the door closed behind him, they heard a police car siren wailing coming up Germantown Avenue. With blood running from his nose, Lenny grabbed Regis by the arm and led him away.

"Why're we turning tail"? said Regis. "He attacked us!"

"Yeah, but he runs the business. Who are the cops gonna believe?"

"But—"

"No buts, Reege, they have it all on video. I put my hand on him first, he can claim self-defense. And you threw a punch before he decked you. He can use the footage to make the case that he was defending himself. We'll be the ones charged with assault, not mister business man."

"Yeah, I know, I got pissed off. I'm sorry, man, but what else was I gonna do? I got t' stick up for my union brother."

"Of course, it's not a criticism," Lenny said, reaching his car. "It's just the way it went down. That guy's slick; he waited for us to make the first move."

Lenny opened the trunk, pulled out a roll of paper towels from the back shelf and pressed it against his nose, stanching the blood, which had stained his blue work shirt. "Are you okay? He hit you pretty hard."

"I'm cool. I'm thinking maybe I should drive you to the ER."

"I'm not going to the ER, I'm going home." He opened the front door and settled in behind the wheel.

"Your nose might be broken," said Regis, slipping into the passenger seat.

"They don't set the bone, they just tape it and it heals all by itself. I'll drop you."

As he drove Regis home, Lenny went over the incident again in his mind. He couldn't believe a guy as thick and muscle bound as Brunner could be so fast. From his physique the guy had probably been a professional weight lifter. No doubt he'd studied martial arts as well.

"That bastard probably thinks he's some kind of Claude Van Damme," said Lenny.

"Yeah, he did have some kinda accent. What was it, Russian?"

"No, it wasn't Russian. German, maybe. I'll get his name and Google him. We'll need to know as much as we can about him if we're going to convince the workers at the spa to sign union cards, he probably scared them to death."

By the time Lenny arrived home his nose had stopped bleeding, but his worries only continued. He was afraid that the confrontation might sink his chance of winning the workers to sign union pledge cards. Maybe they would be angry by Albert's pushing them around. If he was that tough on union representatives, he was probably doubly tough on the workers in the gym.

The campaigns was going to take some serious planning.

TWENTY-SIX

At home Patience crushed some ice in the blender and made a pack for Lenny's nose. Lenny was on his cell phone grumbling to Moose about how much he hated being pushed around when she pressed the ice pack to his nose.

"*Ow!* Hey, I'm on the phone!"

"Lenny, you need to lay down and let the ice work or you'll be all black and blue."

He held the pack to his nose and continued. "I should have asked you to go with me to the gym. Brunner wouldn't have pulled that crap if you were there."

"I told you I don't mind helping. I told you."

"I know, Moose, I should have listened to you."

"The thing you got to get out of it is, you have to know your enemy's strengths. Know your enemy, know yourself."

"You're right, I should have investigated the place before I took on the creep that runs it. I wasn't thinking."

"A good fighter plans for a fight, even when he hopes there won't be one. Next time you go out, I'll be with you."

"Next time I'll have a court order. I called the union lawyer. He's gonna file some papers tomorrow and make sure we have a right to give out our stuff."

"Court order's okay, long as you can back it up with strength."

They discussed where to go next with the murder investigation. Lenny thought finding the father of Briana's unborn child was a priority, although neither he nor Moose had an idea how to find him. Lenny told him what Tony O had said about losing five hundred dollars to a client who was "beyond his reach." Moose agreed it sounded like Briana.

"You got to have something to give Tony if you want information," said Moose. "What have you got?"

Lenny admitted he had nothing to trade. They agreed to keep that option open should a piece of information come their way that Tony would find valuable.

With Patience staring at him, Lenny told Moose before hanging up, "You know how you've been bugging me for years to take up some weight training?"

"You finally wanna get serious about it?"

"I think it's time."

Moose chuckled. "Nobody likes bein' pushed around, I hear that. We can start next week."

When Lenny finally hung up, Patience turned off the ringer and led him upstairs to the bedroom.

"Sorry, babe, I'm not in the mood for sex right now," he said.

"Shut up and take off your clothes," she ordered, pulling back the sheets and piling the pillows together. "You're calling out sick tomorrow, aren't you?"

"I'll be all right."

"*Mister* hard head. How many sick days have you accumulated, anyway?"

"I don't know; a hundred, hundred-twenty. I lost count."

"So why don't you use them?"

"I'm saving them up in case I get really really sick."

"You *are* really really sick. In the *head!*" She kissed his bald spot and closed the door behind her.

Lenny settled back into the pillows and turned on the TV. The news came on. Larson Flood was back reporting from Carlton's home, this time, the back yard. Flood reported that police dogs searching for evidence located several jars filled with money buried in the yard. A forensics team was examining the jars, after which they would be opened and the cash examined further.

"Asked if this new evidence would strengthen the District Attorney's case further, one police officer said, with a little irony, that Carlton had dug his own grave, and it was only a matter of time before he was buried in it. This is Larson Flood, for FIX News."

Disgusted, Lenny turned off the set and the light, closed his eyes, and tried to get some sleep. His nose ached and his ego was bruised from being beaten by a Neanderthal. Moose was right, he should have planned the leafleting better. He made a note to do a computer search of Albert Brunner in the morning. Right now all he wanted to do was sleep and let the whole murder investigation dissolve into nothingness.

TWENTY-SEVEN

Like a drill sergeant checking his new recruits, Joe West looked over the four security guards standing at attention in his office with a stern face. "Men, you have all been issued side arms for this mission. We will be facing a wanted killer. He is skilled in survival and in lethal weapons. Be ready for traps. For subterfuge. For any kind of trick. We hope to take him by surprise, but he will probably have defensive devices that will warn him of our presence."

Checking his watch—it was exactly four am—West released the strap on his holster, then watched as the other guards followed his example. "Let's go."

They walked single file down the steps to the basement, and then down deeper into the bowels of the hospital: the musty, poorly lit sub-basement. Their footsteps echoed in the dark hallway. When they came to the row of cages, West peered through the mesh into the first cage. The single fluorescent lamp barely illuminated the boxes stacked in uneven rows.

West took out his master key and quietly unlocked the cage. Two guards remained outside the cage, the other two followed West in. They peered into the rows between the boxes, shining their flashlights. There was no sign of human habitation, and no box large enough for Carlton to hide in.

West led his team to the next cage, but instead of going in, he gazed down the row of storage facilities. The light inside one of the cages was out; all the others were lit.

West made a sign for silence and pointed at the dark cage. He moved silently along the corridor to the cage, inserted the key and unlocked the cage. He drew his weapon, waited for the others to bring their guns out, and then stepped silently inside.

He sent one guard along one side of the cage, a second down the other. Two others remained at the open door to block any escape. West stepped down the center of the cage, shining his light along the rows of boxes. Many were old and mildewed, with layers of dust on them. Looking down, he could see footprints in the dusty floor.

Behind the last row of boxes he saw the long box that Carlton was using for his sleeping quarters. It was a new box; there was no mildew or dust on it. One end abutted a row of boxes, the other end was free of obstruction. Obviously the entrance to the hiding place.

West pointed at the box. He signaled to the guards to have their flashlight ready to illuminate the interior. The two guards took up positions at the head of the box with guns drawn. West grasped the flap and ripped it open while the two guards aimed their flashlight into the dark interior of the long box.

The box was empty.

Cursing, West bent down and crawled part way into the box. He found a hospital blanket neatly folded with a pillow on top. There were boxes of breakfast cereal sealed in a Ziploc bag, a bowl and spoon, and fresh fruit. The Daily News was two days old.

"You want us to check the other cages?" asked one of the guards.

"You might as well, but he's not here. He's set up a new hiding place somewhere else in the building."

Leaving the four guards to complete the search, West stalked out of the cage and barked into his walkie-talkie, "Rogers is in the hospital somewhere. I want two officers at the video desk watching the monitors twenty-four seven." When the elevator arrived, West barked once more into the box, "And let me know the minute Lenny Moss punches in."

"Sir, do you want us to bring Moss to the security office."

"No. Follow his every movement. He's going to lead us to our fugitive."

Nursing Station Four West was under construction. New patient rooms, all private, with Jacuzzis in the bathrooms "for hydrotherapy" (a billable service), movie rentals on the flat screen television, and. state-of-the-art ventilation controls. The rooms could be switched from a positive pressure ventilation for patients with weak immune systems on reverse isolation, to negative pressure, for patients on TB isolation.

The nursing station was half built, the sinks lying on the floor waiting to be installed. The toilets were torn up and waiting for new plumbing. Even the soiled utility room was getting an ultra-modern bed pan flusher that used high speed jets of hot water, followed by steam, then dry heat.

Carlton carried a 4x8 sheet of wallboard into a room marked LINEN. He had already nailed several 2x4 metal studs in place. Now he began nailing the wallboard in place, leaving a two-foot crawl space between his new wall he was constructing and the original back wall.

He added a second sheet of wallboard, cut to reach the ceiling. Soon he had a credible fake wall, with a section that he could pull out at the bottom to crawl through. He planned on completing the taping and spackling another night. But not this night. This night he had serious work to do.

Changing to scrubs, OR cap and stethoscope around his neck, Carlton made his way to the department of surgery. It was four-thirty in the morning: just enough time to do a little breaking and entering before a certain scum bag surgeon came in to work.

TWENTY-EIGHT

After punching in at the time clock, Lenny made his way to the Recovery Room, determined to find out if Briana had gone back to using drugs. Negative urine tests cut no ice with him, he wanted to hear it directly from a co-worker. He found Rose, a nurse whom he had helped when she needed an immigration lawyer to help bring her mother to the US.

Rose confirmed what he had heard, that Briana had been acting erratically. Some days she was peaches and cream; other nights she was moody and silent.

"Were there any doctors who paid her special attention, or that she seemed especially familiar with?"

"Oh, all the surgeons hit on Bree, she was such a looker. But I never heard her say she fancied any one in particular."

"Rose, didn't she lose a lot of weight? I saw a picture of her from Christmas summer and the difference was striking."

"That's what worried me, I was afraid she was back on the drugs. The charge nurse made it a point to not assign her to patients who were going to receive narcotics, we were afraid she'd steal some of the opiates."

"So she didn't have access to drugs."

"Almost never. Nurses on drug probation are assigned to patients who don't need narcotics."

Lenny eyed the two patients in the Recovery Room who had spent the night. He pointed to the urine bags hanging from the stretchers. "Do the RNs empty the Foleys, or do they leave that for the aides?"

"Usually the nurse's aide takes care of that, but we all work together. Nurses empty them when the aide is busy transporting a patient. Why?"

Not wanting to cast aspersions on the nurse who had been murdered, Lenny said he was just trying to get a handle on how the work was broken down. He thanked the nurse for helping him and went on to his station. Rose had confirmed what Carlton said, that Briana was not able to steal narcotics from the patients. Lenny didn't know how Carlton knew it, but if he was living in the hospital he could have access to patient records.

He hoped that Briana had been off drugs. The fact that she wasn't given access to narcotics wasn't proof she was clean, she could have been scoring drugs from somebody in the hospital. Or she could have stolen some blank prescription forms. She had opportunity to steal urine and fake her test results, so her passing the drug tests didn't prove anything.

Lenny had dealt with too many addicted workers to believe that Briana Nearing had kicked the habit, although her being pregnant might have given her the motivation she needed.

If she knew she was carrying the baby.

Joe West had a security guard bring in the Central Stores clerk who was seen on tape with Carlton in the basement. When the fellow came into West's office, the security chief told him to sit in the straight-backed chair in the middle of the room. West pulled the young man's ID badge from his shirt and held it up to the light.

"Darren Spense, Central Stores technician." He eyed the young man, a reedy fellow with straw colored hair and a little fuzz on his chin. Instead of handing the badge back, West tossed it on his desk. "How long have you been working at James Madison?"

"A little over two years."

"Two years, three months and one week," West said. "You like it down there in the basement? All dark and quiet, nobody to bother you."

"It's okay."

"You want to keep your job. Isn't that right?" said West, standing over the young man.

Spense shrugged. Up to that moment he had glanced once or twice at West's face, not wanting to look him in the eyes. With the threat of being fired thrust in his face, Spense felt his anger rising in his chest. He grew up on a rough street in South Philly, and he knew you didn't act scared when a bully threatened you, it could get you killed.

"Keep it, lose it, it all depends," said Spense.

"On what?" said West, leaning into the fellow.

"It all depends on what I have to do to stay put."

West placed a series of photos from the video that showed Carlton walking past Spense in the sub-basement. Spense glanced casually at the photos, saying nothing.

"You can't deny seeing the fugitive in the hallway. Pictures never lie."

"I don't pay no attention who I pass in the hallway. I got my eyes on my packages, make sure they don't tumble off and break something. One time a guy piled his boxes too high, couldn't see where he was goin', ran smack into a little old lady visiting her husband and knocked her down. She broke her hip n' never walked again."

"There are no visitors in the sub-basement," said West.

"Don't matter, the principle's the same. I got to be careful with my load or I get written up for delivering damaged goods."

West pointed to a photo of the cage where Carlton had been hiding. "We know nobody could access that storage facility without a key to the cage, and you're the only one who had a key and had a reason to give it to Carlton.

Spense shrugged. "I ain't got no reason to give nobody no key."

"Then explain to me how a wanted fugitive got his hands on the key to the cages?"

"Simple enough; you gave it to him."

"*I gave it to him?* What the hell are you talking about?"

"Carlton was a floater, yo? He didn't have no regular floor, they sent him to whatever area was short a man, and they had to give him a key to get in the office. Carlton worked in Stores couple a' months ago, he probably copied the key. Shit, I bet he can open every fricking door in the whole damn hospital."

Spense leaned back, clasped his hands behind his neck, stretched out his long legs and smiled up at West.

West didn't let his face betray the fury he was feeling over the young storeroom clerk's story. He wasn't so much furious at the fellow's cheek, but at realizing he hadn't figured out how Carlton could stay hidden in the hospital with so many guards looking for him.

West picked up Spense's ID badge and tossed it to him, telling him to go back to work and adding, "I want you to be perfectly clear on this: anybody working at James Madison who assists Carlton Rogers in any way will be fired immediately and turned over to the police in handcuffs for harboring a fugitive."

Once Spense was out of the office, West called the Housekeeping Director and yelled into the phone, *"Why do you give keys to every locked room in the entire facility to a dishonest, delinquent like Carlton Rogers?"*

"Hey, don't hang this on me, I don't make policy. We give keys to employees on a as needed basis. If you have a problem with our practice, take it up with the Environment of Care Committee, they approve all our policies."

"I don't talk to committees!" West growled and slammed the phone down. He plucked his walkie-talkie from his belt and blared into it, *"WHERE IS LENNY MOSS?!!"*

There was a long silence that made West's anger bubble up even more. Finally a security officer reported, "Sir, Mister Moss has just arrived at his station, Nursing Unit Seven-South."

"*Just arrived?* What was he doing before he got there?"

"Uh, I have no knowledge of that, sir."

"I gave strict orders that someone was to watch Moss every place he went, from the time he stepped into the building until the time he left."

West ordered the guard monitoring the video feeds to go back to six in the morning and watch for Lenny Moss entering the facility and punching in at the time clock. The officer was to track the man's movements until he arrived at the seventh floor.

"*I want to know every place that Moss went. I want to know when he goes for coffee and when he takes a shit! Understood?*"

"Yes, sir." The guard rewound the video from a camera that monitored the basement where the Housekeeping staff punched in at the time card. A few years before one of the custodians squeezed Krazy Glue into the machine, rendering the time clock useless. West had a security camera installed soon after.

Joe West shut the door to his office, settled into his plush chair, and called his contact at the Philadelphia Police Department, hoping that they had uncovered more evidence against the annoying squatter, Carlton Rogers.

TWENTY-NINE

Settling in to start his work, for once Lenny wasn't surprised when he found a photograph in the bottom of his wash bucket in the Seven-South housekeeping closet. Carlton was at it again, finding clues and passing them on. Lenny was beginning to appreciate that his friend, with his ring of keys to every department in the hospital and his living like an outlaw, could find clues that were beyond a shop steward's reach.

He held the photo up to the light. It showed Briana in a bikini posing with Dr. Farr. They were standing on a beach, the ocean behind them. Lenny couldn't be sure, but by the gray color and the lack of surfers, he guessed it was the Atlantic shore. Jersey, maybe. Or the Carolinas. Briana had her hand on the doctor's shoulder; Farr had his hand on her butt.

It seemed to be a summer setting, which made the timing of her pregnancy just right. The autopsy said she was around twelve weeks pregnant. From mid-August to mid-November was the right window.

Lenny considered what it would mean if Farr was the father of Briana's unborn child. He was a married man. Respected. It would mean trouble for his marriage. Maybe even his reputation. But it wasn't as if he was a right-wing politician campaigning on a family values ticket. Fatherhood by itself didn't feel like motive enough to kill Briana, especially since it would mean that Farr had killed his unborn child.

As he filled his bucket with soapy water, Lenny considered how he could manage an interview with the surgeon. It wasn't like talking to one of the union members; they were all used to telling him their problems and their secrets. Farr would have nothing to say to a hospital custodian.

Dipping the mop in the water, his thoughts returned to Tony O and that mysterious client who owed him 'five large" but had "moved beyond his reach." The loan shark knew even more hospital staff than Lenny. If Briana had borrowed the money, Tony might know what she needed it for: drugs, or some kind of trouble.

The kind of trouble that got somebody killed.

Gary Tuttle was worried. Jimmy's urine output had trailed off during the night and was now essentially zero. The kidneys were not functioning. Neither extra intravenous fluids nor large doses of diuretics had jump-started them. If the kidneys didn't start making urine soon, Jimmy would need dialysis, which would eliminate any chance of getting a lung transplant.

Smelling a foul odor, the nurse turned Jimmy slightly to the side and looked in the bed. Sure enough, there was a small pool of black, foul smelling stool. The black color told him instantly that Jimmy had developed some degree of GI bleed. Whether it was an upper bleed from the stomach or a lower bleed from the colon, he couldn't tell. Either way, it was one complication that the fragile patient could not afford.

Dr. Singh came to the bedside with his team and reviewed the latest lab values. "I see his INR is up and his 'crit is down," said Singh, who was not surprised when Gary told him of the black tarry stool. "His coagulopathy may explain his bleeding."

Singh stood a moment looking at the patient. "Tell me, Shira, does melena indicate an upper or a lower GI bleed?"

The young resident said, "Uh, I would expect bright red blood if the bleeding was in the colon."

"In point of fact, there is no way to discern the source from the color. A bleed on the transverse or right colon will mix with stool and become black by the time it reaches the rectal vault. A rapid transit from the duodenum may be bright red as well."

"Do you want to consult GI for an endoscopy?" the resident asked.

Singh pointed to the thick, yellow sputum in the suction canister at the head of the bed. "He is too unstable for GI to scope him, he has pneumonia as well as renal failure. All we can do for the moment is give him blood and correct his coagulation disorder."

When the doctors moved on to the next patient, Gary sat down at the nursing station to write up his initial assessment. He was just affixing his stamper to the note when he heard a familiar voice calling his name.

"Hey, Tuttle! What's happening?"

Gary told Lenny that Jimmy had several organs failing and would need kidney dialysis. "I guess that means you'll have to call off the fund raiser."

"No, we're going ahead. Jimmy's family will use the money, one way or the other." Lenny looked over at his friend. "I see you're looking up lab results. I was wondering if you could help me with something."

"Sure. What do you need?"

"Do you think you could look up lab tests for Briana Nearing?"

"Uh, yeah, I guess I could do that." Both of them knew that accessing a patient's lab work without a medical reason to be reading them was grounds for immediate dismissal. It could even cost Gary his license to practice nursing. Gary logged off and then opened the laboratory program using a different password.

"You still using Mother Burgess's access code?" Lenny asked.

"No way. Not after all the trouble I got in to the last time I tried that. I'm using one of the ICU residents. They leave their programs up all the time." He asked Lenny what tests was he looking for."

"Well, a pregnancy test for starters, although I guess she could buy one of those test kits at any pharmacy. She could have been sick, she lost some weight and she just didn't look like a healthy woman who was pregnant. I'm told she could have been having some kind of hormone disorder."

Lenny leaned into the computer as Briana's lab results appeared on the screen. There were no pregnancy test results, as he expected. Scrolling down, he found one test for liver enzymes and another for pituitary function.

"What do you make of them?" Lenny asked.

"They're all normal. She didn't seem to have any disease of her adrenals or pituitary gland."

"What's the chance she didn't know she was pregnant? She was around twelve weeks, according to the Medical Examiner."

"That's the end of the first trimester," said Gary. "She was a nurse; she would have recognized the signs."

"So why *those* tests?"

"She must have worried she had some kind of endocrine or liver disease. There's no test for hepatitis, so it wasn't your typical liver disease." Gary printed out the labs and gave the results to Lenny. "You're going to have to talk to somebody in endocrine."

Lenny looked at the lab printout, trying to pull more information from the words and numbers arranged in neatly ordered columns. He felt sure he was missing something important. Something beyond the numbers. Then it hit him.

"Who ordered the test?"

Gary looked up the ordering physician at the lab header. It stated: Doctor Jean Farr.

Lenny noted the date of the test. It was mid-September; roughly a month after Briana's time at the shore with the physician. Could Farr have confused her pregnancy symptoms with something else? If she had a false period, she might not have realized she was expecting.

"Tuttle, is it odd for a surgeon to be ordering that test. I mean, wouldn't you expect a medical doctor to do it?"

"Definitely, a medical physician would be the appropriate consult. It would usually be an internist or a family practice doctor, or an endocrinologist. A surgeon ordering it is unusual unless she had an operation. Did she?"

"No, the autopsy didn't report any kind of surgical scar."

As Lenny turned to go, Gary stopped him, saying, "Listen, Lenny, seeing Doctor Farr's name reminded me of something."

"Spill it, Tuttle. You know you can tell me anything."

"Well, last week, it was the day after Briana was found in the park, I was caring for Jimmy Jones in the ICU. I had the Daily News for him to read, although he didn't feel like reading."

"You're a kind nurse, Tuttle."

"I noticed that when Doctor Farr saw Briana's photograph in the front page of the newspaper, he stopped listening to the resident's report and walked off the unit. He hadn't answered a STAT page, he just turned and walked out without a word."

Lenny left the ICU and returned to his unit, wondering what kind of relationship Briana Nearing had had with Dr. Jean Farr, and just how much the cryptic Carlton knew about it.

If he only had a way to reach the crazy guy. It was maddening that the secretive bastard was right here 'in his back pocket' but still so far out of reach.

THIRTY

Lecture Hall B-4 was filling up with physicians, medical students, physician assistants and nurse practitioners come to listen to Grand Rounds. A drug rep stood just inside the entrance beside a table laden with donuts, croissants and stacks of colorful literature. The crowd eagerly reached for the food and coffee, for the most part ignoring the free hand outs.

This day's Rounds included the mysterious case of a patient who had been exposed several times to HIV but who never showed clinical or microbiological signs of the virus. The drug rep was promoting a new AIDS cocktail. His company was reporting extremely low levels of the virus in the blood after treatment, although they were nothing as startling as the patient who seemed to be naturally immune to the disease.

Carlton, dressed in sharply ironed slacks, pale blue shirt and conservative tie, crisp white lab coat and a stethoscope dangling casually around his neck, stopped at the reception table and signed in, scribbling a signature that nobody could read. He saw Dr. Jean Farr seated in the hall wearing scrub suit and a lab coat, chatting with another doctor.

Taking a seat behind Farr, Carlton sipped a cup of coffee and listened to Farr chatter about his difficulty with regulatory agencies burying him with guidelines that restricted his practice. When the speaker was introduced, Farr finally shut up. Carlton spent the hour studying the man and trying to imagine him climbing the path in Fairmont Park with a dead weight over his shoulder.

Lenny pushed his mop and bucket out onto the ward and attacked the marble floor, which was streaked with ugly black strips. Somebody had pushed a stretcher or maybe an x-ray machine with a frozen tire that left a black residue down the corridor. He was scraping a thick spot from the floor with a putty knife when he heard his name ring out in a loud, familiar voice.

"Mister Lenny Moss! The man. The legend!" Tony O was striding toward him, pushing a messenger's cart with actual envelopes in the basket.

When Tony arrived, Lenny pointed to the cart. "What's this, are you doing some actual work today?"

"Props, my friend. Any good performer must have props." Tony picked up a thick padded envelope for Lenny to read the label. "Doctor A. Einstein, Experimental Physics Laboratory, Room MC-2, JMUH.

Lenny burst out laughing. "*Einstein?* You're delivering to *Albert Einstein?*

Tony shrugged his broad, muscular shoulders. "Without a sense of humor, life is a dull and wretched affair." He dropped the envelope back in the basket. "How's the nose feel? I hear you let some muscle-bound creep sucker punch you."

"News travels fast. Yeah, he hit me pretty hard. I should have taken you with me."

"For a fee, I would consider acting as your protector, but you have Moose." Lenny acknowledged his friend would be with him for all future visits to the gym. Tony said, "You know, Lenny, you and I are very much alike in our work."

"You think?"

"I do. We both help people. We're both in the service industry."

"You think?"

"Of course! You help them when they're in trouble over the rules and regs, I help when they come up a little short going into payday."

"Yeah, but I don't charge them."

"Sure you do. You take out union dues every month. Don't you?"

"Yeah, but we don't make a profit on them."

"*No profit?* Who do you think pays for all those conferences and union assemblies? Who pays the bill for the free airfare, free hotels, and all the food you can eat? You get your share of perks, my friend. Not that you don't deserve them."

"I guess that's true. Well, your interest rates are pretty damn high."

"I charge less than the credit card companies do if you miss one little payment. And I won't destroy your credit for seven years if you skip on me."

"No, but your customers might walk with a limp if they don't pay."

"Point taken."

Seeing that Tony was in no hurry to get on with his delivery schedule, Lenny asked, "Uh, is there something on your mind?"

"Just one thing. You're trying to get your boy Luther his job back. Correct?"

"That's right."

"You sure you want him back?"

"Where are you going with this, Tony?"

"My friends tell me Luther does more than use drugs."

"He deals?"

"To feed his habit. And more."

"So why are you telling me this? Aside from our being brothers in arms and all."

"I don't sell drugs, Lenny, and I don't finance drug sales."

"You'd be happy if Luther never came back to work," said Lenny.

"You know it. One less drug dealer in my domain, the better for me. Drugs make people desperate. Desperate people do stupid things, and that brings in the cops. I prefer to loan money to somebody's hard up for the rent, or behind in a car payment. For that I got you covered. But when you're in deep to your dealer, that's a debt I have no desire to cover."

Despite his disapproval of loan sharking, Lenny was finding more and more to like about Tony O. The man always did what was in his best interest, but he was honest about his motives, and his information was always reliable. Lenny hated to admit that winning Luther his job back would be no victory for the hospital workers. On that he agreed completely with his favorite loan shark.

As Tony turned to go, he said in a casual voice, "That's tough luck for your boy, them finding all that money buried in his back yard."

"Yeah, well, you know Carlton, he doesn't trust banks. He's probably been burying the proceeds from his meat sales in his yard for years."

Tony nodded in agreement. "A man after my own heart. Still, the money looks bad to a jury." Tony pushed his cart down the wall, saying as he went, "Tough luck, my friend. Tough, indeed."

As he finished mopping the hall, a dispirited Lenny tried to reassure himself by going over all the goofy ways that Carlton handled money. He didn't have a checking account or a savings. He didn't have a credit card. He paid all his bills with postal money orders, and he paid cash for all his purchases. The buried money was consistent with a lifelong paranoia about financial institutions and credit agencies.

But still, the buried cash was worrisome.

Finishing with the hall, he began mopping the patient rooms. Several patients were gone for tests or procedures or therapy, making it easier to move the furniture and give the floors a good cleaning. He still had a problem with Carlton's claim that he *happened* to be in the park at the time of Briana's murder. But if he wasn't there to hunt deer or to kill the nurse, what was he doing?

When the last room was cleaned, he looked at the clock on the wall, saw it was lunchtime. He hurried down the stairwell to get a coffee and a sandwich to take to the sewing room. As his steel-tipped shoes echoed in the stairwell, he wondered just how much Tony O knew about the death of Briana Nearing, and what it would take to pry the information out of him.

THIRTY-ONE

Lenny found his friends in the sewing room eating lunch. The fragrant smells of spicy beef, curried rice and lemon grass tea filled the room. Settling in a battered old folding chair, he told them that Spense called to tell him how West tried to scare him with the video that showed Carlton passing him in the sub-basement hallway. With a laugh Lenny said, "Spense told West that the hospital gave Carlton keys to every department in the hospital, and it was the boss's own fault they couldn't find him!"

"Heh, heh. Those South Philly street rats have balls," said Moose.

"They ain't never gonna catch old Carlton," said Birdie, holding her mug of tea cupped in her hands. "He has more hiding places than a pack rat."

"He can't stay in James Madison forever," said Lenny. "West has security cameras all over the place. Sooner or later they're gonna catch Carlton on film and nail him."

"I hear West still got the shoot to kill order out," said Regis.

"That's nuts," said Birdie. "I know West is mean, but he can't shoot an unarmed man, can he?"

There was sharp disagreement over what West was capable of doing, with Moose and Regis arguing that West would sooner shoot a man than take a chance he would beat the charges, while Birdie didn't think it would happen.

Lenny showed them the photograph that Carlton left in his bucket. He told them what he'd learned about Briana and Farr having an affair. "Tuttle noticed that Doctor Farr froze up when he saw Briana's photograph on the cover of the newspaper. That goes along with the photograph of the two of them on a beach."

"It don't make no sense," said Regis. "If Farr was the father, why would he kill her? It would mean killing his own son."

Birdie said, "That's the oldest story in the book. He's a married man got to answer to his wife!"

"*If* he's the father," said Regis. "We don't have the DNA tests to prove it."

"It's gotta be him," said Moose. "Why else'd he order her lab tests?"

"Nurses are always asking the docs they work with to write them a prescription," said Regis. "She could've just grabbed him in Recovery and got him to write the order."

Lenny reminded them that he found no evidence that Briana had been using drugs. "She could have faked her urine test, but she was worried about some kind of condition, she was getting tests for her hormone levels. Gary says the tests were off, but not by much."

"That's got to be from her pregnancy," Birdie asked. "Women get all kinds a' imbalance in our hormones when we're pregnant."

"I don't know. I'm going to have to talk to somebody who specializes in it." He added the information from Tony O that Luther was apparently dealing drugs. And he reported on the money the police found in Carlton's back yard.

"That money's from his deer meat," said Moose. "You know Carlton didn't trust the banks. He used to say the banks used our money against us, investing in weapons and dirty energy and stuff. Man was always ahead of his time."

"I hope that's all there is to it," said Lenny.

Regis gave Lenny a look of disbelief. "Don't tell me you think our man's guilty. Don't you tell me that!"

"Of course I think Carlton's innocent. Of the murder. But there's shit he's not telling me, I have no doubt about that."

Moose said, "You mean, like, his just happening to be in the woods the same time the girl got herself killed."

"Right. I don't see him killing another human being, even with him being a skilled hunter. But until he explains what he was doing in *that* section of the park on *that* night . . . "

"We sure could 'a used him and his bow and arrow the day we mixed it up with the creep that runs the gym in Chestnut Hill," said Regis.

Lenny laughed. "Yeah, I'd love to see him plant an arrow in the bastard's leg."

"I'd like t' see it in the side of his head!" said Regis.

"When you goin' again?" asked Moose. "I wanna watch your back this time."

Lenny told him the union filed a petition with the National Labor Relations Board, asserting that the hospital was interfering with their protected activity of promoting the union. "The NLRB will send the hospital a letter saying they're going to investigate the complaint. If they think the complaint is valid, they'll schedule a hearing."

"Man, that could take a long time, couldn't it?" said Moose.

"Yeah, but usually the hospital settles before a hearing. They don't like the publicity." He added that he was planning to go back to the gym today after work.

"That's the way t' do it!" said Moose, holding up a clenched fist. "Don't let nobody push you around." He and Regis agreed to meet Lenny at the parking lot. They didn't put much stock in the paper the lawyer filed for the union. When it came to dealing with a thug like the one who managed the Chestnut Hill gym, they had more faith in muscle and street smarts.

Albert Brunner was looking over his list of gym employees, considering who among them might be weak and gullible enough to sign a union membership card. He was strict with them on occasion, of course, but strict discipline made for efficient employees. Efficient employees made for a successful business, and success in business gave people jobs. Everything he did was in the best interests of the employees. Deep down, they knew that.

Still, a few might be dumb enough to believe the foolishness that the unions told them. Brunner was circling the names of three workers he had doubts about when the call came from the hospital's Risk Management Officer. Risk Management defended the hospital against lawsuits and advised the administration on ways to avoid sanctions from the various regulatory agencies, especially the state Department of Health, which could shut the hospital down if they found sufficient evidence of noncompliance with accepted practice.

The officer told Brunner that the hospital had received a fax from the National Labor Relations Board about a complaint from the union that the hospital was preventing members of the Hospital Service Workers Union from distributing literature in a public place. He explained that the Board would conduct an investigation if the hospital did not come to an understanding with the union over the disputed activity.

The hospital representative finished by explaining to Brunner that neither the hospital nor any of its representatives may block union members from carrying out their work in a public space.

"You may restrict them to an area at least fifty feet from the entrance to your facility," the officer explained. "But should any union member block entrance to or egress from the facility, you are not to take matters into your own hands, you are to summon the police and allow them to enforce the law. Do you understand?"

"I understand. I will personally do nothing to prevent the union rats from giving out their poison."

"Remember, getting in a fight is bad publicity for the union. It's better to let the law protect our interests."

"I can assure you that none of my people will sign the union cards. They are loyal to me one hundred per cent. This I guarantee."

When the Risk officer hung up, Brunner looked over his list of employees one more time. Deciding that some of them might be vulnerable to the union's empty promises, he considered other methods available to him for stopping Lenny Moss. Mulling over one or two attractive options, he was pleased to have the opportunity to prove his managerial expertness in his own unique way.

THIRTY-TWO

Lenny, Regis and Moose crossed Germantown Ave and approached the New Body Spa and Fitness Center. "Remember," said Lenny. "We stay fifty feet away from the entrance, and we can't block the sidewalk. Right?"

"We can ask people if they work at the gym, can't we?" said Moose.

"That's fine, but most of them will be wearing their name tag. We offer them the literature and ask them can we talk to them after work. We can go to their home, or hook up at a cafe or whatever."

As he pulled out literature from his backpack, Lenny saw Albert Brunner glowering at them from inside the gym.

"I don't want any trouble with the cops," Lenny told his friends. "If the Neanderthal comes around, let me do the talking." He and Moose took up positions up the street from the entrance; Regis stood on the other side, so that they could greet people from either direction.

The slender young blonde who had greeted Lenny at the reception desk walked down the street toward the entrance. Lenny offered her some literature and a card, saying, "Hi, Lenny Moss with the Hospital Service Workers Union. I have some information about the benefits of joining the union."

"No thank you!" she said, walking past with her chin up in the air and entering the gym. As she passed Brunner, the manager gave her an affectionate pat on her ass, then he walked to the front door, shoved it open and strode toward them, an iron horse plunging full steam ahead.

"You must stand yourselves at least fifty feet from the entrance and you can not block the pedestrian way," he said. He backed up to the front door, then took goose steps, counting by three's, until he had gone sixteen paces, stopping a foot away from Moose.

"You stand here, no closer, and you do not block the sidewalk or I will have the police take you away in chains."

As Moose and Albert eyeballed each other, Lenny said, "I hate to tell you, but if you're thinking that one step is equal to three feet, three doesn't divide into fifty evenly, so, you're probably some ways over the fifty feet limit."

Albert turned to Lenny. "You think you are a funny man. You will not be funny when you are in the prison."

Albert turned and strode back to the entrance. At the door he turned, pointed at Lenny, and said, "Fifty feet!" Then he stepped back into the gym.

As a young man with a New Body ID came out of the gym, Brunner watched them from inside, glowering. The worker declined the literature from Regis and was unwilling to stop and talk to him. Another female worker also left without taking the literature.

"They're scared to be seen in public taking it," said Lenny. He called his friends together. "You guys follow the next two to their cars and put a leaflet in their windshield. I'll stay here."

"You sure you want to be alone with the cave man?" said Moose.

"Yeah, I'll be okay. As long as I don't make the first move, he's all mouth."

Moose followed the next worker out, explaining that all the service workers in James Madison were in the union and that the workers in the gym deserved the same rights. At the young man's car, out of sight of the gym, Moose slipped him a piece of literature and offered to visit him at home if that was all right. The worker was polite, but noncommittal.

When Brunner saw Regis and Moose following the staff to their cars, he rushed out of the gym and stomped up to Lenny, now alone on the sidewalk.

"You are harassing my people. I will not put up with harassing, you will stop immediately!"

Lenny didn't answer Brunner, but he didn't back down, either. He put an innocent look on his face, saying, "Hey, if anybody's causing a problem out here, it's you. I think you should stay fifty feet inside your god damn gym."

Seeing Brunner eyeball to eyeball with Lenny, Moose hurried back to his friend. He stood to the side of the manager, knees slightly bent, hands balled in fists, ready to take on the bastard if he touched Lenny.

Brunner looked at Moose. He saw that Lenny's friend was muscular and ready to fight. A smile curled his lips as he considered mixing it up with a worthier opponent. "I can wipe the sidewalk with all three of you without even making a sweat," he said. "But I don't believe in hitting children." Brunner turned and walked slowly back to the entrance.

After two hours greeting the few workers who came and went to the spa, Regis went up the street and returned with a pizza. Lenny was chewing on a slice of pepperoni when Laticia came out of the gym. As she walked past him she declined his offer of literature but threw him a wink, whispering, "I gave cards to four of my friends."

Encouraged that they were making inroads at the spa, Lenny looked at his watch and considered if they should call it a day. He was about to suggest they leave when he saw a familiar unmarked police car pull up. Detective Joe Williams got out and walked toward him.

"Hey," said Lenny. "If you don't put any quarters in the meter, you're gonna blow your cover."

"Cut the crap, Moss, I heard you were blocking the entrance to the gym."

"No way. The manager was kind enough to mark off the fifty feet we were supposed to stay from his door. He actually urinated at three points on the sidewalk to mark his territory." Lenny pointed to a dark stain on the pavement.

"You're as funny as a corpse on a rope." Williams opened the door to the gym, saying, "Just keep the sidewalk clear," he added and went inside.

Lenny watched customers come and go, but no more workers came through the entrance. He figured the late shift was all inside and would not come out until the gym closed at ten PM—later than he planned to stay that evening.

Detective Williams came out and approached Lenny. "I need to talk to you. In private."

Lenny suggested they call it a night. Moose offered to drop Regis at home, having come in his own car. Williams took Lenny by the arm and led him to his car.

"You sure you want to put me in the front seat?" he said. "Won't that hurt your image with the guerilla in the gym?"

Williams ignored the crack. He took a sip from a cup of coffee in a cup holder. The spot beside it was crammed with gum, pens and crumpled napkins.

"Get this straight, Moss. You're protecting the wrong man this time. Carlton is going down for the murder, and if you don't stop interfering with our investigation, you'll be sharing a cell with him for the rest of your life."

"I don't think so."

"*You don't think so?* We have evidence linking Carlton Rogers to the dead girl."

"What evidence?"

"You know I can't tell you that."

"Than don't ask me to stop trying to help him. And don't even bother giving me any shit about the money in his back yard. Carlton was paranoid about banks. He only dealt in cash."

"Oh, yeah? What about his running from the police and refusing to come forward to answer questions? Does that sound like an innocent man?"

"He's running from you because he's innocent and he doesn't want to be convicted on a lot of circumstantial evidence."

"Circumstantial, eh? We found a gold chain in Carlton's house that belonged to the deceased. And we have forensic evidence that she was wearing that chain the night she was murdered!"

Lenny had no answer for this new piece of news. He decided to try a different approach. "Have you found out who the father of her baby was?" he asked.

"No, not—"

Williams stopped in mid-sentence. "How the hell do you know about the baby? We haven't released that information to the press." He felt a grudging admiration for the persistent fellow, having seen Lenny uncover the identity of more than one killer in cases where the police were on the wrong trail. The one thing Williams didn't want was to look like a fool again and let Lenny solve another case on his own.

"She told one of her co-workers, word gets around," Lenny lied with a perfectly innocent face. "Did you know she was having an affair with a doctor Jean Farr, and that doctor Farr ordered lab tests for her? Not pregnancy tests, but something to do with her hormones."

"We know about that, yeah."

"Do you think it's related to her murder?"

Williams crumpled his now empty cup of coffee and tossed the paper cup on the floor at Lenny's feet. Lenny liked that.

"Your guess is as good as mine," said Williams. "What else have you got?"

"Well, I know Briana was usually assigned to patients who weren't getting narcotics. She passed all her drug tests, but she could have taken urine from her patients and used it for the tests. What did her tox screen from the autopsy show?"

"You'll know when we release the information at your buddy's trial," said Williams.

"Hey, I gave you everything I know. You've got to give me something in return."

Williams reached across Lenny's lap and pulled the handle, opening the door. "I'm surprised the great Lenny Moss hasn't figured it out already." The detective flashed a satisfied smile.

"Figured out what?" said Lenny, stepping out of the car and then leaning back in.

"Didn't you wonder what I was doing here at the gym?"

"I was a little surprised to see a detective responding to a complaint from Brunner."

"You're right, that piss-ant stuff is for the beat cop. I investigate murders."

Lenny looked into the cop's eyes, trying to figure what he was driving at. The realization hit him like one of Albert's iron fists.

"You're here for the murder investigation!"

"Took you long enough," said Williams, starting the engine. "Briana Nearing was a member of the Chestnut Hill New Body Spa and Fitness Center."

Watching the unmarked police car pull away, Lenny cursed the fact that he missed the connection between the gym and the dead nurse. So many staff members from James Madison belonged, it was right up the street and the hours were good.

But the fact that upset him the most was that Laticia, the trainer at the gym, had not shared with him that one important piece of information.

THIRTY-THREE

In his office, Dr. Jean Farr changed from his scrub suit into a charcoal gray suit, silk shirt and cuff links. He was scheduled to speak at a dinner in Bala Cynwyd, paid for by one of the big pharmaceutical companies. The honorarium was useful, but the chance to spend the night with the drug rep was far more seductive. He would need all his charm for this one, she was a tall beauty with a body to die for. All the physicians had their tongues out when she left their offices, even the female ones.

He knew from the Daily News articles and the television reporting that the police still hadn't managed to pick up their prime suspect, the wild man who hunted deer in the park. Farr had to give the fellow credit, it took guts to pull of something like that. The papers had shown photos of night vision goggles and an exotic looking bow and arrow, explaining how easy it would be to bring down the prey silently and haul the carcass out of the park.

Farr realized that the police might stumble on his love affair with Briana, if they didn't know about it already. He had been careful, paying for hotel rooms with cash, never going to places where they would see anyone from the hospital. As careful and calculating he had been, he couldn't be sure that Bri had been equally secretive. You could never be sure with a wild, untamed creature like her.

Remembering what she was like in bed, he conjured up images of her face, her eyes wide and glistening, her mouth spitting cries of rapture, her fingernails digging into his back, drawing blood.

Memories were safe to hold on to, but he knew that mementoes could land him in a pile of trouble. He decided to destroy the photos he had of their days together. Unlocking his desk drawer, he pulled out a stack of files and reached deep into the drawer for the envelope with the photographs. Feeling the bare wood and the back of the drawer, he bent low to look into the dark space.

The envelope was gone.

Feeling a rising sense of fear, he opened the file folders, thinking the envelope may have been inadvertently slipped into one of them, but the files were empty. His heart pounding in his chest, he opened all the drawers and pulled out the contents, scattering them on the desktop, the chair, even the floor.

The photographs were nowhere to be found.

He tried to recall if he had removed them after Bri's death. Had he taken them home? Or left them in his attaché case? No, he *always* kept them locked in the bottom drawer, safe and secure. He was sure of it.

Bending down once more, Farr examined where the lock interfaced with the deck frame. There were scratches in the wood and the metal surfaces. New scratches, it appeared. Somebody had broken into his desk and taken the shots of him and Briana.

He had no idea who would have the nerve to violate his personal space. It didn't sound like the sort of thing the police would do. They would get a court order for a search warrant and come barging in en masse.

There was that annoying union fellow who was always butting his ugly nose into people affairs. He had a reputation for breaking the rules when he defended his low-life associates. Farr thought anyone who mopped floors and picked fights with supervisors was capable of the most despicable crimes. It had to be that scruffy Moss fellow; he was sure of it.

It was time to put an end to that meddling pest.

The dinner over, Patience sent the children to their rooms to finish their homework, then she put on rubber gloves and washed the dishes. When she was done, she hung the gloves to dry and looked at her hands. She had slim fingers, clear polish on the neatly trimmed nails, and a scar along one thumb from a broken glass years ago.

She joined Lenny in the living room where he was reading the Daily News. Patience ran the back of her hand over Lenny's cheek. "You need a shave," she said.

"I *always* need a shave."

She tapped the bald spot on the top of his head with a finger. "Can you get me more of that cream from the gym? I really like it, it's done great things for my skin. My rash is cleared up. Look." She held up her hands in front of his face.

"Somehow I don't think the girl at the desk is going to be giving me any more free samples."

"That's a shame," said Patience. "I guess you'll just have to join the gym."

"Good idea. Let me just make out my last will and testament before I go back there." He held the newspaper up to his face, adding, "Let's see, what sort of obituary will you write about me?"

THIRTY-FOUR

At five in the morning Sherri Ann, an ICU night nurse, began drawing up her six am medications. She wanted to have everything checked off and all her numbers added up by the time the day nurse arrived for report. It had been a quiet night: her GI bleeder's hemoglobin stopped dropping after the third unit of blood and the frozen plasma, and Jimmy Jones—that poor suffering man —didn't get any *worse*. Although Sherri Ann knew that in Jimmy's case, worse was a trip to the morgue.

She looked up when a stranger passed silently by the medication cart. It was Dr. Farr, who looked briefly over Jimmy's vital signs recorded on the flow sheet. The surgeon scanned the monitor, then he studied the readings on the ventilator. Watching to see if the surgeon needed her assistance, Sherri Ann noted, as she had so many time before, that when Farr examined a patient who was sedated and had the breathing tube in place, he never looked at the patient's face.

Farr turned and walked past the nurse to the exit without a word. He had no team of residents and students with him, which was unusual. Sherri Ann guessed that they hadn't arrived at work yet. Leave it to the workaholic to get to work before anyone else.

In the Carpentry Shop Carlton ran the plane along the strip of maple wood, shaving it over and over until it had the gentle tapering shape of a bow, with notches at the ends for the string. He held it up against the strip of ash he had already cut and planed. The match was good. Not as perfect or as elegant as his Mongolian bow. Not as strong or resilient, either. But the Mongols had perfected the art of laminating over hundreds of years. They even used animal skin in the laminate.

He laid down a bead of glue, backed two sides with extra strips of wood, and pressed them solidly together with clamps. Wanting to speed up the drying, he carried the bow to the boiler room in the basement and set it on top of one of the big hot water tanks, where the gentle heat would hasten the curing.

Now all he needed was a piece of strong gut. His choices were limited. The sewing room might have some thick thread, but he doubted it could be woven into a hank strong enough to string a bow that would propel an arrow with deadly force.

He thought about objects that contained strings. The string from a stand-up bass or a viola would be perfect, but he didn't know of any musical instruments in the facility. He decided to go with surgical sutures, there were plenty of them in the OR store room. He made his way to the storeroom adjoining the operating theatre. Inside, he selected a heavy silk suture, taking a half dozen packs. He added six scalpels. They would make perfect tips for the arrow. Now all he needed was something to replace the feathers that would stabilize the arrow in flight, seeing as how he would be hunting once again.

As he drove into the employee parking lot Lenny waved to Sandy, the old security guard, who shot him a curt military salute. Lenny drove to the far end of the lot, where a line of evergreen trees shielded the lot from the apartment building and its private driveway next door.

He turned off the engine, engaged the parking brake, got out and enjoyed the crisp sound of the heavy door as it closed. They really didn't make them like they used to: four thousand pounds of iron and chrome. Who needs air bags when you have that kind of steel cage surrounding you? True, there were rust bubbles along the rocker panels. Some day he'd have to sand the metal down to good steel and pack it with putty. Some day.

He had the key in the door lock and was just turning it when he heard a *crack*. A split second later he felt a sharp stab of pain in his gut. Doubling over with pain, he pressed a hand over his belly, felt something warm and wet. He raised his hand and stared at it, dumbfounded. His palm was smeared with blood.

"Fuck." He pressed his hand against the wound and staggered toward the guard station. When he had driven into the lot it had taken only seconds to cross that distance, but now the shack seemed like a mile away. He felt an overwhelming urge to vomit. The urge scared him. He was afraid that retching would make the wound even worse.

Half way to the station he felt dizzy and reached out to a parked car to steady himself. He tried to call out, but his voice was weak. The effort of taking a deep breath raised the pain to an unbearable level.

He waved his free hand, but Sandy was facing away from the lot, watching the entrance as cars came in. Cursing silently, Lenny begged for Sandy to turn around.

Reaching the first car in the lot, Lenny stumbled. His vision was growing blurry and his legs were shaking and weak. A woman who worked in the laundry drove past the guard station and stopped to say hello to Lenny. As she pulled up beside him she smiled and waved, but then, seeing him doubled over, a hand pressed to his abdomen, she lowered the passenger side window and asked was he all right.

Unable to speak, Lenny shook his head. He fell to his knees, his strength giving out. As he tumbled down onto his side, the laundry worker pressed her hand on the horn and held it there, filling the air with wailing, desperate to get the guard's attention.

Sandy turned to the car, annoyed at the rude employee and ready to curse her. When he saw Lenny doubled over lying on the driveway, he rushed out of the booth toward the stricken man.

Seeing the blood oozing between Lenny's fingers, Sandy ripped the walkie-talkie from his belt and called Control. "Call a Code Red in the parking lot, we got a gunshot victim! Repeat, Code Red in the employee parking lot! Gunshot victim! GUNSHOT VICTIM!"

A sleepy voice crackled in the radio. "Did you say Code Red? You sure 'bout that, Sandy?"

"You idiot, of course I'm sure! Somebody shot Lenny Moss! Tell the Code Team to get their ass out here *now!*"

Not sure what to do, Sandy bent down and asked Lenny to keep his eyes open. "Look at me, Lenny, just keep looking at me," he said. "Don't punk out on me, man, keep looking at this ugly old face. You hear me? Lenny?"

Lenny's eyelids felt so heavy, as if he would need a winch to keep them open. As much as he tried to look up into the face of his old friend, he found the gray fog of sleep stealing over him. As darkness descended, the last thing Lenny heard was the voice of his friend begging him to stay with him. He hoped his friend would forgive him for punking out.

THIRTY-FIVE

Dr. Rick Holden was interviewing a woman with chest pain when he heard the call on the overhead intercom: *"Code Red, Employee Parking Lot. Repeat. Code Red, Employee Parking Lot."*

He cursed the announcement. A cardiac arrest in the parking lot was a royal pain. There were no electric outlets. No oxygen or vacuum ports. Resuscitating a patient in the field was usually a disaster.

As he released the brake on an empty stretcher and shoved it toward the ambulance bay, a respiratory therapist grabbed an oxygen tank and an Ambu bag and threw them on the stretcher, while a nurse unplugged the crash cart and pushed it out the door. Together the makeshift team rushed down the ramp to the sidewalk and hurried around to the side of the building and the employee lot.

As he pushed the stretcher, Holden said, "Why couldn't the employee have the decency to arrest on the public sidewalk? That would leave it to EMS to try and resuscitate him,"

"Very thoughtless," the nurse agreed.

"Hey, at least we're getting out in the fresh air!" the respiratory therapist chimed in.

Dr. Holden saw Sandy standing near the guard station frantically waving his arms. When he reached the stricken employee and saw who it was, Holden let out a string of curses.

"He was shot," said Sandy. I didn't hear it, but..."

The physician ripped open Lenny's shirt and examined the wound, estimating the likelihood that the bullet had perforated the aorta, which would have been rapidly fatal, He palpated Lenny's neck, feeling for a pulse, and was relieved to find it, thready though it was. "Give me a large bore catheter," he told the nurse."

"Do you want a groin line?" she asked, ripping open the drawer of the crash cart.

"I can't take the chance, if he's got an injury to his inferior vena cava, anything we run into his groin will just leak out into his belly."

Wrapping a tourniquet around Lenny's upper arm, Holden hastily jabbed a fourteen gauge needle into the big vein in the crook of the elbow. He smiled

139

grimly to see the dark blood come oozing out of the end of the catheter and quickly attached an intravenous line.

"Run the saline wide," he told the nurse, who had already opened the roller clamp. He began inserting a second line in Lenny's other arm. The nurse slapped electrodes on Lenny's chest while the respiratory therapist placed an oxygen mask over Lenny's face. Holden filled a syringe with blood from the second IV line and handed it to the nurse before running in a second liter of saline. The oxygen bottle hissed as it released its gases while the heart monitor let out its reassuring *beep-beep-beep.*

"He needs blood and a fast track to surgery," said Holden as the team lifted Lenny onto the stretcher. He pushed the stretcher back toward the ER with one hand and barked orders into his cell phone with the other. "Get the trauma team down here NOW! Send somebody for two units of O-Negative blood, and have them type Lenny for six more units. *What's his blood type? How the fuck am I supposed to know his blood type? Lenny donates blood every year, they'll have it in their database!"*

He snapped his phone shut and pushed the stretcher through the automatic doors. Coming to a stop in the first bay, Holden called to the clerk, "Tell the OR to prepare for an emergency ex lap!" He cast his eyes about the ER. *"Where the fuck is the trauma team?"*

"Trauma's on their way!" the clerk yelled back as she dialed the number to the Operating Room.

After cutting away Lenny's shirt, Holden palpated his abdomen, trying to assess whether the bowel had been ruptured and was pumping air into the ab-dominal cavity. His belly wasn't rigid, but Holden knew it was too early to see signs of an acute abdomen.

"You want me to call for a flat plate?" the clerk called to him.

"We don't have time for an x-ray, we need blood and a surgeon!" the physician called back.

Just then Dr. Farr, on call that morning for the trauma team, entered the ER with his cohort of residents and students. The team swarmed around the stretcher, palpating Lenny's feet for pulses and pressing on his abdomen while Farr listened to Holden's report.

"I called the OR and told them to get a room ready," Holden said. "He's got a CBC and chem panel pending."

Farr agreed the patient needed an emergency exploration of his abdomen. "Have you ordered blood?"

"I sent down for six units. The first should be up any second."

Whoosh! A new transport canister was spit out of the vacuum system that fed departments throughout the hospital. The nurse hurried to open it and retrieve the first unit of blood. As she spiked the bag and squeezed it hard, forcing the cold, viscous cells into the tubing, she said to Holden, "You know we need an ID band on this patient before I can hang the blood. I have to have two identifiers. It's the law."

"*Jesus H Christ,*" Holden snapped, "there's only one Lenny Moss! Besides, the blood's for a universal donor." Seeing the nurse still hesitating, the physician grabbed the line and connected it. The deep red liquid flowed into Lenny's vein.

"Get the registrar back here and print out an ID label," he called to the clerk. "Lenny was stuck with a needle a while back, he's gotta be in the system."

The rapid infusion of saline and the first volume of blood quickly elevated Lenny's blood pressure, removing some of the clouds from his mind. He realized he'd been shot. More to the point, he realized that the shooting was tied to the murder of Briana Nearing. His spirits lifted when he saw Dr. Holden standing above him.

"Hang in there, my friend," said Holden, putting a hand on Lenny's shoulder. "You're going to surgery, but no worries, the surgeon will have that little piece of lead you caught out in no time."

Lenny smiled, comforted by the ER doctor's confidence. Then his smile soured as he looked past Holden and saw Dr. Farr conferring with his team.

"Fuck," Lenny muttered. "Is Farr my—"

"He's a good surgeon, Lenny. You'll be fine."

As Holden turned to give the nurse more orders, Lenny reached for his hand. "I need to talk to Regis. Regis Devoe. In the morgue. It's about the nurse who was killed."

"Mister Moss," said Farr, stepping between Holden and Lenny. "You have no time to talk to anybody or you will end up in the morgue." Farr released the brake on the stretcher and called to his residents to move the patient. "I am going to scrub. I will meet you in OR Seven," he said and hurried off.

Riding the stretcher toward the elevator surrounded by the surgical team, Lenny tried to call out to Dr. Holden, but at that moment a patient started screaming, and Holden hurried across the ER to find out what the problem was.

When the Emergency Room doors closed behind him, Lenny felt as if his life was closing as well. As if the murderer was coming to finish the job, and nobody was able to stop him.

THIRTY-SIX

Joe West stared at the section of the parking lot where Lenny was shot. He saw Sandy at the guard station talking to a police detective. Several employees were crowded around the entrance watching the investigation unfold.

West approached Lenny's car, now cordoned off by yellow crime scene tape and guarded by a young uniformed officer. When the patrolman asked West to stay outside the perimeter, West told him he was the chief of hospital security. Seeing that the young cop was unmoved, West pointed to the detective at the guard station talking to Sandy.

"You see that detective down there?" West said. "His name is Williams. Joe Williams. You have any questions about me, you call your superior officer, he'll tell you I have full police authority within *my* jurisdiction."

West strode past the flummoxed cop and ducked under the crime tape. He noted the blood on the macadam beside Lenny's car, as well as the drops of blood forming a trail toward the guard station. Another line of police tape cordoned off the trees on the edge of the lot. This was presumably the place where the shooter had stood. West looked back toward the surveillance camera mounted high on a pole. The trees provided good cover for the shooter.

At the guard station, Sandy looked over Detective Williams' shoulder and saw West examining the crime scene. Puzzled, the old guard looked around the grounds of the hospital. He hadn't seen West come out of the hospital entrance. West hadn't passed him to get to the sight of the shooting. That could only mean that West approached the lot from off the grounds.

Sandy knew that West was *always* inside the hospital giving out the morning assignments at the morning shift change. If West had been out in the street at the time of the shooting, it would have been a break from his routine.

He could have been running late to work. He could have been called in on a day off. But Sandy's suspicions leaned toward a darker kind of explanation.

In the OR the residents lifted Lenny from the stretcher and gently settled him on the operating table. One scrub nurse stripped off his clothes while another wiped his abdomen and groin with an antiseptic. While they wiped the skin, the anesthesiologist stood at the head of the table, his face upside down in Lenny's eyes.

"Sir, are you allergic to any medications?"

Lenny shook his head no.

"Did you eat breakfast this morning?"

"Cup of coffee," Lenny croaked.

"Nothing solid?"

Lenny shook his head once more.

"Sir, I'm going to put a tube down into your stomach and suck out the fluids. But first I'm going to put you to sleep. Okay?"

Lenny reached his hand up and grabbed the anesthesiologist's wrist. "I have to talk to Regis. Regis Devoe in the morgue. Please. It's a life and death matter."

"You can talk to him all you want when you get out of surgery." The physician released Lenny's grip and took up a syringe and bottle. Drawing a milky white fluid from the bottle, the anesthesiologist injected a bolus of the opaque fluid into the intravenous tubing. Lenny watched, fascinated, as the creamy stuff oozed along the tubing toward his arm.

As the anesthetic entered the blood stream and reached his brain, Lenny fell into a dream. In his dream he was in bed with a book, but he wasn't reading, he was thinking about the case. His wife Patience was going through her regular nightly routine, asking him to rub lotion on her back, brushing her hair and piling up her pillows to make herself comfortable.

The pieces of the puzzle seemed to float through his mind. Images and names floated in and out, like letters in a Scrabble game searching for a seven-letter word.

Suddenly, the images snapped together in a simple pattern and the entire case became clear. Briana's secret. The identity of the killer. The face of the person who shot him. In his mind he laughed at the simplicity of it. All along the clues had pointed to the answer, just like one of Carlton's arrows finding its mark.

Lenny felt blackness wiping out the images. He struggled in vain to remember them. To hold the name and face of the killer in his mind. His minded clawed and fought to stay awake and *remember,* but it was hopeless. In the end darkness erased it all.

Once the anesthesiologist had the breathing tube inserted and anchored, Farr approached the patient. The anesthesiologist asked him what pre-op antibiotic the surgeon wanted him to administer.

"We don't need any, he was loaded with antibiotics in the ER," Farr said, slipping on a pair of sterile gloves. He held out a large, strong hand palm up. "Scalpel," he said.

The scrub nurse slapped the handle of the scalpel into his hand. Farr gripped it easily. Comfortably. He jabbed the tip into the soft flesh of Lenny's abdomen and pulled it smoothly from right to left, opening a deep gash. Blood oozed from the margins of the wound. The surgery resident took a Bovie and used the hot tip to sear the capillaries, stanching the bleeding. The smell of burning flesh tickled the surgeon's nose.

In seconds Farr had the abdomen open and was exploring the cavity with his fingers. A stream of bright red blood spurted into a pool and mixed with bowel contents that had oozed out of the perforated colon, forming a black, foul smelling pool.

"The bullet tore the superior mesenteric vein," Farr said.

"You want I should call the vascular service?" the first scrub nurse asked, stepping toward the phone on the wall.

"No need, I can do it," said Farr. "Give me some 4-O silk, I'll repair the vein."

While the OR tech tore open a suture set, the resident alternately irrigated the cavity with sterile saline and suctioned out the fetid black stew. He continued irrigating and suctioning until the organs were clean of stool and Farr had a clear view of the ruptured artery.

Once he had the vein repaired, Farr turned his attention to the colon. He cut through the bowel on either side, leaving clean margins.

"I don't think he'll need a colostomy," said Farr.

Exploring the area around the bowel, he felt a small, round, hard object wedged in the retroperitoneal space. He smiled behind his mask as he felt the bullet's smooth, hard surface. After taking a few seconds to caress its slippery surface, he pushed it into a snug place, then began to sew the margins of the colon together.

Finishing the bowel repair, Farr told the resident to irrigate the abdominal cavity one more time. He looked into the wound, saw no sign of bleeding or leaking from the bowel, and stepped back from the OR table, indicating that the senior resident would close the wound. Farr pulled off his gloves and stepped out of the room, cheerful and pleased with himself for leaving the little memento inside his lucky patient.

THIRTY-SEVEN

Moose hurried into the Morgue and found Regis labeling specimens to send to the pathologist. "Reege, Lenny's in trouble. Somebody shot him."

Regis froze in place, a current of fear coursing through him. If Lenny was dead, the whole world was turned to shit. *"What the fuck happened?"*

"They got him in the hospital parking lot. He took a hit to the belly."

Regis felt the fear recede a bit. He'd assisted in enough autopsies to know that as long as the bullet didn't tear the aorta, abdominal wounds were usually less deadly than chest or head wounds. Belly wounds left the lungs, heart and brain untouched. Regis found a little extra hope in the lucky chanced that the shooting was just a stone's throw from the ER.

"Did the bullet hit the aorta?" he asked Moose.

"I don't know, Sandy just said he was bleeding from his gut. They took him to the OR."

"If he was alive going into the OR he'll be alive coming out," said Regis. "Did you get to radiology and tell Patience?"

"Yeah, I told her. Birdie's gonna take care of the kids after school."

Regis pulled off his gloves and ripped away the rubber apron. "Whoever shot Lenny killed the nurse. That's for sure."

"You right," said Moose. "We got to stay close to Lenny soon as he's out of the OR, the bastard might want t' try again."

They agreed to meet in the sewing room over break, by which time they hoped Lenny would be out of surgery and they would know what his condition was.

Joe West returned to his office with silent elation. *Lenny Moss shot and critically ill.* In a single selfless act some Good Samaritan had accomplished what West had been unable to do for years. It meant no more tiresome arguments over a termination. No more challenges over the contract. Best of all, without Moss helping him, Carlton Rogers would be unable to elude his security forces for long. That would make two trouble makers eliminated.

He went to the dispatcher. "Who's covering Sector Seven?"

"Officer Teasedale."

"Station him in the Recovery Room. I want to be informed if Moss survived the surgery."

"Yes sir."

West had a bottle of single malt Scotch in his desk drawer. It was early in the day to begin drinking, but this was a banner day. A festive occasion. He unlocked the drawer, poured himself a stiff shot of whiskey, and held the glass up to his face, inhaling the exquisite brocade. The first taste was always the most satisfying.

Albert called the staff from the gym together in the middle of the gym, interrupting the early customers getting their workout before going on to their jobs. "I'm sorry to interrupt, ladies and gentlemen, but I have to talk to my staff. It will be just for one moment, please to continue your workout."

Brunner told the staff that a hospital employee had been shot that morning. "The reason I tell you this, he is the one who was giving out union propaganda yesterday evening. The news people will find out about him coming to our facility. They will try to ask you questions. *Do not talk to them.* Do not let them call you at home. Leave any communication with them to me. Is that understood?"

When the staff all nodded their head in silence, Brunner told them to get back to work and not to think about the "tragic event." He checked the schedule to see when Laticia was due in to work. She would be the only potential problem in an otherwise perfect day.

Laticia was in her car was on her way to the supermarket on Germantown Ave, having dropped her daughter off at school. She needed to pick up something for dinner before going on to work at the gym. KYW played on the radio. As she pulled into the supermarket parking lot, the announcer came on with a late breaking story about a hospital employee shot in the parking lot of James Madison University Hospital. Even before the radio released Lenny's name, Laticia knew who it was.

Bringing the car to a stop in the lot, she listened with horror to the few details released to the press. Lenny had been shot by an unknown assailant as he left his car to go to work. He was undergoing emergency surgery; his condition was critical. At this time the police had no suspects and no theory about the reason for the shooting.

Shaking, with tears running down her cheeks, Laticia sat behind the wheel letting the radio play, with no desire to leave the car. She felt as if the patrons in the store would stare at her and accuse her if she ventured out of the car. Could guilt be so heavy that it radiated off of someone, like heat or light?

Laticia took her cell phone out of her purse and called the gym to tell them she would not be coming to work. There was no way she would be able to go through that front door and let Albert Brunner stare at her with his cold, dead eyes. She would rather live in a shelter with her daughter than go back to work for that monster.

THIRTY-EIGHT

Gary was listening to Dr. Singh's plan for Jimmy Jones that day. Singh explained to his team that if the GI bleed continued, he would ask the gastroenterologist to do a colonoscopy in the hope they could cauterize a bleeder.

"What about dialysis?" one of the residents asked.

"Renal medicine will place a catheter today. If the patient's blood pressure doesn't bottom out, they'll try dialyzing him without taking off any fluid. But dialysis and bleeding aren't his biggest problem, are they?"

Singh told his team they were walking on a tightrope with the patient's lungs. "You have to do a high wire act in cases like these," he said. "Jimmy's lungs are so badly scarred, he needs high levels of peep to maintain an acceptable level of oxygen in his blood." He looked at the medical student on the team. "What is peep, Charlie?"

The student swallowed. "Peek end expiratory pressure?" he said.

"Very good. Now what does it do?"

The student looked to the anesthesia resident for encouragement, since anesthesiologists dealt with issues of ventilation every day. When the resident blew out his cheeks and held the air in his mouth under pressure, the student said, "Peep prevents the alveoli from collapsing at the end of expiration."

"Correct," said Singh, ignoring the anesthesia resident's assistance. "Remember that we all have some degree of peep. Our epiglottis closes and the pressure within the lung parenchyma does not drop to zero. When you have the endotracheal tube keeping the airway open, the pressure in the lung will drop to zero and collapse the alveoli. The alveoli will stick closed, and that will prevent them from transporting oxygen to the blood stream."

"High peep, you blow the lung. Moderate peep, your brain dies from hypoxemia. A high wire act like no other."

While Dr. Singh was lecturing to the residents and students, a respiratory therapist coming to draw Jimmy's blood gas asked Gary if he heard about Lenny being shot. Gary felt the news hit him almost as if he had taken the bullet. The therapist explained that her co-worker from nights who worked in the ER helped bring Lenny into the hospital and rush him to the operating room.

"What sort of injury did he sustain?" asked Singh, who overheard the therapist's remarks.

"I heard he was shot in the abdomen," said the therapist. Singh pointed out that an abdominal wound was not usually fatal, especially if the victim can be brought to the operating room in a timely fashion and explored.

Gary asked another nurse to cover for him and rushed down to the surgical suites. He found Patience in the OR waiting room pacing back and forth. As he put his arms around her she burst into tears.

"My poor Lenny!" she cried. "How bad is he, Gary? Tell me the truth!"

"I don't know, I just heard he was shot in the abdomen. They're doing an exploratory lap."

Gary led her to a chair and sat beside her. "It could be worse," he said. "It could have been a gunshot to the head. Or the heart."

"That's not comforting. They said it was emergency surgery. They said he was critical!"

"He got to the OR alive, that's a good sign," he told her. "And he's strong and healthy, that's a plus. He—"

Gary stopped speaking as a young physician in scrubs with a surgical mask hanging from his neck stepped into the waiting room.

"Uh, is there a Missus Moss here?"

Patience jumped up. *"I'm Lenny's wife; is he all right? Can I see him?"*

"We just brought him into Recovery. Doctor Farr said you could come in for just a quick look. He's still under anesthesia, so he won't respond to you."

"Will he be okay?"

"The operation went well. We had to repair his colon, it was ruptured from the bullet. And the renal vein was torn, that was a little tricky, but the repair went well."

Gary said, "Was there a lot of fecal material in the peritoneum?"

"Some. We washed him out good. He should recover nicely."

Patience grasped the young doctor's hand and squeezed it. *"Thank you!* Thank you for everything. And thank Doctor Farr for me, please."

She and Gary hurried into the Recovery Room, where they found Lenny in a corner slot. The first thing Gary noted was that Lenny's head wasn't elevated and that he was receiving a unit of blood. That could mean he was bleeding and his blood pressure was low.

Patience took Lenny's hand. "He's cold! Why is he cold, Gary?"

"That's normal, the temperature in the OR is kept low. He'll warm up."

The Recovery Room nurse, who knew Patience, came over and offered reassuring words. Gary asked if Lenny was receiving pressors: adrenaline-like medications that supported the blood pressure. He was relieved to hear that Lenny was not receiving any drugs for his blood pressure, which meant there was no sign of shock. He was also glad to see that the oxygen concentration on the ventilator was only fifty per cent, which meant Lenny's lungs were working well.

When the nurse told them they couldn't stay, Patience kissed Lenny on the forehead and gently stroked his hair. "I love you, Lenny," she whispered in his ear, then followed with, *"You better not die on me, you hear me, Leonard?"*

She told the nurse she was staying in the waiting room in case there was a change in Lenny's condition. As she walked out of the Recovery Room with Gary, she kept saying, "He's so cold . . . *he's so cold.*"

Suspended in a dense fog, Lenny fought to find his way out, but there was nothing to guide him. No lights to lead him home. He heard murmurs in the distance, but he couldn't tell what direction they came from or what they were saying. As he struggled to clear his mind, he felt there was something he needed to remember. Some crucial fact that would make a big difference in a crucial task, but he couldn't make out what it was. Couldn't even fathom what he was supposed to be doing.

He thought he felt something touching his hand, but he couldn't move his fingers to try and feel what it was. He couldn't open his eyes to see if it was someone he knew. The sounds drifted away and he became the fog that surrounded him, a lifeless figure without thought or feeling. A creature that was not quite alive, not entirely dead.

THIRTY-NINE

Detective Joe Williams was seriously pissed off. As he surveyed the crime scene one last time, he confirmed what he had found in the initial examination: *nothing*. He had uncovered no forensic evidence of any kind. No footprint beneath the trees, no shell casing, no fresh cigarette butt. No tire tracks in the driveway. Even worse, the old guard at the entrance to the lot hadn't heard a shot or seen anyone lurking about in the area where Lenny parked his car. The laundry worker who first saw Lenny hadn't seen anyone, either.

So Williams had squat, and that pissed him off royally. He thought that Carlton was unlikely to shoot Lenny, since Lenny had been fighting to clear him of the murder. *Unless* Carlton *was* guilty and he believed that Lenny was the one person who could find proof of his guilt. On the other hand, Carlton didn't seem to use guns very much, his shotgun had rust inside the barrel, telling him it hadn't been used in years. Rogers clearly liked more primitive weapons.

He needed to take possession of the bullet that wounded Lenny and preserve the chain of evidence. If the bullet *was* fired from the same gun that killed Briana Nearing, it would simplify the investigation. If it was from a different weapon, he knew he might have two different suspects, working together. Or one employing different guns.

As he walked across the parking lot to the hospital entrance he saw the news van pull up. A blonde reporter was in the passenger seat fixing her hair in the mirror. That gave him time to slip behind the van and enter the hospital without having to deal with her. He wanted to get to Lenny Moss as soon as he was awake enough to answer questions.

Once she had her makeup done and the cameraman was set up on the sidewalk outside the hospital entrance, the news reporter flashed a dazzling smile. "This is Candy Calloway outside James Madison University Hospital, where a hospital employee, Mister Leonard Moss, has been shot in the hospital parking lot. Over there—"

She pointed to the employee parking lot. The camera panned to the area and zoomed in on the section cordoned off by crime scene tape. "Over there we see the spot where Lenny Moss was shot by an unknown assailant. At this time the police have no suspects and no leads in the shooting."

The camera returned to the reporter. "Mister Moss is a close personal friend of Carlton Rogers, the man wanted for the murder of Nurse Briana Nearing. He was apparently investigating the murder in the hope that he would find evidence that would clear his friend's name. It doesn't take a Sherlock Holmes to realize that whoever killed nurse Nearing may have also been responsible for this shocking incident right on hospital property.

The camera panned to the hospital entrance. "Leonard Moss is at this moment undergoing emergency surgery. We don't know at this point in time the extent of his injuries or his chances of recovering, but we will remain here at the hospital until we have answers to this and to other questions. The camera turned back to the reporter. "This is Candy Calloway for FIX News at James Madison Hospital."

As the cameraman lowered his camera, Candy said, "Are we going to stay here all day? Christ. Let's get something to eat, I missed breakfast."

When the administrative assistant to the hospital president picked up the ringing phone, Albert fixed his eyes on the leggy brunette's fantastic legs. He imagined her sprawled across her desk, her long legs wrapped around his hips as he made her cry out in pain and rapture, a fitting reward for the promotion he was about to receive.

"You may go into the conference room now, Mister Brunner," she said, hanging up the phone.

He left his seat without thanking her and entered the room, where he nodded slightly to President Lefferts, seated at the head of the long mahogany table. Albert pulled the chair back but remained standing. He believed that since height was not one of his best attributes, he would appear to better advantage if he remained standing while the others were seated.

"Thank you, President Lefferts," he said, being sure to use the CEO's title. "As you are no doubt aware, my New Body Spa and Fitness Center has brought James Madison a net profit of eighty-five thousand dollars in the past fiscal year. More important, my enrollment has increased every quarter by fifteen to twenty per cent since you appointed me manager of the Chestnut Hill enterprise."

He paused to see the effect of his impressive statistics. The old gray-haired suits sat with impassive faces. They mistrusted a foreign born manager who didn't grow up in a rich family out on the Main Line.

"I have a plan to bring the other four Spas up to the same level of growth that I have accomplished." He handed a raft of papers to the man beside him.

"I will turn the entire enterprise around in six months if you make me the director. After that, I will implement a plan to take the franchise national and grow the business beyond your wildest dreams."

Doctor Slocum, the Chief Medical Officer, asked, "What makes you so sure you can do so well in the other facilities? Chestnut Hill is a prime location."

"There are two reasons that my plan will bring success. First, I know how to inject *motivation* in my people. When employees are motivated, they charge into their work with the greatest enthusiasm! Second, my employees always treat every single client like *royalty.* I tell them to always act like they are serving a Princess Di or Prince William. This high level of respect ensures that the clients not only return for more sessions, but they spread the word far and wide about how good they are treated."

He paused to see if the CEO or Dr. Slocum had any more questions. Nobody spoke, and nobody looked at the handout he had provided. Albert's self-confidence began to falter. He provided them with all the information they needed to give him the position that he clearly deserved, so why was there no discussion? *Why was there no praise for his accomplishments?*

He hastily added, "I should tell you that the hospital union is about to launch a campaign to enlist the employees in the spa into the union. I can assure you that this effort will die a quick death. My employees are supremely happy with their working conditions. I will *crush* the union's puny efforts. I will *tear* them out by the roots and leave them to die in the street like the weeds."

He waited to see if the board was swayed by his last remarks, but instead found the members looking vacantly at each other or at President Lefferts. After an uncomfortable silence, Lefferts said, "Mister Brunner, we are all gratified for the hard work you have put into the facility at Chestnut Hill. No one doubts your qualifications as an exercise trainer."

"Thank you, sir. I believe that I—"

"*But* . . ." Lefferts interrupted Brunner with a raised finger. "To grow a business on the scale which you are suggesting requires someone with a thorough knowledge of business practice. Of financial policies. Regulatory agencies. State guidelines. The board is not convinced that you have that sort of expertise."

"I have a masters of business degree. I am fully qualified to handle any issue that comes to me." Albert saw the smirk on Dr. Slocum's face at his reference to the business degree, which was from an online college.

"We will be considering another candidate from outside James Madison who has more substantial expertise in *all* these areas," said Lefferts.

"An outsider will not know Philadelphia as I know it."

"This gentleman was born and raised in the Delaware Valley and attended Penn. He is quite familiar with our city. In addition, we need someone with the temperament to handle difficult issues without engaging in thuggish behavior on a public street. It is lucky for you that the incident was not picked up by K-Y-W."

"I see," said Brunner, fighting within himself to remain calm and civil. "When will you make the decision?"

Lefferts looked to Slocum, who said they were interviewing the last candidate this afternoon and would announce their decision by the end of the week.

Raising himself to the fullest height he could attain, Brunner gathered up his unread papers, turned and walked out of the room. He had suspected the board would look for someone with the credentials they found so reassuring. Someone with a Main Line background. But he hadn't anticipated that his encounter with Lenny Moss, far from bringing him favor among the board, would poison them against him. That idiot president did not realize that the only way to deal with vermin like union organizers was to beat them into the ground and bury them.

Brunner knew he was not going to get the position he craved, and that Lenny Moss was the reason for his failure.

In his hiding place behind the false wall in the linen closet on Four-West, Carlton settled into his makeshift hammock. A flashlight hanging from a string was his lamp. He looked over his cache of arrows, each tipped with a scalpel blade. The blades were not as wide as a true hunting arrow, but they would penetrate skin and muscle just as well. Maybe better.

Carlton unwound six strands of surgical suture, tied the ends to a hook anchored in the wall, and began patiently weaving them together. It was slow work, but not at all tedious. He enjoyed the rhythm of the weaving, alone in his hiding place. It gave him time to think and to plan how he would kill his next prey.

As much as he loved hunting deer in Fairmont Park at night, eluding the police, dragging the dead animal out to his van and carrying it back to his garage, this was way better. This was the greatest hunt he had ever been on. To escape Joe West and his flat-footed guards, moving from unit to unit, invading offices and departments . . . To stay two steps ahead of the police, who were dying to pin the murder on him . . . And to keep feeding Lenny the information as he uncovered it—here was a hunter-warrior of legend. Here was a hero whose name would be spoken with reverence and awe at James Madison for years. Centuries.

His fingers nimbly weaving the silk strands, Carlton felt at peace with the world. He was at one with the universe.

FORTY

Moose got up from the folding chair in the sewing room, too restless to stay seated. "Whoever killed Briana knows Lenny is on his tail. It's gotta be the same person that shot him."

"We don't know that," said Gary. "Lenny has pissed off enough people in the hospital over the years, there are any number of people who would like to see him dead."

"Yeah, but look at the timing!" said Regis. "The killer saw Lenny closing in on him and *bam!*, he tries to take him out. I say it's Brunner. That creep has a stone for a heart."

"You're just pissed 'cause he put you on the mat last week," said Moose.

"Yeah I'm pissed, but look at the son of a bitch. He hates the union and he knows Lenny was the one started the campaign at the gym. Kill Lenny and the workers'll be too scared to even think about joining the union."

Birdie said, "I agree, Brunner is greedy and mean. He could've shot both of them. Maybe he had the hots for her and she turned him down. The man is disgusting. What decent girl would want *him?*"

"I'm puttin' my bet on Farr," said Moose. "He killed her 'cause she was carrying his baby and he shot Lenny knowin' he was on his trail."

"Unless he loved Briana," said Gary. "The look on his face when he saw her photo on the front page, I wouldn't be surprised if he really did want to marry her."

"People kill for love as much as for hate," said Regis. "People do all kinds a' bad things when they can't have what they want."

"Nobody thinks it was Carlton that did it," said Birdie. "Ain't that right?"

"No way was it Carlton," said Moose. "One thing's sure. We got to carry the weight, now that Lenny's out of the ring. And we got to watch his back, too, the cops sure ain't gonna do it."

Birdie said, "I think he's pretty much okay s'long as he's in the Recovery Unit. Somebody's always there to see who comes in and goes out."

"When he gets to the ward he'll need a private duty nurse or companion," said Gary. "I can take the night shifts, I can take some days off from work." Moose and Regis agreed to cover the first night Lenny was transferred out of Recovery. Gary would come on the second night.

"What about the benefit for Jimmy Jones?" said Birdie. "Should we postpone it?"

161

"I say let's keep it going," Moose said. "Lenny wouldn't want us to cancel just on account of him. And if Jimmy don't make it. . . " Moose turned to Gary, who confirmed that Jimmy's chance of surviving was not good.

"We got everything ready," said Birdie. "The food, the music. If it turns out to be a wake, so be it."

"All right," said Regis. "The fund raiser is on. Now what about Briana's murder? That's what started this whole thing. What have we got on it?"

"Well, we know Briana was on probation for drug use, and she was clean on all her tests," said Regis.

"But she could've substituted urine from her patients," said Gary.

Regis said, "Lenny found out that the Recovery Room assigned her to patients who didn't need narcotics, so it looks like she wasn't scoring from the narcotic cabinet."

"She might a' had a script" said Moose. "Or she took street drugs. We know there's drug sales in the hospital, and security's on the take."

"Her drug dealer could've done it on account she owed him big time," said Regis.

"I'm still puttin' my money on Doctor Farr," said Moose. "He was sticking it to her, and he was probably her baby's daddy."

"But what's his motive?" said Gary. "Having an affair? Being the father? Is that enough of a reason to kill her?"

"Depends on what kind 'a wife he's got," said Birdie, with a sly look at Regis. "'Member the time Salena threw all your clothes out on the street and changed the locks on the doors 'cause you stayed out all night drinking?"

"Birdie's right," said Regis. "Except Salina would kill *me*, not my girlfriend. If'n I had one."

"We can't exclude Carlton," said Gary, to loud objections from everyone. "I know Lenny believes in him, but look at the facts: he was in the park when she was murdered."

"That was 'cause of his hunting," said Regis.

"But was he in the park to hunt for deer or for Briana?" said Gary. "Remember the police found that gold chain and locket in his house. He might have taken it from her after he killed her."

"Kill a girl and rip the chain off of her neck?" said Moose. "No way Carlton's gonna do something evil like that. And no way did he shoot Lenny, I *know* that."

"What makes you so sure?" asked Gary.

"'Cause if it was Carlton did the shooting in the parking lot, he would've nailed him in the heart."

The meeting ended with the group agreeing to try and determine where the suspects were at the time of the shooting. Returning to the pathology lab, Regis passed the autopsy room, with its stainless steel table and scale. He couldn't help imagining assisting with Lenny's autopsy. The thought sent a chill through him. Ain't gonna happen, he told himself. *Ain't no way my boy's ending up on that table.*

But he couldn't shake the image of Dr. Fingers holding out his hand for the scalpel to make the first incision in Lenny's chest.

Standing outside the Operating Room, Detective Williams saw the big red stop signs and the warning that only those in full scrub attire could enter. He had confirmed Lenny's information about Farr having an affair with Briana Nearing. No surprise that Lenny knew about it, the annoying fellow had the ear of every employee in the hospital. Even some of the administrators. Williams asked one of the anesthesiologists going into the OR if Dr. Farr was still in surgery.

"I know he finished the emergency case. I'll see is he free."

A few moments later Farr stepped out of the operating suites, a mask dangling from his neck.

"Someone asked to see me?"

Williams introduced himself and asked if there was a place they could talk. Farr led him to an interview room for pre-operative evaluations. The detective began by asking if the surgeon had been able to remove the bullet from Lenny's abdomen, explaining the importance of having it for forensic evidence.

"I was unable to retrieve the bullet."

"Why is that? Wasn't it visible on the x-ray?"

"You have to understand, the bowel that's coiled in the stomach runs for over twenty feet. Any time you manipulate it: lift it out of the peritoneum, pull it to the side, explore around it, you cause damage. Inflammation. After you close, that inflammation can lead to the bowel shutting down and becoming obstructed. In addition, you risk damaging the liver, kidneys, the nerves coming off the spinal cord. No, I was not willing to risk harming my patient for the sake of some evidence at a trial that may never even take place."

"I see. Well, just for the record, where were you at five forty-five this morning?"

"I was making rounds in the hospital. I was on call last night for trauma. Any number of nurses and physicians saw me." Farr crossed his arms and cocked his head back. "Why do you want to know where I was this morning? Am *I* a suspect?"

"It's routine in this kind of investigation to rule out anyone who knew the murder victim."

"I did not know Mister Moss. I undoubtedly walked past him from time to time as he mopped the floor or took out the trash, but I never even spoke to the man."

"But you *did* know Briana Nearing, didn't you?"

For the first time Farr's smooth poker face showed a crack of irritation. "Briana was a nurse in the recovery. I worked with her when she was caring for my patients."

"Did you see her outside the hospital?"

"I ran into her at staff parties. At Christmas time we put up some money and threw an affair at a club; all the nurses came to that."

"What about a more personal encounter? Did you ever, say, visit her at her home? Or a hotel?"

"No, of course not. *What are you suggesting? I'm a married man!*"

"I can see the wedding ring, doc. I noticed you didn't say you were a *happily* married man."

"I'm as happy as any married man has a right to be. And I resent your insinuating I was involved with Miss Nearing or any other girl in the hospital."

"So you wouldn't mind taking a paternity test, since you're such a stranger to the dead girl. Right?"

Farr's face sank. For a moment he was speechless. "Briana . . . Miss Nearing was *pregnant?*"

"Yup. She was around twelve weeks along, as far as the Medical Examiner could determine."

Farr snapped back into the impassive surgeon's role. "If you want to invade my personal privacy you will need a court order." He pulled the mask up over his nose and punched the plate on the wall that opened the doors to the OR. "I have a case on the table waiting for me. If you need to speak with me again, contact my attorney."

As Detective Williams watched the big automatic doors with the giant stop signs on them close behind Farr, he wondered if Farr left the bullet in Lenny's belly because it could be linked to him. Williams knew he didn't have enough evidence to request a search warrant of Farr's home and office, but he could find out if the man had a gun registered in his name.

The detective looked up and down the hall, saw the sign with an arrow pointing to the Recovery Room, and knew who he had to interview next.

FORTY-ONE

When Patience returned to the Recovery Room, she was relieved to see the anesthesiologist had removed the breathing tube and Lenny was awake, more or less. He had an oxygen mask over his face and another unit of blood was infusing into his vein.

As glad as she was to see him alive and seeming to recover, she was angered to see a familiar, unwanted figure standing beside him. Detective Joe Williams was questioning her husband. She understood he had a job to do, Lenny *had* been shot after all. But she had about as much faith in the Philadelphia police as she did in the tooth fairy making their next mortgage payment.

Approaching the stretcher, she heard Lenny say, "It's all a blur; I don't remember any of it." He paused to take a few breaths. "I felt this sharp pain in my gut, that much I remember. And I kind of remember Sandy, he's one of the security guards. He was standing over me saying something, but that's about it."

"You didn't see anyone suspicious in the lot? You didn't hear a car drive off?"

"No, but I wasn't exactly studying the landscape. I was hoping I wouldn't die in the parking lot. I mean—" Lenny stopped to catch his breath.

"Excuse me," said Patience, stepping between Williams and Lenny. "Do you *have* to do this right now? I can see my husband is short of breath. Why don't you come back tomorrow?"

"Ma'am, the sooner I gather as much information as I can about the shooting, the sooner I can catch the individual who did this."

Lenny held up a hand. "It's okay, I can take it." He pulled off the oxygen mask to speak. "Tell me, what did the security camera pick up?" Lenny knew that the hospital kept continuous video surveillance of all the parking lots. One of the workers had been caught on tape keying his supervisor's car, and Lenny had lost the case.

"We're checking the videos," said Williams. "I'll let you know."

"Have you dropped the idea that Carlton killed Briana Nearing?"

"Not at all. Nothing that's happened today changes the dynamic."

"Carlton would never hurt Lenny!" said Patience. *"Never!* He looks up to Lenny. He *loves* him!"

The detective remained unimpressed. "Let's wait to see if he has an alibi for the time of your shooting. We already know he has none for the murder of Briana Nearing." Leaning in over Lenny's face, Williams added, "I don't suppose you know where your boy was at the time of the shooting, do you?"

Lenny looked into the detective's eyes, wishing he had enough breath to curse him out one more time.

Joe West marched into the security office and bore down on the officer at the monitors. "Why didn't you page me STAT the minute Rogers came into view?" he said, freezing the young guard with his shark eyes.

"I didn't actually see him, sir. Not in real time, that is. It was the facial recognition program that identified him. There's a time lag from feeding all the different videos from all over the hospital. The program only looks at one frame at a time. It's very slow."

"You were supposed to identify him on the video when he first showed up!" West watched as the guard rewound the video clip. It showed Carlton dressed in a carpenter's outfit complete with a set of tools hanging from his belt walking out of Four West. The time stamp was five-ten AM.

West summoned a half dozen officers. "There are no patients on Four West at this time, are there?" he said.

"No sir," said a guard who covered the area. "It's under reconstruction."

"That's a perfect place to establish a rat's nest," said West. He instructed the guard at the video monitors to focus his attention on Four West. "Page me STAT the minute Rogers is in the area. We will close off the exits and search the rooms until we find him."

"Yes, sir!" The guard made a silent vow to not screw up his assignment a second time around.

He assigned two guards to watch the video monitors, one to watch the suspicious area, the other to watch the rest of the hospital.

Lenny lay on the stretcher, his face turned to Patience. He was looking past her into the distance, not focusing on his wife.

"Are you okay?" she asked, anxiety gripping her.

"Yeah, yeah, it's just, I'm trying to remember something important. At least I *think* it's important. When I was under, I had a dream. I dreamed I saw the guy that shot me, only . . Now I can't for the life of me remember . . . what it was I saw."

"Don't talk so much, you'll tire yourself out!" Patience told him. "Just try to rest and get better. Let Moose and Regis and the rest take care of the investigation. *You need to take care of you for a change!*"

"I don't *think* it was Carlton I saw. If I could just . . . Remember."

Patience watched his chest rising and falling. He was breathing too fast and his color was growing dusky. She didn't like it. "Are you sure you're okay? You seem more short of breath."

"Is the oxygen. . .turned on?"

She checked the flow meter in the wall, confirmed the oxygen was on.

"You should be home to meet the kids," said Lenny.

"Birdie is picking them up from school, they'll be all right. I don't want them to see you until you're better."

Her anxiety rising, Patience was relieved to see a surgical resident come into the Recovery Room. She hurried to him and asked would he examine Lenny, she was worried, he seemed out of breath. The resident assured her that some degree of dyspnea was expected after bowel surgery. "Doctor Farr will be here in a few minutes. He'll explain it to you."

Patience returned to Lenny, still anxious about his breathing. She asked the nurse if she could give Lenny more oxygen. The nurse agreed that Lenny's breathing was labored and increased the flow of oxygen to his mask.

Moments later Patience was relieved when Dr. Farr and his team came into the Recovery Room. Relieved. She waited while the team went from patient to patient. When they arrived at Lenny's bedside, she waited again while the resident made a brief report of Lenny's post-operative course.

Satisfied, Farr turned to go on to his next case without examining his patient, when Patience said, "Excuse me, doctor, my husband is awfully short of breath. Is he all right?"

Farr turned to her, not looking at Lenny. "His abdomen is distended from the trauma. That pushes up his diaphragm, making it hard for him to draw a full breath. He'll be better in a few days."

"But his color isn't good, is it?"

Farr gave Lenny a quick glance. "That's nothing unusual, he will pink up soon enough. He's fine."

"Oh, okay. Thank you, doctor." She watched as the team left the Recovery Room, trying to believe that Lenny was on the road to recovery. But her experience told her that Lenny's rapid, shallow breathing and his difficulty saying a full sentence were not the normal course for a post-operative patient.

She knew from talking with Lenny that Farr was connected with Briana Nearing's murder. Lenny was investigating her death. Was Farr really looking out for Lenny's well being, or was he pushing him into a grave? The thought made her shiver with fear. She went to the phone at the desk and called the one person she knew would not hesitate to drop everything and help her.

FORTY-TWO

Detective Williams showed the smiling, nubile blonde at the reception desk his identification and told her he was there to speak to Albert Brunner. "I'll tell him you're here!" she said in her perky voice. Williams noted that her smile remained pasted on her face, even when she saw his police badge. She had been well trained.

Brunner came out to the desk and shook the detective's hand, applying enough pressure to let Williams know he could crush the bones in an instant if he so desired.

"How can I be of help to you?" he asked, showing beautiful white teeth.

"Is there someplace we can talk in private?"

Settling in the manager's office, Detective Williams asked if Brunner was the manager of the spa. Brunner told him that he was not only manager of the Chestnut Hill spa, but his spa had the best record of growth and customer satisfaction of any gym in the entire Delaware Valley.

"I have doubled the number of clients at this facility in less than a single year!" Brunner stuck a stubby finger in the air to punctuate his sentence. "I have brought new health and vigor to hundreds of people. I have inspired my employees to become the best physical trainers in the city of Philadelphia. In the whole of the United States! They are the best of the best because I am the superior fitness specialist."

Williams took a moment to take in the grandiosity of the man. His ego was bigger than his biceps. The man had illusions of grandeur and was supremely ambitious. The big question was, how far would Brunner go to get what he wanted?

Williams said, "I'm investigating the shooting of a James Madison employee this morning. The shooting occurred. . ." Williams referred to a small, dog-eared notebook. "It was at five forty in the morning."

Brunner kept his smile intact, saying nothing. The detective noted that Brunner expressed neither shock nor concern about the health of the shooting victim. He hadn't even asked if the victim survived.

"I need to know where you were between five-thirty and six this morning," Williams prompted.

"I was right here." Brunner waved his hand, indicating the office, then he slapped the arm of his leather chair. "In this chair!"

"Do you usually come to work that early?"

"Yes, I do. I am always the spa early. You can not leave a business to run by itself. It will be a disaster. Good companies need a strong hand at the wheel all the time."

Williams had no doubt about Brunner's strength, judging by the muscles in his arms and chest and his bull neck. But as to being an effective manager, that looked doubtful, given his gigantic ego.

"Did anyone see you here at that time?"

"No, not that early. We open for business at seven. My first shift employees do not come to work precisely at seven and not one minute later."

"So nobody actually saw you at five-forty."

"Not a body saw me," said Brunner. "But a *thing!*"

A huge smile on his lips, Brunner pointed to a bank of monitors suspended above his desk. "I have security cameras that show me everything that is happening in the gym. That camera records the parking lot. I can rewind the tape and show you the time of my arrival. You will see that my car did not move from its spot since I arrived."

Brunner pointed to another monitor. "That camera watches the entrance. You will see that I have not left the spa since I came in to work this morning."

Williams asked if he could have the tapes to review. Brunner pulled them from the recorders and handed them to the detective, smiling broadly. He was happy to establish his alibi. Too happy, the detective thought. Somebody who cooperates with the police so enthusiastically is either as innocent as a newborn baby or confident that his alibi will never be broken, even when he was guilty.

Williams left with the conflicting impressions that Brunner was slick and egotistical enough to do anything that advanced his career, and that he had a solid alibi that would take some serious investigation to break.

Patience felt a surge of relief when she saw Gary Tuttle come into the waiting room. Rushing to him, she said, "Gary, I don't like the way Lenny is breathing! Doctor Farr told me it was normal for his kind of injury, but I've seen a lot of patients, and I don't like it."

"Let's take a look," said Gary, leading her into the Recovery Room. He asked Lenny how was his breathing—did it hurt when he took a deep breath? Did he feel like he couldn't get a full breath?

"I don't know, Tuttle." Lenny took a number of shallow breaths. "It just feels like. . . the oxygen is turned off."

Gary took out his stethoscope and listened to Lenny's chest. "Sit forward," he said, helping to pull Lenny into an upright position. He listened to all the lung fields. "Say 'E' several times," Gary said.

"Eee!" A pause. "Eee!" Exhausted, Lenny fell back into the stretcher.

Gary examined Lenny's fingernails, which were dusky rather than a healthy pink. He looked up at the monitor and saw the heart rate was one-eighteen. Too fast for someone at rest. His oxygen saturation was ninety-two. With the oxygen mask in place delivering one hundred per cent oxygen, the saturation should have been one hundred as well.

"This isn't normal, is it?" said Patience.

"I don't think so. What exactly did Doctor Farr say?"

"He told me Lenny's abdomen was pushing up on his diaphragm and preventing him from taking a full breath. He said it would all go away in a few days."

"He has crackles in both lower lobes of his lung. That doesn't come from a restricted diaphragm. I wonder if he had a post-op chest x-ray." He spoke to the Recovery Room nurse, who told him Dr. Farr had not ordered any x-rays for Lenny.

Returning to Patience, Gary said, "I've seen a lot of people with a distended abdomen. Liver failure patients, bowel obstruction patients. They weren't as dyspneic as Lenny is unless they had cardiac or pulmonary complications."

"I knew it! I knew he wasn't right! That damn Doctor Farr didn't even examine Lenny." She looked past Gary at her husband. "What do we do?"

"I'm going to call Doctor Singh in the ICU."

Gary called the unit and explained the situation to Doctor Singh. As soon as Singh heard that it was Lenny Moss who was developing acute respiratory failure, he promised to come to Recovery right away.

Gary watched Lenny's chest rising and falling rapidly. "It's a shame we don't have a post-operative chest x-ray for him, that's the first thing Doctor Singh is going to ask for."

Patience put her hands on her hips and stuck out her jaw. *"Gary Tuttle, have you forgotten what department I work in?"*

Realization led to satisfaction as Gary watched Patience rush out of the Recovery Room headed for Radiology. Five minutes later she returned pushing a portable x-ray machine.

"Do you want an A-P *and* a lateral, Doctor Tuttle?" she said.

"I don't think we need a lateral, but could you get a flat plate of the abdomen, too?"

"Whatever you want, sir." She pulled a cassette from the box and Gary helped pull Lenny upright to place the film behind him. Lenny looked from Patience to Gary.

"We're just checking your lungs," Gary explained.

Lenny closed his eyes, too tired and short of breath to care.

After taking the two x-rays, Patience wheeled the machine back to radiology to dump the digital data into the department's computer. When Gary saw the respiratory therapist checking the flow rate on Lenny's oxygen meter, Gary said, "Say, Chrissie. Would you mind very much drawing a blood gas?"

Chrissie looked at Gary, puzzled. "Have you got a doctor's order?"

"Doctor Singh is on his way down from the ICU right now. He told me he wanted it."

"Oh, okay, Gary. Anything for Doctor Singh."

As he watched Chrissie draw the blood gas from Lenny's wrist, Gary felt that all he had to do was wait for Doctor Singh to come down and Lenny would be in good hands.

FORTY-THREE

By the time Dr. Singh arrived in the ICU, the chest and abdominal x-rays were available for viewing on the computer and the blood gas results were entered on the bedside flow sheet. While his team of residents reviewed the chart and lab results, Singh examined Lenny, listening for a long time to his lungs, heart and bowel sounds. He read the lab results, then sat at the station to review the x-rays.

"The belly has a lot of fluid and small amounts of free air, but that is to be expected after repairing a perforated colon," he said. "There is the bullet. You see?" He pointed to a small white spot in the abdomen. "Curious that Doctor Farr left it in situ. I would think he'd want to remove it."

"Maybe it was out of reach," said Gary.

"Perhaps," said Singh. "His lungs have significant fluid collection. You see all the fluffy infiltrates?" He pointed to the patchy areas scattered across the lung fields. "He is developing pulmonary edema, I'm afraid."

Patience asked how serious was it.

"It can be very serious. Lenny has peritonitis from the bowel contents that spilled into his abdominal cavity. When the body reacts to the foreign matter it releases large amounts of anti-inflammatory substances that inflame the lungs, causing them to become edematous."

"Will you have to intubate him?" she asked.

"Hopefully not. Diuretics will draw off some of the fluid. We may be able to avoid the tube by using external Bipap." To Gary he said, "Of course, I can't order medications or ventilatory support myself in the Recovery, he is under Doctor Farr's care."

"Can you talk to him?" asked Patience. "Can you get him to see he has to *do something?*"

"We can only try," said Singh. Paging Farr, Singh explained his findings and suggested the surgeon order diuretics and the positive-pressure external breathing support known as Bipap. Farr told him that there was no need, the patient would mobilize his fluids on his own.

Singh said, "If you would review the latest chest film, I am sure you will agree the patient requires more aggressive management."

"Chest x-ray? Who the hell ordered a chest x-ray?" Farr barked.

"I have no knowledge of that," said Singh. "I only know that the post-operative chest x-ray and the flat plate are extremely troubling."

"I didn't request any x-rays and I didn't ask for an ICU consultation!" said Farr in a brittle voice. "You have no business interfering with my post-op patient. Stick to the patients in the ICU and leave my Recovery patients alone!"

Singh heard Farr slam down the phone. Hanging up, he went back to Lenny's stretcher, where Patience and Gary waited.

"Doctor Farr does not seem as concerned as I about the patient's pulmonary status. He does not agree that Lenny needs diuretics and ventilatory support." Singh watched Lenny's breathing pattern for a moment, worried and feeling powerless to help him.

"*Somebody has to do something,*" said Patience. "He's getting worse and worse!"

"I agree. If he were in the unit, I could take over his care. Unfortunately, he is in Recovery. I have not even been consulted."

Gary looked from Patience to Singh. "Why don't we move him to the unit?"

"I can't do that, Gary. Not unless he coded."

Patience looked at Gary, begging him with her eyes to do something, but Gary was helpless against the strict rules of the hospital. Farr was the physician of record, and his word would have to be followed.

Unless. . .

Gary leaned close to Dr. Singh. "As the ICU Attending, you're on the code team. Right?"

"Correct."

"And you could take over Lenny's care if he coded. . . Or *pre-coded.*" Gary gave Singh a conspiratorial look.

Singh's eyes lit up. "Brilliant, my friend, totally brilliant." He knew of the hospital's new policy of calling in the "Pre-code" team for patients who were crashing but had not yet suffered an actual arrest, a tactic that provided aggressive treatment to unstable patients before they actually coded. The new policy was already saving many lives.

Singh grabbed a consultation sheet from the desk. "What is his blood pressure?" he asked, scribbling a quick note.

"Eighty over fifty," Gary said, making up the number.

"I can see his respiratory rate is over thirty."

"It's forty and labored," Gary prompted. Singh winked at his team and wrote down the number. "His arterial oxygen concentration is eighty-six. That's on what per cent of oxygen?"

"One hundred," Gary lied.

"I believe he meets the criteria for a pre-code," said Singh, signing the con-sultation with a flourish. He told a resident to call the unit and tell them they had a patient on the way.

Gary slipped a portable oxygen tank in the stretcher's holder while Patience unplugged the intravenous pumps and coiled the wires at the back. The Recovery Room nurse saw the flurry of activity and came over asking what was going on.

"We're transferring Mister Moss to the ICU," said Singh. "I am calling a pre-code."

"But, but, shouldn't you clear it with Doctor Farr? It's his patient."

"I just spoke with him," Singh assured her.

"Oh, well, In that case let me get you the chart." Patience grabbed the chart from the nurse's hand as she and Gary pushed Lenny's stretcher out the door and on the way to the ICU.

FORTY-FOUR

In the ICU Dr. Singh ordered Gary to give Lenny forty milligrams of Lasix and instructed the respiratory therapist to put him on the Bipap mode of ventilation. He was concerned that Lenny's oxygen level was so low. There had been no injury to the lungs, and the patient had no pulmonary disease. So why did he look like crap?

The therapist strapped the special oxygen mask over Lenny's face with elastic straps that wrapped around his head as tightly as a scuba diver. Each time Lenny started to take in a breath, the ventilator forced air into his lungs under pressure, much as it would if he had the breathing tube anchored in his airway.

Singh said to Patience, who watched her husband struggling to breathe with rising anxiety, "In many cases we can avoid intubating a patient by using the external Bipap. It give us time to draw the fluid off the lungs."

"But you may have to put the breathing tube down, isn't that right?"

"That is correct," said Singh, who looked almost as worried as Patience. "If he fails to respond to medication, I will intubate him myself."

Looking past Lenny to Jimmy Jones in the next bed, Patience said, "Jimmy's not doing well, is he?"

"No, his condition is deteriorating. Doctor Singh says his prognosis is poor." Seeing the fear in her eyes as she compared the two patients, he added, "Lenny's problems are no comparison to Jimmy's. He's young and healthy, he'll pull through; you'll see."

"He has to, Gary, I don't know what me and the kids would do without him."

When she told the nurse she planned to spend the night in the waiting room, Gary told her she would be a lot more helpful to Lenny if she went home and got a good night's rest. "The kids will be scared for Lenny, too. They need you home with them," he told her. "Really. Go home, rest up and you'll be in better shape for him tomorrow."

"You have the number?" she said, eyeing Lenny one more time.

"In my cell phone."

"Okay. But only because I trust you, Gary." She kissed Lenny, hugged Gary and dragged herself out of the ICU.

Once Patience left, Gary returned to caring for Jimmy Jones. From Jimmy's bed he saw Lenny reach up to his oxygen mask and try and pull it down from his face. "Don't touch the mask, Lenny!" he called to him, hurrying to the bedside.

"I can't breathe with that thing squeezing my face."

"If you take it off your breathing will be worse. Just relax and let the machine help you." Gary cringed at having told Lenny to relax, it was the worst cliché in the hospital. How could anybody stay calm when their lungs were filling with water and they felt as if they were suffocating?

Not wanting to tie Lenny's hands down, which would make him even more anxious, Gary asked the resident to add a sedation order to the morphine already prescribed. The nurse was soon spiking Lenny's IV tubing and pushing a healthy dose of Ativan, saying, "I'm giving you something to help you stay calm and cool."

"I didn't know you could give Jack Daniels in the IV," said Lenny, struggling for an air of levity.

"Just keep your hands off the mask," Gary cautioned, returning to his other patient's bed.

Dr. Singh sat at the nursing station studying Lenny's latest lab results. "Any response to the forty of Lasix yet?" he called to Gary.

"He's put out a little over two hundred cc's so far," said Gary.

"I want a liter of urine by midnight." Singh opened Lenny's chart to see what antibiotic Farr used for the pre-op coverage. He wanted to continue the course for at least twenty-four hours after the surgery. Leafing through the chart to the operative section, he searched the anesthesia form, but saw no record of any antibiotic. He went to the surgeon's report, which likewise showed no evidence of an antibiotic. Finally he reviewed the circulating nurse's Time Out form. No one had administered an antibiotic before or during the operation. That made no sense, it was the standard of care for any surgery. Even in an emergency operation they gave antibiotics to prevent a surgical site infection, and when there was a ruptured bowel spilling its contents into the abdomen, antibiotics were absolutely required.

Singh called the OR and asked to speak to the anesthesiologist who assisted in the case earlier that day. "Luang, you intubated the emergency gunshot case, didn't you?"

"Yes, yes, I was on early call."

"I don't see a record of a pre-op antibiotic. Didn't you give it?"

"Doctor Farr say antibiotic was given in the ER. He say not to give again."

"What in holy hell is going on?" Singh said aloud as he hung up the phone. He turned to the Emergency Room notes, which were neatly typed, the ER having gone to a computerized chart. As hard as he scrutinized the record, he could find no evidence of anyone administering an antibiotic. With no antibiotic given in the ER or the Operating Room, the bacteria and fungi spilling out of the bowel had hours to establish themselves in the open abdominal cavity. No wonder Lenny was presenting a septic picture.

Singh hastily ordered STAT coverage with broad-spectrum antibiotics and handed the orders to Gary. As Gary faxed it down to the pharmacy, he said to Singh, "I hate to sound suspicious, but perhaps Doctor Farr didn't *want* Lenny to receive the antibiotic."

"What are you suggesting?"

Gary filled Dr. Singh in on Farr's connection to the murder investigation that Lenny had been leading. Singh was not shocked by the romantic connection between the murdered nurse and the surgeon. "Farr's a preening narcissist," he said, "although I would never have thought him capable of murdering someone. Not with a gun. But failing to give a pre-operative antibiotic in a patient whose bowel contents are spilling into his abdominal cavity and spreading through the lymphatic into the lungs is a very clever way of dispensing with somebody you don't like."

Gary pointed out that Farr could have left the bullet in Lenny's abdomen in order to prevent the police from identifying the gun that fired it. "If it was the same gun that killed Briana Nearing and shot Lenny, and if Doctor Farr was involved with the nurse . . ."

Calling up the latest x-rays, Singh scrutinized the films searching for early signs of pneumonia and peritonitis, now doubly more likely since the abdomen and lungs had not been protected from infection at the time of the operation.

"I'd like so much to know what Farr was doing in the OR," said Singh, gazing at the x-ray.

"Perhaps you'll want to ask him," said Gary, looking over Singh's shoulder.

Surprised, Singh looked up and saw the surgical team pouring through the automatic doors, Farr in the lead and bearing down on him like a general leading an armored cavalry.

"How dare you kidnap my patient and take charge of his care! *How dare you!*" Standing over the seated Singh, the tall, thick-waisted surgeon looked ready to crush the slightly built ICU physician with a blow of his fist, while his residents spread out on either side to guard the flanks.

Singh rose from his chair and looked up into Farr's contorted face, his Buddhist training the only thing keeping him from cursing the arrogant surgeon.

"Your patient, I fear, was in acute respiratory distress. His vital signs and his blood gas all pointed to an impending arrest. As the hospital's Code Team leader I am responsible for responding to all codes and pre-code situations."

"Blood gas? Who ordered a blood gas?"

"Of that I can not enlighten you," said Singh, sneaking a quick look at Gary, who stood silently outside the group. "I can only tell you that, were it not for the quick actions of the nurse and the respiratory therapist, *your* patient would most certainly have coded and quite possibly expired."

Farr argued that he had the situation firmly in hand and that the patient's condition was not even close to critical. "I examined him myself in the Recovery Room. He was not in any kind of respiratory distress."

"Did you? What was his respiratory rate? What was his oxygen saturation? What were his breath sounds?"

Farr turned to his team, shouting, *"Who assessed the patient post-op?"*

A prematurely balding young resident with a stubbly beard stepped forward. "Uh, the nurse didn't say anything to me about the patient being in distress."

"Did you examine the patient?" Farr's face was becoming increasingly distorted.

"I didn't actually *listen* to his lungs. But I thought his color was good. His urine output was within normal limits."

"I don't give a shit about his urine, I want to know was he in distress!"

The resident told him as far as he saw, the patient was in no distress. Farr bellowed, *"How can I make a sound clinical judgement if I don't have all the pertinent information?"* He barked at the surgery Fellow to call up the chest x-ray. Giving it a quick look, he told the resident to order Lasix IV."

"That will not be necessary," said Singh, "I have already ordered a diuretic and put him on external Bipap. I started him on triple antibiotic coverage as well."

"You have no right to order medications on my patient!" declared Farr.

"On the contrary, sir, it is you who are lacking in rights. The patient is in *my* ICU, and as such he is under *my* care. Your team of course is always welcome to enter a note in the chart as a consultant, but they will write no orders on this patient while he is in my ICU."

"We'll see about who's in charge," said Farr. "I'm going to Slocum on this."

"Be my guest. When the Chief calls me for an update, I will be sure to tell him that you failed to order pre-operative antibiotics on a patient with incipient peritonitis."

"He was covered in the ER!"

"No antibiotics were administered in the Emergency Department," said Singh. "Failing to administer antibiotics to a patient with a perforated bowel is gross malpractice, as I am sure you are well aware."

Farr glared at his team. "I'm surrounded by idiots!" he yelled, stomping to the exit and punching the metal plate to open the doors hard enough to break it. "How can I care for my patients when I'm surrounded by *idiots?*" he said, dragging his team into the hall.

When quiet finally returned to the unit, Gary went to Lenny's bed to check his vital signs. Lenny, drowsy and weak, pried the Bipap mask an inch from his face and looked at Gary. "What was all that yelling? Was I dreaming, my mind is all fucked up."

Gary gently pulled Lenny's hand away and centered the mask over his face. "It was just some surgeon decompensating. Go back to sleep."

"Oh. Okay." Lenny closed his eyes and drifted off, riding a cloud of morphine and Ativan.

FORTY-FIVE

After receiving her shift-to-shift report and sending Gary home, Becka settled in for her twelve-hour tour in the ICU. She began by introducing herself to Lenny and doing a quick assessment: just a check that his vitals were within normal limits and he was responding to questions.

"Hi, I'm Becka. I'll be your nurse tonight," she told him with a smile.

Lenny opened his eyes. "Do I have to have this thing on my face? It makes it hard to breathe," he said, reaching for the Bipap mask.

"The mask is actually *helping* you breathe," she said, gently moving his hand away from the mask. "Doctor Singh will discontinue it as soon as your lungs are stronger. Okay?"

Lenny shrugged and closed his eyes. He didn't like the idea of spending the whole night in this place, wherever it was. He didn't now who this Dr. 'Singh' was. The name sounded like some guy out of a B movie. He decided to bide his time and watch for an opportunity to split.

Becka went on to Jimmy Jones, who was heavily sedated and so did not respond to her question or her touch. She lifted his top sheet and looked between his legs. There was no blood. She hoped his GI bleed had finally stopped, Gary had transfused three units already. Poor Jimmy. His Foley bag was empty. No urine out meant the kidneys had shut down. The bad news just kept getting badder.

She went to the station and began checking doctor's orders, calling pharmacy for STAT drugs, and gathering the supplies she would need to get through twelve hours with two critically ill patients.

Lenny's nurse was so focused on reviewing the doctor's orders at the station, she didn't notice the custodian coming through with the big trash container. The custodian pulled the liners from the trash receptacles, tied them up and dragged them to the dirty utility room. Walking past Lenny, Carlton saw that his friend's eyes were closed. Carlton didn't like the mask with the straps over Lenny's face. Still, he figured it was better than having the tube down his throat like poor Jimmy.

Carlton looked at the ceiling. He saw the camera focused on the bed, but couldn't tell if the images were recorded. Probably they were just set up for the nurses to watch the patient from the station. Which meant that any effort to hurt Lenny could be seen by somebody at the station. Plus, the curtains in the open unit were all pulled back, so a nurse at the far end could see Lenny clearly. It looked like Lenny was safe from harm as long as he stayed in the ICU.

Finishing with the trash, Carlton went to the boiler room to retrieve his new bow, now nicely dried in the heat. He bent the bow, testing the adhesion of the glue. It looked good: no gaps or spaces between the layers of wood. It would serve him well, at least at short range.

Wrapping the bow in a long trash bag, he made his way out of the boiler room to take it to his hiding place and stow it with the arrows.

Regis pulled up in front of the house on Horter Street. He double-checked the address on the union card. *Laticia Gordon. Apt. 2.* The second floor must have been converted to an apartment.

He rang the bell and waited. Someone came down the stairs, slowly. A tremulous voice asked who was there.

"It's me, Regis Devoe, from the hospital. Is that you, Laticia?"

A long silence. Then, "What do you want?"

"Just give me five minutes. Please. It's really important. Please."

"I can't. I have my daughter. I'm not really—"

"Lenny's been shot. He's in critical condition. He needs your help, girl. Nobody else can do this 'cept you!"

Regis waited quietly, as Lenny had taught him to do so many times before. Eventually he heard two locks turning. When the door opened a crack, he saw that she was crying.

One of the security guards monitoring the video feeds spotted a familiar figure stepping out of the elevator on Four-West. Excited, he began yelling, *"I got him! I got him on camera!"*

"You got Rogers?" asked the second. "Lemme see!"

"Sure I'm sure, check it out!" He rewound the tape. The figure exiting the elevator was clearly Carlton Rogers.

"Hot shit! I'm paging West! I hope he lets me go on the raid."

When Joe West took the call, his first question was did the guard spot Carlton from the facial recognition program or was it in real time. The security guard assured him it was in real time, less than a minute ago.

"Did Rogers exit the other side of the ward?"

"I can't tell that from the monitors, sir, we don't have a camera on the far hallway."

"*Christ!* Send two officers up there STAT! One to watch the entrance to the ward, the other to watch the exit at the far end. I don't want him to slip through our fingers again. I'll be there in five minutes. And keep watching the monitors!"

Clipping a Glock pistol to his belt, West called two of his officers to join him. He rushed up the stairs, the younger men trailing behind him. With a little luck they would trap the fugitive in his new lair. There would be no escape for him. And if he showed any kind of a weapon, he was authorizing his men to shoot on sight.

·

FORTY-SIX

Regis sat in Laticia's living room on a lumpy chair with an old rug covering it, waiting for her to stop crying. When the sobs died away, he said, "I don't much like putting this stuff on you. You're a nice person, I could tell that first time we met."

"It's all right, I heard about the shooting on the radio anyway." She blew her nose and wadded up the tissues. "How did you find where I live?"

Regis grinned. "You filled out a union card, remember?"

"Oh, I forgot," she said weakly and almost smiled.

"Here's the thing," said Regis. "I figure whoever shot Lenny also killed Briana Nearing, and you didn't give us the whole story when we talked that time at the diner. I mean, like, that she was a member of the gym. That's a cold hard fact right there."

He looked into her eyes. Saw fear and sorrow. Like Lenny had taught him, he waited, not pushing.

After a long moment of silence, Laticia said, "I'm sorry I didn't say anything. I'm really, really sorry. I wanted to tell you everything, but I was so scared! I can't afford to lose my job, I have a daughter I'm raising all alone. And I'm here on a work visa."

"Is that what your boss has on you? Your visa?"

Laticia sadly nodded her head yes. "I told the police detective about it. I was afraid to not tell him about Bri, he could *really* make trouble for me."

"That's fine, talking to the cops. But Lenny and me got a better shot at catching the real killer, so if you tell me what happened to Briana at the gym, we'll bring that sucker in. You want him caught, don't you?"

Laticia nodded again. "All I know is, she had a big fight with Albert about a month before she was killed. She came in yelling and waving her arms. I thought she was going to pick up a weight and smash something, she was really wild."

"What was she saying?"

"I couldn't make any sense of it. Something about you messed me up, *you fucked me over.* They went back to his office and I guess she stopped yelling because we didn't hear her through the door."

"She ever come back to the gym?"

"No, I don't think so. That was the last time I saw her."

187

"What do you think she meant: 'you messed me up?'"

Laticia shrugged. "Maybe the weight training was damaging her musculo-skeletal system. That happens when people just starting lift too much weight."

Regis asked if she knew where Brunner was the morning Lenny was shot. She told him she couldn't go to work when she heard the news and called out sick, but that Brunner was usually there before the early shift arrived at seven. "That way he can short our pay if we're five minutes late," she said.

"It's the same with us, only we have to punch in a time clock."

Regis knew the gym had surveillance cameras, but only the cops could get access to them, they were no help to him. "Do you know someone who was at work early this morning? Could you call them?" Laticia said she was friendly with one of the trainers, she would call her later and see what she could find out.

When Regis got up to go, she asked if Lenny was going to be all right. He told her he got through surgery okay and looked like he was going to make it.

"Tell Lenny I'm sorry. Really sorry. Will you?"

"Sure."

He heard the two locks turn as soon as the door closed behind him, and knew that the dangers Laticia faced could not be kept at bay by any locked door.

At nine o'clock it was time for Patience to send the children to bed. She told them to put on their pajamas and brush their teeth, then it was lights out. Takia complained, arguing for more TV time, but Malcolm quietly went upstairs to get ready.

Patience felt a powerful urge to hire a babysitter so she could return to the hospital and keep watch over Lenny. But Gary had cautioned her that if she became exhausted she would be of no help to him. Although the nurses had her phone number and promised to call if there was a change, she knew there were a thousand ways for a hospital to kill a patient, and that the best chance for a full recovery is to have an advocate at the bedside who watched *everything*.

It wasn't long after she'd told them "Lights out!" that the two of them came into her bedroom, Takia, the older, was in the lead, with Malcolm standing just behind her, hoping for the best but not sticking his neck out.

"Can we sleep in your bed tonight?" she asked.

Before Patience could tell them *No*, Takia pointed out that Patience was sleeping alone. "That's lonely!" she declared. "You don't wanna be lonely."

"Lonely!" Malcolm chimed in.

For once Patience hadn't the will to be the disciplinarian. She pulled back the covers and made room for them. As they snuggled up on either side of her, she told them she was going to read for awhile, but they should close their eyes and go to sleep.

Takia closed, then opened her eyes. "Lenny gonna to be all right, ain't he?" she asked.

"Of course he will," she said, not bothering to correct her grammar. "He'll be out of the hospital and back here before you know it."

"Lenny is *strong!*" Malcolm declared. "Ain't nothin' can stop him!"

"That's right," Patience said, kissing the tops of their heads. Returning to her book, she felt a pang of worry return, thinking how her children's hearts would be broken along with hers if Lenny didn't make it. If the evil person who shot him worked in the hospital and was even now planning another attack.

Lying in his bed with the mask pressing hard against his face, Lenny felt as if he was floating away on an ocean. All around him he saw dangerous-looking machines and strangers moving back and forth. The mask strapped to his face kept blowing on him, making him feel trapped. It smelled funny, too. *It's poison gas, they're trying to kill me, he thought.*

He reached up and pulled the mask away. When he tried to sit up he felt a piercing pain in his gut. The pain terrified him. An alarm sounded just above his head, raising his fear even higher.

A strange woman came to his bed and stood over him. "Remember what I told you about keeping the mask on? *You have to leave it in place. It's very important.*"

The nurse pressed the mask over his face and tightened the straps. "Listen, hon, I don't like to tie my patient's hands, but if you take the mask off again, I'm gonna have to tie you down. Understand?"

Lenny didn't understand, but he didn't want to antagonize this woman who was threatening to put him in bondage, so he nodded his head, yes.

"Are you having any pain?" she asked.

"Yeah, when I try to sit up it hurts really bad."

"I'll give you a shot of morphine." She went away and returned with a syringe, which she stuck into some kind of tubing. "There. That'll help you relax, too. It's nine o'clock. Close your eyes and try to get some sleep. *Okay?*"

189

It wasn't okay, but Lenny was too scared to tell the strange woman for fear she would carry out her threat to lash his hands to the bed. She might even gag his mouth. He watched until she disappeared behind a nearby curtain.

Nine o'clock. The time meant something important, but he couldn't recall what it was. He knew he was supposed to be somewhere at nine o'clock. That he had a *responsibility*. But he could not remember it to save his life.

He put the effort to remember aside. Right now he had much more serious issues to deal with. These people were obviously trying to kill him. He had to figure how to get out of wherever the hell he was without setting off all the alarms and bringing that evil woman back.

FORTY-SEVEN

Lenny pulled on the straps holding the Bipap mask tight against his face until he could lift it from his face. A machine beside his bed began to bleep loudly. He looked around for the woman who had threatened to tie him up, but there was no sign of her. He grabbed the funny rails that penned him in with both hands and pulled himself to a sitting position, moaning at the pain exploding in his gut. The pain was bad, but staying in this death trap was worse.

He saw a woman at a desk writing in a book and ignoring the alarm. That was hopeful. Another woman was doing something to a guy in a bed way down at the end of the room. There were people lying in beds with the same rails keeping them prisoners.

He threw off the top sheet, saw that he was barefoot but didn't care, he had to get out. Fast. He tried to push the bars on the side of the bed down, but they were solid. Cursing, he pushed himself crab-like down to the end of the bed. As his feet dangled off the end, he felt something pulling on his chest. There were wires attached to his skin!

Jesus Christ, what kind of gouls are running this prison? He ripped the wires from his chest, feeling twinges of pain as they pulled away. As he scooted farther down in the bed a slender plastic rope of some kind sticking to his neck held him fast.

They're not keeping me tied down. He grasped the smooth line in his strong hand and yanked. Felt a pop in his neck. He tossed the rope away and continued scuttling down the end of the bed, while a new alarm began ringing. Despite the loud clanging, the woman at the desk didn't look up and the other woman at the end of the room paid no attention.

When he felt the cold hard floor on his bare feet he knew he had to move fast. *Got to get to the door without them seeing me!* But as he took a first step, a feeling of nausea and dizziness began to take hold. *Don't get sick! Don't throw up!* He reached for a table standing a few feet from the bed to steady himself and tried to keep from vomiting as the alarms sounded all around him. His legs began to shake and the room spun in a dizzying circle of madness.

West emerged from the stairwell onto Four West with his team behind him. A security guard at the entrance to the ward reported that no one had come in

191

or out since he arrived. West received confirmation on his walkie-talkie from the other end of the unit that Rogers had not exited there, either.

"All right, this is how we'll do it. You two start with the first room on the left. Examine it carefully. Look for any kind of hiding place, this guy is an experienced hunter, he has a bag of tricks. The rest come with me."

West led his team into an empty patient room. The wall cabinets had been pulled down and were sitting on the floor in the middle of the room. Otherwise, the room was bare. West opened the door to the tiny toilet. No room for a man to hide in there, there was barely enough room for the commode.

"Next room," West muttered. By the time he got to the last patient room his frustration was boiling over. He told the guard at the end of the hall, "You must have let him slip by you."

"No, sir, I didn't let so much as a mouse go past my nose."

Furious, West crossed to the other side and began searching those rooms.

"Sir," said one of the guards, "we searched all these rooms already. There's no place for him to hide in any of them."

Ignoring the junior guard, West went from room to room, looking into bathrooms, under tarps covering furniture. He pushed open the dirty utility room and looked at the large sink. He even opened the hopper where the staff cleaned the bedpans with hot steam and looked in there, though it was barely large enough to hide a newborn baby.

He kicked open the door to the linen room, looked inside, saw the wire carts lined up against the rear wall were empty of linen. He was turning to go when the smell of fresh spackling compound filled his nose. *He sniffed again. It was an odor he not had picked up in any of the other rooms.*

West examined the sealing tape and fresh compound on the rear wall. The workmanship was poor, the edges not as smooth and feathered as he expected from the hospital's construction team. Something felt wrong about the room. There was no obvious place to hide, but something was definitely off.

He looked at the room. What was it? What disturbed him?

Then he got it. The room was shallower than the dirty utility room. It had the same width, but the depth was not as great by a foot or more.

He pulled the wire linen carts savagely from the wall and tossed them into the hall, where they fell over with a crash. Bending down on his knees, he saw that the freshly spackled wallboard was marked at the floor level by a line forming a two-by-two foot square. He kicked the square. It fell inward. He called to one of the guards.

"Get me a sledge hammer!"

"Sir?"

"A hammer. *Get me a big god damned hammer!*"

Moments later the guard returned with a large claw hammer. "This was all I could find," he said sheepishly.

"Pull down the wall board."

As the guard lifted the hammer above his head, West pulled his Glock from the holster, held it in two hands and pointed the barrel at the wall.

One guard broke through the wallboard, a second tore the broken pieces away, revealing the crawl space behind. West stepped closer, pointing the pistol into the hiding place. He savagely ripped another big chunk of wallboard away. Light from the overhead fixture pushed back the darkness, revealing a hammock hanging across the space. The hammock was made of hospital sheets three layers thick. A loaf of bread and a jar of peanut butter were on the floor. Carlton was not.

Cursing, West spun and stalked out of the room, growling, "You lost him! You let him slip right through your fingers!" He strode toward the elevator, the gun still in his hand, wanting to shoot somebody. *Anybody.*

FORTY-EIGHT

Behind the curtain, Becka and the nurse's aide cleaned and diapered Jimmy Jones. The foul odor of bloody stool filled the air. The aide sprinkled spirits of peppermint about the fresh linen to mask the odor.

"Turn him on his back, quick!" said Becka, seeing Jimmy's oxygen level drop when he was turned to his side. Jimmy was so deeply sedated that his limbs flopped limply on the bed whichever way he was turned. Once the patient was repositioned and the top sheet pulled up neat and crisp to his chest, the aide wrapped the bloody linen into a ball and stuffed it into a waterproof laundry bag.

When the aide pulled the curtain back, Becka looked across to Lenny's bed and saw with horror that it was empty. That was when she became aware of the alarms from the Bipap machine and the heart monitor, which had been wailing for she didn't know how long.

Looking around, she saw Lenny standing buck-naked a few feet from the foot of the bed. He was swaying back and forth, his face was pasty white, his lips dark scarlet, and his eyes were bulging. Scarlet rivulets of blood pulsed from the hole in his neck where the central venous catheter had been. The blood ran down his chest and dripped onto the floor.

"Oh my god!" the nurse screamed. "Call a code! Somebody call a code!"

She reached Lenny just as his knees buckled. Becka pressed her own knees against his and wrapped her arms around his lower back, keeping him upright. The aide joined her and the two picked Lenny up and tossed him back onto the bed.

Ripping the Ambu bag from the from the wall, she turned the oxygen on full blast, pressed it over Lenny's face and began squeezing the bag hard, forcing pure oxygen into Lenny's airway.

"Put some pressure on the IV site!" she ordered as a second nurse came rushing to the bedside with the crash cart. While the aide connected the cardiac leads to Lenny's chest, the other nurse tore open some sterile dressings and pressed them hard against the insertion site in the neck to stop the blood that was running down Lenny's chest.

As the code team rushed into the unit, Becka told the senior resident, "He pulled out his central line! He lost a lot of blood!"

The resident ripped open a central line insertion kit, calling for a blood pressure and oxygen saturation. He hurriedly wiped Lenny's groin and took out a large bore needle. When the resident stuck the groin, Lenny began to kick up his legs and grab at the Ambu bag pressed onto his face.

"Somebody sit on his legs!" the resident yelled, desperately trying to keep the needle in the femoral vein. An intern climbed up on the bed and sat on Lenny's knees just as an Attending physician came in to take charge. The resident quickly slapped tape over the new femoral catheter while the Attending looked at the monitor on the crash cart. The oxygen level was ninety and the blood pressure was one-ten over eighty.

The senior physician, calm and looking bored with no actual cardiac arrest to take charge of, asked the night nurse if Lenny had shown any overt signs of delirium.

"The nurse on days didn't say anything about him being confused!" she declared, afraid of being blamed for the incident. She admitted she had not yet done a complete neuro assessment, she had to clean up the GI bleeder in the next bed first.

"Well he's obviously suffering from ICU psychosis," said the Attending. "Give him five of Haldol and two of Ativan." Becka hurried to the medication cart for the anti-psychotic drug and the sedative while Lenny continued to writhe in the bed. He grabbed the resident who was holding his legs down and pulled hard, nearly throwing him off the bed. The Attending grasped Lenny's wrists. "I want this man in four point restraints!"

"I'm sorry, doctor," Becka said, injecting the Haldol. "We're not allowed to restrain more than three limbs. Four point restraints are considered an assault."

"Fine," said the Attending, already heading for the exit. "Tie up both his wrists and one leg and assign a fat aide to sit her butt on the other. I don't want him pulling out any more lines!"

FORTY-NINE

Pedaling along dark, empty streets, Carlton pulled off at the Chestnut Hill New Body Spa and Fitness Center on Germantown Ave and concealed his bike behind a dumpster in the back. He'd heard from a worker in the hospital how Brunner knocked Lenny down and swore to stop the union drive. As far as Carlton was concerned, Brunner was suspect numero uno in Lenny's shooting.

He stayed in the shadows, walking silently around the building, careful to stay out of sight of the security camera. He was looking for places a person could sneak out of the building and avoid being caught on tape. On one side of the building a small parking lot was in the line of sight of a video camera mounted on the wall. The other side of the building butted up against a pizza shop.

A sidewalk running along the back of the building was bordered by a low row of neatly trimmed hedges. Past the hedges he found a narrow parking lot with a sign saying PRIVATE PARKING—VIOLATORS WILL BE TOWED. A space marked MANAGER in bold letters told him where Brunner kept his car. Another security camera mounted on the back wall pointed directly at the manager's parking spot. Carlton pressed his back against the rear of the building and looked up. It was clear that the surveillance camera would miss him, as it pointed toward the manager's parking spot across the lot, not the rear exit.

Which meant that Brunner could skip out the back way and take off on foot any time he wanted, and there would be no recording.

Bending down beside the hedges, Carlton saw that the ground was soft and moist from yesterday's rain. He took out a penlight and worked slowly and methodically along the row, searching for footprints just as he searched for deer prints in the park.

He found nothing that surprised him, and everything he expected.

Walking unnoticed through the ICU, Dr. Farr saw the red code cart in front of Lenny's bed. He noted the three-point restraints and the Bipap mask over the patient's face. Going to the desk, he said to the young resident making out his note, "I see your code survived."

"It wasn't a full blown code, he had a pulse the whole time," said the resident. "He pulled out his central line. It looks like full ICU delirium."

"He's probably suffering from delirium tremens from alcohol withdrawal. His liver felt a little gnarly when I was in the abdominal cavity."

"We've got him on Haldol and Ativan. It's calmed him down pretty well."

Farr asked, "His wound didn't dehisce from all the agitation, did it?"

"No, sir, the wound is well opposed. I pulled the dressing after we had him stabilized. There's minimal erythema. The sutures are intact."

"Well then I won't have to open the dressing tonight and examine the wound."

As Farr walked casually out of the unit, the young resident wondered what Farr was doing making rounds alone so late at night. Well, he was the Attending. He could do whatever he wanted.

Carlton leaned back in the plush leather chair belonging to the chief of neurology, kicked his legs up onto the broad red cherry desk, and closed his eyes. He was dressed as a physician again: clean shaven, crisp white shirt and boring tie, pleated dress pants and polished shoes. The stethoscope hung from one lab coat pocket, a paperback book about diagnostics filled the other.

He set the alarm on his watch for five am, knowing that no one would be coming into the neurology office until eight in the morning. Maybe nine, neurology wasn't like surgery, these physicians kept banker's hours, with every holiday off.

Five in the morning would be time enough to retrieve his new bow from its new hiding place.

There were eyes on Lenny twenty-four/seven as long as he was in the ICU. That was all right. Eventually they would move him to a private room on the wards. After that, there would be a night when he was alone and asleep, and as vulnerable as a deer in the park unaware of the hunter bringing silent death.

FIFTY

After seeing the children off to school, Patience hurried to the hospital to check on Lenny. When she entered the ICU she was relieved to see him sitting up in bed talking to Gary and Regis. He still had the Bipap mask strapped to his face, but at least he didn't seem to be struggling for air, as he'd been the day before.

She kissed the top of his head. "How are you feeling?" she asked.

"A lot better," said Lenny. "They were just filling me in on what they found while I was out of it."

"You don't need to go into all that crap!" said Patience. "You just need to relax and get better."

"Yeah, but the case is really getting hot," said Lenny. He told her that Briana Nearing had a big blowout with Albert Brunner at the gym before she quit the program, and that Doctor Farr had an affair with her. Regis pointed out that Farr left the bullet inside Lenny, which would make it harder to prove who the shooter was, and Gary added that the surgeon didn't give Lenny any antibiotics before the operation, which could be an innocent mistake, or could be something else.

"I never trusted that man," said Patience. "I want you to get yourself another doctor."

Gary said, "Lenny made quite a commotion on the night shift. Did you hear he tried to elope last night around midnight?"

"*Elope,*" said Patience. "As in, go AMA?"

"That's right. Lenny had a bout of sundown syndrome. He became delirious and jumped out of bed. He even pulled out his central line. The night staff came within a hair of coding him."

"*What do you have to go and do a fool thing like that for?*" said Patience, punching him in the arm.

"Ow! Hey, don't blame me, I was in La-La land! Isn't that right, Tuttle?"

"Sepsis often causes confusion," Gary agreed, "especially in the mentally unbalanced." He reached into his pocket and removed a neatly folded slip of paper. "Are you together enough to consider another clue? Somebody left this pinned to your pillow."

Lenny unfolded the paper and read the neatly printed words. "*Foot prints neath the window tell the tale.* Now what the hell is that supposed to mean?"

Regis said, "Carlton's gotta be talking about the gym up in Chestnut Hill. If Brunner was the shooter, he might've left footprints where he sneaked out of the building and came to the hospital. I'll go on up there after work and check it out."

Giving the note back to Regis, Lenny suggested that Brunner hated the union enough to do something crazy. "I'm not sure the administration would give him a promotion for shooting a union rep, but Brunner might be insane enough to think so. Maybe you should take Moose with you."

"I was thinking I should be packing," said Regis. When Lenny gave him a look of reproach, he promised to leave his piece at home.

Just then Dr. Singh came toward them with his team on morning rounds. "Well, Mister Moss, you certainly made my resident's night a challenging one."

The on-call resident told the team how they had to wrestle Lenny down in the bed and insert a femoral IV at the same time. "The way his jugular site was pumping out blood, I thought he was going to exsanguinate right in front of me. I got the nurse to tamponade the neck while I stuck a new line in the femoral vein."

Singh said, "Mister Moss's ICU psychosis probably developed as a result of his blood loss and a period of hypotension prior to surgery. He likely has a mild degree of hypoxic encephalopathy."

"You mean my brain is fried, is that it?" said Lenny.

"In a manner of speaking, but I have high hopes your full mental capacity will be restored in time." Listening to Lenny's lungs and reviewing the latest blood gas results, Sing told the respiratory therapist to discontinue the Bipap and put him on a forty percent oxygen mask.

"The Haldol has him oriented times three," the resident added. "Do you want a CAT scan of the head?"

"That won't be necessary unless he develops focal signs," Singh said. "We will continue to treat him with anti-psychotics, opiates and benzo's for a few more days."

Lenny said, "Yeah, doc, I don't know what drugs you're giving me, but whatever they are, they're *grrreat*. Can you send me home on them? Even better, can you put my wife on them?"

Dr. Singh patted Lenny gently on the shoulder. "To be serious for just a moment, climbing out of bed that way, if you had dehisced your abdominal wound, your colon would have been dragging on the floor. That would be ugly."

"Doctor Farr must have used stainless steel sutures," Lenny said,

"No doubt." Singh told his team that the diuretics and antibiotics had resolved the patient's pulmonary edema, and that if Lenny continued to be calm and oriented, he could go up to the wards in the afternoon.

"What's the chance I can be home by Saturday? I helped organize a fundraiser for Jimmy Jones. It was supposed to be for his transplant, but I guess, the way he's going. . ."

Singh said, "Indeed, the money will doubtless help to pay for the funeral services. As to discharging you Saturday, that is most unlikely. But this afternoon you will be back under Doctor Farr's care. It will be his decision."

"Can't you still be his doctor?" asked Patience. "We don't trust Doctor Farr."

"Alas, I only care for patients in the ICU." Instructing his team to go on to the next patient and begin reporting to the Fellow, Singh quietly asked Patience, "Have you some specific reason for not wanting Doctor Farr to care for your husband? I understand Lenny was involved in an investigation of some kind, and that Farr may be implicated in some way."

Gary said, "When Lenny was In Recovery fighting to get a breath, Farr blew it off. He said it was *normal* in cases like his to be short of breath. It was some bull crap about the diaphragm pushing up on the lungs."

"His point is correct as far as it goes. However, if he did not read the postoperative x-ray as pulmonary edema, that is worrisome."

"That's part of the problem," said Gary. "Farr didn't order the chest x-ray. I did."

"You did?"

"Yes. I told Patience you would want to see an x-ray when you came to see Lenny, so she went to Radiology and brought back the portable machine."

Singh smiled at Patience, delighted at her resolve. "I only hope my wife is as proactive on my behalf as you are, my dear, if ever I am admitted to a hospital."

Gary said, "I told them what you said about the surgeon leaving the bullet in Lenny's abdomen. That sounded suspicious."

"And I understand that you believe Farr had a relationship with the murdered nurse, which Lenny was investigating," Singh added. "I can see why you wouldn't wish him to be your primary physician."

Patience said, "I want another doctor handling his case."

Singh considered the issue a moment. Finally he said, "If you really want to change doctors, I can recommend a surgeon for your follow-up care. Doctor

Farr won't like it, but that's his problem, isn't it? I'll ask Doctor Stone to come and evaluate you."

As Singh went to join his team, Lenny called after him, "Yo, doc! What does a fellow need to do to get some breakfast around here?"

FIFTY-ONE

Shortly after Dr. Singh finished rounding on the ICU patients, Detective Williams came in and went to Lenny's bedside, pleased to find him awake and lucid. Williams said, "They tell me you were one mixed up mess yesterday."

"Really? How'd you hear about it?"

"Like you, I have my sources." Williams rolled one of the nurse's chairs to the bedside and sat down. "Did you remember anything more about the morning you were shot? Before you went into surgery you couldn't tell me much."

"No, it's still a blank. I remember feeling the pain when I was hit, and I sort of recall the security guard calling for help, but that's all."

"You didn't hear the shot?"

"If I did I don't remember it. Did Sandy hear anything?"

"No, nothing unusual." The detective stared at Lenny's abdomen. "It sure would be nice to retrieve that bullet. Any chance you'd go under the knife once more so I can process it?"

"Go fuck yourself! I don't want any more doctors working on me."

"That's too bad. It makes my job a lot harder." Williams sat a moment seeming to listen to the many sounds filling the room. Finally he said, "Heard from your buddy Rogers?"

"Not a word. I think he's gone back to the deep woods."

Williams laughed. "Don't give me your bull shit stories, you know he's still in the hospital. And the longer he stays in hiding, the worse it's gonna go for him when he goes to trial."

"He didn't do it. He couldn't. He's a gentle soul."

"Oh, sure. He's a gentle soul who kills deer, skins them, cuts away the meat and packs it neatly in his freezer. I wouldn't be surprised if he drank the blood."

"Neither would I," said Lenny, starting to chuckle and then grimacing at the pain in his belly. "Admit it. You don't have any real evidence against him."

"You don't think the cash buried in his back yard is suspicious?"

"Of what, that he doesn't trust banks? No, I don't think it's suspicious. Could you even tell where the money came from? Did it have anybody's fingerprints on it?"

"Now there you raise an interesting point," said William. "We dusted some of the bills for prints, along with the glass jars, of course. We found Carlton's prints on all but one of the bundles. On those bills we found—"

"Briana Nearing's."

Williams looked at Lenny with admiration. "How'd you figure that one out?"

"Simple. Briana had to have been into something dangerous enough to get herself killed. The pregnancy, maybe, but I don't think so. If it was drug sales or something like that, she'd need to hide her income. Carlton probably told her he buried his money from the deer sales in his yard, and she decided to take advantage of the safety deposit boxes."

"You admit your friend had an intimate relation with the dead girl."

"I don't know how intimate it was, but if they had more than a passing acquaintance, it's still not a motive to kill Briana."

"I've broken up enough lovers quarrels to know a guy that's dumped is capable of anything," said Williams. *"Although. . ."*

"Although what?"

"Did you hear that Miss Nearing had a big fight with Albert Brunner right before she dropped out of the gym?"

'No, I didn't know about that."

"You mean for once I'm a step ahead of Lenny Moss?"

"Hey, I've been a little busy fighting for my life, ya know?"

Chuckling, Williams told Lenny that Brunner had a solid alibi for the time of the shooting. He explained that the spa had video cameras covering the front and rear entrance. "The rear camera looks right at Brunner's car."

"He could have sneaked out the back underneath the security camera's field of vision, it doesn't pick up the rear door."

"Jesus H. Christ," said Williams, "is there *anything* you don't know about this case?"

"Brunner could have ridden a motorcycle he stashed down the block and rode to the hospital, it's not far. Or a bicycle, even."

"Like the one Carlton rode all the way from French Creek," said Williams with a look that implied *he* knew that *Lenny* knew all about it.

"I was too short of breath to tell you about that," Lenny said with a laugh, then he groaned from the pain in his gut. "What about for the night Briana was killed? Where was Brunner?"

"I can't talk about that, I've already told you too much already."

"You only tell me stuff I already know!" When Williams didn't respond, Lenny said, "Did you know that Jean Farr ordered the lab work to test her hormone level?"

"Yeah, that's old news, tell me something I *don't* know."

"I'd like to tell you Farr was the father of Briana's baby, but I haven't got the DNA evidence. Yet."

Since Williams had seen Lenny come up with evidence that even the police couldn't find, he didn't doubt Lenny could actually obtain the DNA signatures of Briana's unborn child and Jean Farr, given enough time.

"We'll have to see which one of us gets that one first," said Williams, rising from the chair. He dropped his business card on the bedside table and left the unit, wondering how he could convince the District Attorney to compel a DNA sample from Dr. Jean Farr.

When the detective left, Lenny had to admit to himself that Carlton was a lot more involved with Briana Nearing than he admitted. Probably they were lovers. Had she used him, or had he used her? What was that money buried in his back yard about—a getaway stash they had together or was it Briana's alone? And why was Carlton in Fairmont Park at midnight in the very place where *somebody* dumped her body.

Lenny had defended too many workers for too many years to expect every one of them to tell the truth, the whole truth and not a pile of crap, but this was *Carlton,* the man whose handshake was as solid as a contract with Tony O.

Could I be defending the killer all along? The thought made him feel as low as when he looked at Jimmy Jones in the adjoining bed and considered what he would say at the funeral.

FIFTY-TWO

Lenny was still struggling with the idea that Carlton could be the killer after all when he spotted another threatening figure coming into the ICU. Dr. Jean Farr, looking even more pissed off than usual, was leading his team in a German-style blitzkrieg, and they were heading straight for him. Dr. Singh saw them, too, and stepped toward Lenny's bad.

"I am told you want me taken off your case," said Farr, standing over Lenny. "Where the hell did you get a suicidal idea like that?"

Before Lenny could speak Dr. Singh told Farr that Lenny had doubts that came out of the lack of antibiotics administered in the OR, and the fact that the surgeon had left the bullet in the abdomen.

"The quack in the ER told me he gave a full court press of antibiotics," said Singh. "And leaving the bullet in place was a clinical decision that only the surgeon who has his hands in the wound can make. Second guessing from an x-ray is folly."

Singh said, "Nevertheless, the patient has a right to switch doctors, as I am sure you have read in the Patient Bill of Rights. It is posted outside the unit on the wall beside the elevator, if you would care to review it."

"He can't request a change if he's not competent!" snapped Farr. "Have you forgotten the patient was delirious last night and nearly *killed* himself?"

Before Singh could respond, Farr turned to Lenny. "Tell me your name, the place you're at, and the date. When Lenny answered all three questions correctly, Farr continued, "What brought you to the hospital?"

"I was broke and I needed a job," said Lenny.

"Don't get cute with me!" snapped Far. "I mean, as a *patient.*"

"I heard they were short of cadavers in the med school so I hired a guy to shoot me," said Lenny.

"Do you realize you're asking to replace the surgeon who *saved* your *life?* Would a rational man make that decision?"

"My wife's been telling me for years that I'm nuts. Get in line." Seeing Dr. Singh smiling at the interchange, Lenny added, "Thanks for the operation, but I'm changing doctors."

Farr declared that he would not be held responsible if Lenny suffered any complications from the surgery and stormed out of the ICU, cursing and vowing to appeal Lenny's decision. Singh looked back at Lenny and said, "Do you believe, I have to deal with that asshole every day?"

Later in the morning Gary was telling Lenny to hold a pillow across his abdomen, take a deep breath and cough vigorously. Lenny tried a weak cough, wincing at the pain. Gary brought him an injection of morphine and told him to try the exercise again.

"I used to like you, Tuttle," he said, pressing the pillow to his belly once more.

Doctor Alex Primeaux came to his bedside, smiling and shaking his head at the site of his friend. "My o' my, you sure gave me a scare, goin' an' getting' shot an' all. Ah been worried sick about you, Lenny."

"I've been kinda worried about me, too." Lenny chuckled, then groaned in pain. "How are things in Employee Health?"

"We're fine, except I don't have anybody to negotiate with Human Resources for an employee returning on light duty. Nobody bargains like you."

"Modesty forbids me from responding, but, thank you, Alex, it's much appreciated."

"I've been following your lab reports and x-rays an' such. You're making beautiful progress. Your lungs have lost most of the fluid overload, and your signs of infection are going down."

"Yeah, that's what Doctor Singh tells me."

Alex looked Lenny up and down, assessing his degree of swelling, his skin color, his chest expansion and breathing rate. All together, the signs were encouraging.

"Ya know, ever since you came to talk to me about Briana Nearing, I've been puzzling about the change in her body image you told me about, but I couldn't for the life of me think of a prescription drug she would take that would do that. So I looked over those labs that Doctor Farr ordered. Remember those?"

"Yeah, they had something to do with hormones."

"That's right. Her blood glucose level was way up. So was her estrogen. Her body was stressed big time, and I think I know why." Primeaux leaned close to Lenny, his face serious as a terminal prognosis. "Was she by any chance into competitive weight training or long distance running?"

"She belonged to one of the new gyms the hospital bought up. At least she was up until a month before she was killed. What's the connection?"

"I called the Medical Examiner, ah have an old friend in the department, and I told him of my concern. I asked him to test for performance enhancing substances, and he found traces of anabolic steroids. Her hair had concentrations of them, too. It looks like she stopped taking them not long b'fore she was killed."

"That makes sense," said Lenny. "Probably somebody in the gym was selling black market drugs."

"But the timing is off, don't ya see?" said Primeaux. "Since she was around three months pregnant, she would almost certainly have known she was pregnant two months ago."

"She was a nurse, she'd know the signs," Lenny agreed.

"So I asked myself why would someone who knew she was pregnant keep on taking steroids, and *then* stop them a month later?"

Realization seeped into Lenny's drugged-up mind. He recalled how his wife's irritated hands calmed down completely when she used the cream from the spa. "Briana didn't stop taking the steroids right away because she didn't *know* she was taking them!"

Primeaux nodded, happy that his friend agreed with his analysis. "Ya see, her woman's body was at war with itself! The anabolic steroids were trying to *masculinize* her while her pregnancy was trying to *feminize* her."

"No wonder she was so moody and unpredictable," said Lenny.

"That's right. When she applied the cream, the male hormones kicked in, and when she didn't, the female hormones took control."

The solution was so simple and obvious, Lenny wanted to kick himself for not seeing it long ago. Primeaux reminded him that his mind had been clouded by drugs and swelling of the brain, but Lenny found little consolation in the remarks.

"This explains why she had the big fight with Brunner and why she quit the gym."

"Her being pregnant would tear any woman up," said Primeaux. "The risk to the baby of congenital abnormalities is enormous."

"No joke. She must have been spitting bullets." Lenny thanked his friend, who had to return to Employee Health, then he settled back in bed, oblivious to the pain and the fatigue. He was getting close to the solution to the murder. He could feel it. Taste it. The end was in sight.

He felt guilty for putting all the work on his friends. He would have preferred to be out in the field tracking down the clues and confronting the suspects, but he'd taken the bullet and there was no choice but let his friends pursue the case without him. What would he do without such good friends to lean on?

"Tuttle!" he called. "What does a man have to do to get a bed upstairs?"

FIFTY-THREE

By the late afternoon Lenny was breathing comfortably on oxygen by nasal cannula and showed no signs of confusion. Dr. Singh gave his consent to send him to the wards. He even wrote an order for a clear liquid tray for supper.

"Mmmm, Jello. My favorite," said Lenny.

"I'll see they make it with some Jack Daniels," said Moose, who had brought up a snack tray to the ICU and was hanging out with Lenny. Regis took a late lunch break to join them as well.

Gary wanted to transfer Lenny on a stretcher, but Lenny would have nothing to do with it. "Leave me a *little* dignity, Tuttle," he said. Regis said if Lenny didn't want to be seen lying on a stretcher he'd be willing to take him upstairs on the morgue cart. "It's got a canopy so nobody'd know it was you. Smells a little funky, though."

"Gee, thanks, Reege. Why don't you zip me up in a body bag while you're at it?"

Moose brought a wheelchair, and he and Gary helped ease him out of bed and into the chair. Gary wheeled Lenny out of the unit to the elevator. When they arrived at the room on Seven-South, they found Patience waiting for them.

"It's about time you got here," she said. "I was beginning to think Doctor Singh was going to keep you another day." She helped Lenny out of the wheelchair and settled him in bed, plumping the pillow and pulling the blanket up to his chin.

"Hey, I'm not an invalid, you don't have to baby me."

"Do too," she said and smacked him on the top of the head.

Once Lenny was made comfortable, Regis told him that their suspicions were falling more on Dr. Farr. "Farr didn't give you any antibiotic before your operation. That's standard operating procedure."

Gary pointed out that Farr thought the medications were given in the Emergency Room, but Regis threw the idea out as a lame cover.

"Don't forget he left the bullet inside you!" Moose said. "Without it the cops can't trace it to the gun that he used."

"*Christ,*" said Lenny. "Don't tell me I had a murderer for a surgeon. No wonder I got so sick."

"He wanted you dead, plain and simple," said Regis. "Just like he wanted Briana Nearing and her baby dead, on account he was the father."

Lenny agreed Farr's actions were suspicious. But he had trouble believing that the unborn baby was reason enough to commit murder. Patience argued that a married man like Farr in a position of authority couldn't afford the scandal of a baby born out of wedlock. But Lenny remained skeptical.

Regis said, "When you look at who's capable of cold blooded murder, my money's on Albert Brunner. He hates Lenny's guts and he hates the union. Killing you would scare the piss out of the workers at the gym. No more union."

"But don't you think he'd be more of a hands on kind of guy?" said Lenny. "Don't you think he's prefer to strangle me with his bare hands?"

"Shooting's safer," said Moose. "Besides which, Laticia told me Briana went into the gym a month before she was killed and had it out with him. They had a big old fight. She was cursing up a storm."

"Do you know what they were fighting about?"

"Nope, Laticia couldn't hear the details. Briana kept saying 'You fucked me up!' Then she quit the gym"

"I wish I knew from the get-go Briana belonged to the spa," said Lenny. "It would have got us a lot farther along."

"She feels bad about that, Lenny. Real bad. She wanted me to tell you she was sorry. But Brunner threatened her visa; she was scared for her little girl as much as for herself."

Lenny told them about Alex Primeaux's suggestion that Briana could have been taking anabolic steroids without knowing it. "That fits with her going into the gym steaming mad. She must have found out what they were doing to her."

"Yeah, but how did they dope her?" asked Regis. "Injections? Pills?"

Gary said, "A number of the athletes who were charged with doping claimed the steroids were in their lotion and that they weren't aware of it. Brunner could have added it to a bottle of lotion."

"We need somebody to go to the gym and try and get some of their cream. They gave me a tube of—" He stopped in mid-sentence, recalling what his wife said about how her irritated hands were doing so much better since she rubbed in the free cream from the gym.

"Son of a bitch! Patience, do you have any more of the cream I brought from the gym?"

"No, I finished that last week. It's in the trash."

"Today is, what—Wednesday?" asked Lenny.

"It's Thursday," said Regis. "The trash was picked up already."

"Damn!" said Lenny. "Now we'll never know for sure if he was doping the lotion they give out to get his customers bulked up and coming back for more. That's reason enough to kill Briana."

"She'd sure as shit want to blow the whistle on him," said Regis. "Especially her being pregnant."

Gary adjusted the nasal oxygen on Lenny's face, which had fallen down around his neck. "You know, Lenny, you do need to keep Carlton on the list of suspects. They found that gold chain that belonged to Briana in his house, don't forget. And he was in the park the night Briana was killed."

"I'm going to get a straight answer out of him, Tuttle, if it's the last thing I do. Carlton's going to explain why he was in the park or I'll turn him in to the cops myself."

Moose slapped his thigh and chuckled. "Know what that crazy mother did? He built his self a hidey-hole up on Four-West."

"The place that's under reconstruction?" asked Lenny.

"That's it. He put up new sheet rock in the linen room with a trap door just big enough to crawl through. He even had a hammock hanging from the walls made out of bed sheets. West just about tore that room apart when he found old Carlton wasn't in there."

Lenny laughed, then moaned and grabbed his belly. "Don't make me laugh, *please!* It hurts too much. Oh, man, I wish I could have been there to see the look on West's face."

Moose turned serious. "Listen up, there's something we got to settle before everyone goes their own way."

"What's that?" said Lenny.

"While you was in the ICU you were safe and sound, no problem. But up here, especially at night, you're unprotected. Vulnerable. I don't like it."

"I'm with Moose," said Regis. "It's not like the cops or the security guards are gonna give you round the clock protection."

"I'm worried, too," said Patience. "Really worried. What are we going to do to protect him?"

"It's wonderful you're all so concerned about me, but I don't think whoever shot me is dumb enough to come back into a place like this and finish me off. I mean, they have pretty good security at the doors, the ward is under video surveillance twenty-four seven. I don't think I'm in any danger."

"You don't know squat," said Patience. "Of *course* you're in danger! You're just too thick headed and full of that fake humble pie to ask for help is all."

"It's not that, it's—"

"We got to sit on the room and watch for trouble," said Moose. "It's the only way."

"I'll take the evening shift," said Regis. "I can be here at four."

"I'll cover nights," said Moose. "I can go home, catch a few hours sleep and be back here at eleven."

"I can be here at four AM and cover the end of the night shift," said Gary.

"Thank you, guys, but you really don't have to—"

"They're staying over and you're going to keep quiet about it!" Patience snapped. "They're your friends, they worry about you, they're staying."

When everyone but Patience returned to work, Lenny lay quietly in bed, marveling at what his friends were willing to do for him. He knew he was the richest man in the hospital. Wealthy with friends. He didn't exactly understand *why* they were willing to sacrifice so much for him, but his wife told him to accept it, and that was that.

"How do you feel?" she asked him.

"Exhausted, but pretty happy. You know, I have some great fucking friends."

"Yes you do," she said.

"There's one thing that's nagging at my mind, though. I have this sense that I already solved the case."

"Really?"

"Yeah, but I can't remember who the killer is. I wonder did I dream it or was it just my imagination?"

"You were awfully confused upstairs in the ICU," said Patience.

"Maybe it was a dream. But I feel like I had the case in the palm of my hand, and now I can't for the life of me remember what it was."

"It'll come back," said Patience, kissing him gently on the cheek. "When you least expect it, when you're thinking of something completely different, it will pop into your mind, and this time you won't forget it."

She left to meet the children after school, leaving Lenny to try and reach into the jumble of images the delirium had produced to see if one of them would yield the solution to the case and take him out of danger from the one who wanted him dead.

FIFTY-FOUR

Joe West received the word that Lenny Moss was being transferred to the ward with deep satisfaction. Having come up empty each time he tried to apprehend the suspect, West vowed he would not be fooled again. Let the fugitive have his secret lairs. Let him sleep in the president's office for all he cared. This time he was going to set a trap for Carlton, and Moss would be the bait.

He ordered two guards to watch the video monitor for the elevators that served the Seventh floor continuously. "Never take your eyes off that screen," he said. "If one of you has to take a piss, the other sits and watches that screen. Understood?"

He went to the Admissions department and demanded to speak to the director. The director of admissions, a short, stocky man with a bald head and a weak chin came out of his office and looked warily at Joe West as if he expected to be slapped in the face at any moment.

"I want the patients moved out of the room directly across from Lenny Moss's room," West said. "And I want you to leave that room empty for an undercover operation."

The Admissions director complained that the hospital was full and that moving the patients would be an undue burden on the nursing staff. West removed the handcuffs dangling from his belt and pulled them taut between his two hands. "I am trying to apprehend a cold blooded killer who is concealing himself in this hospital. You will assist me in my duties as director of Hospital security or I will arrest you for obstructing a police investigation."

"You're not the police, you're just—"

West snarled, *"I have full police powers within the institution."* He grabbed the director's wrist in an iron grip. "You *will do everything you can to assist my operation. Do you understand?"*

"Okay, okay, I'll clear the room."

The director went to one of the admissions clerk to explain what had to be done. As he went over the census, he looked back and saw that West had left silently, like a ghost. He took out a handkerchief and mopped his brow, hoping he had seen the last of Joe West for the day, and wondering where in hell he could put the two patients coming out of the room.

At dinnertime Patience and the children visited Lenny in his room while Regis stood in the doorway keeping watch. Malcolm climbed up into the bed and immediately began to test its springs.

"Don't bounce on the bed, Malcolm!" Patience said. "It's very painful for Lenny."

"Sorry!"

"And whatever you do, don't make him laugh, that hurts even worse."

Malcolm looked at Takia, who started to giggle. The children started making animal noises, bending their noses to the side and staring up as high as they could to make their eyes look all white.

"Zombies ain't gonna make me laugh," said Lenny.

Giving up on the humor, Malcolm eyed the dinner tray, which Lenny had barely touched. "You gonna eat your pudding?" he asked.

"Nah, it's got artificial flavoring. You can have it."

"Lenny, you need the calories!" said Patience. "How are you going to heal if you don't take in some protein?"

"I had a glass of soy milk before you came."

"Bull, you hate soy milk."

"This one was strawberry flavored. It was delicious."

"Yeah, right."

Malcolm watched his mother as he slowly reached for the cup of pudding. When he saw she wasn't going to object further, he pulled off the lid and plunged a spoon into the soft delight.

"I think I should leave the children with Moose and Birdie and I'll stay with you tonight."

"Nothing's gonna happen to me here. Look, they've got surveillance cameras outside the elevators, and the nurses are all trained in hand-to-hand combat."

"That's not funny," said Patience. "I'm going to spend the night. The kids can stay at Birdie and Moose's again."

"We're goin' to a slumber party? On a *Thursday?*" said Takia.

"Can I skip school tomorrow?" said Malcolm.

Lenny told her he was going to be fine, she should take the kids home and get a good night's rest. After more back and forth between them she agreed to go home, despite the loud complaints from the children.

In the Chestnut Hill New Body Spa and Fitness Center, Albert Brunner pushed up against the fearsome weight, the veins in his neck bulging from the strain, sweat running down his face and chest. The last repetition was the one that tested his mettle. He tightened his abdominal muscles, clenched his jaw and pushed up before the barbell could come crashing down and crush his chest. With a Herculean effort he locked his arms and swung the bar onto the holder.

Rising to a sitting position on the bench, he looked out at the empty room, the clients and staff having finished for the night. It was *his* domain. *His* fortress. He had worked hard to instill discipline and professionalism among the staff. Had made his spa the premiere body building establishment in Philadelphia. He had even stopped the union in its tracks, as he promised President Lefferts he would.

If the president would only give him control of *all* the gyms, he would whip them into shape and return huge profits for the hospital inside of a year. He would elevate the health and longevity of the entire population of Philadelphia. He would bring his message of hard work and discipline to the schools—god knows they needed discipline more than they needed textbooks. The students would revere him like a famous athlete.

But deep in his soul Brunner knew that Lefferts didn't like him. The fool was loyal to his own kind: Main Line blue bloods who played golf in their exclusive country clubs and went to the opera together. That was why Lefferts was sure to turn him down for the director of the entire New Body franchise. It certainly wasn't because he didn't have the skills and the proven track record. He'd proven his abilities in nearly doubling the enrollment at the Chestnut Hill gym.

Lefferts was a blind fool. He was going to place the whole organization in the hands of some Wharton graduate born with a silver spoon up his ass. It would be a business disaster. A travesty of justice!

He stood in the shower beneath a steaming spray of hot water, relishing the sting. Fury pulsed through his body with every beat of his enraged heart. He ran a soapy wash rag slowly over his body, feeling the rippling muscles and knowing they could crush a human being in their grip. Surrounded by clouds of steam, he decided that he had one chance to repay the pest who had ruined his chance of becoming head of all the spas. Let them give the position to some Wharton type who would drive the business into the ground.

It was time to separate the men from the boys. It was time to put a stop to Lenny Moss once and for all.

FIFTY-FIVE

Dressed in a doctor's outfit complete with lab coat and stethoscope around his neck, Carlton walked up the stairs from the basement. He carried his bow and arrows concealed in the blue fabric and yellow tape of a sterile instrument tray that had been through the steam autoclave. Carlton wouldn't have his night vision goggles, but that wasn't important. The dim lights used during the night shift were more than enough to lead him to his prey.

He had been in hiding long enough. On the defensive long enough. Tonight he was going to blow the case wide open. Tonight he was going for one last kill. His arrows were tipped with razors. His bow was strong.

Carlton thought of life as a contest between predator and a pray. Some creatures you ate, others ate you. All animals hunted for their food. Humans were no different, they just thought about it too much.

He believed in keeping things simple. Steal from a blind man, I pluck out your eyes. Violate a young girl, I cut off your balls. Justice was a matter of balancing the scales, and Carlton was determined to set them even on this night, even if it was his last night of freedom. Even if the cops brought him down in a hail of bullets, he was determined to bring down one last prey.

Dr. Jean Farr was used to going long stretches without sleep, but tonight the fatigue was dragging him down, down down. Wednesday he had been on call for trauma and slept only a few hours, awakened at four in the morning for a motor vehicle accident victim who turned out to need orthopedics, not the trauma team. Now it was Thursday night, and after sending his team home he was finally catching up with his charting. Jimmy Jones was the last progress note he needed to read and co-sign before going home.

Home. What was the point? A shrew of a wife, and Briana and her baby dead. Once upon a time Briana provided compensation for his miserable marriage. Those rare intoxicating nights alone with Briana. Now every return to his home reminded him he had no antidote for the poison of his toxic home life. Even the dog hated him.

He wished he had a reason to visit the Medical Examiner's office and view her body one last time. But he had no claim on her, he wasn't her husband; he wasn't ever her physician. Nor could he make a claim on the baby, a paternity test would only give the wife a winning hand at the divorce table.

Farr wondered if it was a son who died with her. The news reports had not mentioned the sex of the baby, and Bri didn't tell him. Perhaps she didn't know. Or maybe she held it back, like she held back so much from him. Give and take. Please and tease. It was always like that with Briana. Long interludes without contact but for the secretive touch, the glancing contact in the Recovery Room, interrupted by periods of trembling joy, when she made him howl at the moon and laugh like a madman.

Tonight as he sat in the ICU writing a note on Jimmy Jones, he felt as if his future was as bleak as his patient's. Jimmy's blood pressure was supported on maximum infusions of stimulants. For all intents and purposes, a continuous chemical code. Even on one hundred per cent oxygen, his blood gas was horrific. The man should have a DNR order, but the family wanted "everything done." The simpletons still believed in miracles.

Finishing his note, Farr went to his office, not caring if he fell asleep in his leather chair.

When Lenny's nurse came into the room at ten PM and turned on the overhead light, she was surprised to see he was wide awake, and even more surprised to see Moose Maddox, who had replaced Regis, seated in a chair in the corner.

"Can't sleep?" she asked Lenny.

Lenny shrugged. "My friend there snores and keeps me awake."

Moose chuckled. He put down his sketchpad, where he had been drawing Lenny in tights and a cape, a figure he would give Malcolm, and watched as the nurse hung an antibiotic and plugged it into his IV line. She lifted Lenny's gown to check his abdomen, looking for signs of bleeding or infection in the wound. The dressing was clean and dry. Satisfied, she lowered his gown and pulled the sheet up over his chest.

"Everything okay?" he asked.

"Everything's fine. I just needed to check your wound."

Lenny watched her make a notation in his bedside record. "I had no idea this place got so quiet at night. It's spooky." Asked if he needed any pain medicine, he said, "A bourbon and coke would go down very nice."

"Sorry, you don't have a doctor's order for spiritus fermenti." She asked if Moose was going to spend the whole night. He told her another friend would be taking over at midnight. "Private duty," she said." Nice."

The nurse turned off the overhead light, leaving just a dim lamp above the sink casting long shadows across the room. Lenny settled back in bed trying to get comfortable. He turned on one side, then the other, then lay on his back. *I should have taken another shot.* He comforted himself with the thought that he could always press the call button and the nurse would come back for him. He closed his eyes and tried to relax his body, but when he shut his eyes he was still haunted by violent images that flitted through his mind. The anti-psychotic medicine beat them back, but paranoid thoughts still cascaded around in his head.

The facts in the case swirled through his mind. Briana's body dumped in the park; Carlton *happening* to be there for the dump; her apparent steroid use and pregnancy; and the prescription being written by Farr. He remembered Brunner knocking him down and *enjoying* it. And Tony O mentioning the deadbeat who was "out of his reach." He had bits and pieces but no thread. No rhyme or reason.

There was Briana's gym membership and her abrupt resigning from the club in a burst of anger. That seemed to connect her death to Brunner. But why would he dope her lotion? She wasn't a competitive athlete. She didn't play any sports, she was just a nurse trying to stay in shape.

Lenny thought about Patience home without him. She wouldn't have him to help put the kids to bed. Or to spread lotion on her back the way she liked. He would kiss her lovely slender neck when he was done, and maybe more, the sexy wench.

He closed his eyes. As he drifted off to sleep, he remembered the moment he was taken into the operating room and the anesthesiologist prepared to put him to sleep. He had asked to speak to Regis. It was important. It was critical. As the doctor put him under he was going to tell Regis something important, but what was it?

As sleep smothered him in its arms, the face of the killer appeared in his mind, just as it had before the anesthetic took it all away. He smiled in his sleep, because this time he knew when he awoke the next morning he would remember who killed Briana Nearing. And in that morning he would see that the killer was arrested and brought to justice.

As the skeletal crew on the graveyard shift struggled to carry out its duties, nobody noticed the silent figure moving along the corridor. No one questioned the figure with no medical reason to be there. The figure that had lumbered up a moonlit trail with a dead woman over his shoulder. The figure that brought only death.

FIFTY-SIX

At midnight Lenny was sleeping fitfully. The stitches in his abdomen pulled whenever he turned over, bringing him half awake. He turned onto his back, a position he normally avoided, preferring to lie on his side with his arm wrapped around Patience. But he was in a hospital bed and his wife was far away.

Moose poured himself a cup of coffee from a thermos and took a swallow. He looked over at his sleeping friend, feeling a mixture of anxiety and affection. Lenny was always rattling the cages, pissing people off, making enemies. But he made a lot of friends, too. That was what kept him going. And alive.

He settled back in the chair and drank his coffee. Only four hours until Gary came in to relieve him for the last two hours of the shift. A piece of cake. He'd go home and catch a few hours of sleep, be back on the job by seven.

Across the hall and two doors down from Lenny's room, Carlton stood behind a curtain drawn across the bed. The old man in the room gurgled and gasped as he slept. Carlton was surprised the guy didn't wake up, with all his spluttering, but he never opened his eyes. Probably had a stroke or something.

The night nurse came in making her hourly bed check. She cast her flashlight on the old man's chest to be sure he was breathing, although you could hear him sputtering from the doorway. Carlton folded himself into the curtain and held his breath. The narrow beam of the light whipped past him, but the nurse was only interested in the patient and saw nothing else in the room.

As she turned and left, Carlton leaned out from behind the curtain. He could see Lenny lying in bed and the feet of somebody sitting in a chair in the corner. Probably it was Moose. Or Regis. Carlton shook his head at the feeble effort of Lenny's friends to protect him. They wouldn't interfere with his plan, he could still hit his target from the doorway and be down the stairs and out of the hospital before anyone knew what had happened.

He glanced at the luminous dial of his watch: two am, the heart of darkness. The time for nocturnal predators to satisfy their needs.

"Help me, help me! Nurse, help me!"

223

Moose sat up in the chair when he heard a patient down the hall calling for help. He hurried to the door and looked out. The voice was coming from the end of the hall. Looking in the other direction, he saw a nurse poke her head out from behind the nursing station looking annoyed. Moose looked back into the room, saw that Lenny was sleeping soundly.

"H-e-l-p!" The voice filled the hallway.

Moose cursed under his breath and stepped out into the hall. The irritated nurse came around the nursing station and walked toward Moose.

"What's goin' on?" he asked when she came abreast of him.

"Mister McGoochie is always making a fuss. He probably has his head caught between the head board and the side rail again."

"Is he a big guy?"

"Two hundred fifty pounds of stiff Parkinson's. He just about breaks my back if I have to position him by myself."

Looking up and down the hall to see that no one else was around, Moose said, "I'll come with you." The two made their way to the end of the room at the far end of the hall, where they found the patient sprawled on the floor on his back.

"Oh for god's sake!" said the nurse. "What are you doing on the floor Mister McGoochie?"

"H-E-L-P!!!" The patient cried even louder when he saw the nurse standing in the doorway. Sighing, the nurse strode into the room with Moose beside her. They put on gloves, lowered the side rails of the bed, and bent down to examine the patient.

"You gonna put him back in the bed, aren't you?" said Moose.

"I guess we should. I'm just thinking, if he broke his hip it might do more damage to lift him." She stood up and studied the situation. "Why don't we double up a sheet, roll him onto it, and lift him with that? It will support his frame in case he has a fracture."

Moose didn't like to spend too much time in the room, but it seemed cruel to leave the old man flailing on the hard floor. As he pulled the sheet from the bed and began folding it in half, the nurse stood over the patient and said, "Mister McGoochie, how did you get over the side rails?"

"I don't know, I must have been walking in my sleep!"

"But you can't walk, your tremors are too severe!"

Moose held the sheet out to the nurse and said, "Okay, now what?"

Lenny was dreaming of a peaceful place where nobody asked him for help and the kids did their homework without complaining. He felt a stir in the room. Half opening his eyes, he saw a shadowy figure standing over him. "Moose?" he asked in a groggy voice, "is that you?"

A steely hand clamped over his mouth. Lenny tried to reach his hands up to free himself, but found both his wrists were tied to the bed frame. He looked down, saw the soft cloth restraints the hospital used on confused patients pinning him. Fear rode his spine like an out of control roller coaster plunging downhill. He pulled at the straps with all his strength, desperate to reach the iron hand pinning his head down and muffling his voice.

The figure bent low. In the dim light, Lenny saw the leering face of Albert Brunner. The creature's eyes burrowed into his. They were crazed, laughing eyes; eyes dilated by madness. Whether it was all the steroids he'd taken or some long simmering insanity, it didn't matter. Lenny could see his impending death in the crazed eyes.

In his peripheral vision Lenny caught the glint of metal. He saw a surgical scalpel in Albert's free hand. The razor-sharp edge was poised high above his face.

"You have put a roadblock in my path for the last time, Lenny Moss. Your wound is going to open and you are going to bleed to death right in your own bed. When you pass out from losing all of the blood I will remove the restraints, and no one will even know I was here."

Albert ripped the dressing from Lenny's abdomen. "They will think you went crazy again and ripped open your gut." He jabbed the wound with the tip of the blade, slicing through the sutures in one swift motion.

"I am going to enjoy watching you die even more than I enjoyed watching Briana." Brunner turned the scalpel around and dug the blunt handle deep into the wound. Lenny felt a bolt of pain burning into his belly. He looked down, saw to his horror a river of blood gushing out of the yawning wound.

Lenny jerked frantically on the straps, his feeble cries muffled by the iron hand over his mouth. The leering face hovering above him began to swim in a haze. Lights flickered about the room. He felt a wave of nausea coming over him. He had been close to death before, but never this close. Never teetering this far over the edge. His mind froze in terror as he stared up into the face of death.

"ARGHHH!"

Suddenly Brunner released Lenny from his grasp and staggered back from the bed, his face contorted in pain. In agonizing slow motion he turned around to face the doorway, revealing the arrow sticking out of his back. He reached behind for the arrow and grasped at it, trying to pull it out.

Bound to the bed, Lenny watched Carlton notch a second arrow in the bow, take aim and send it flying. The arrow drove deep into Albert's neck. Albert gurgled, brought his hands to his throat, and sank to his knees, blood bubbling out of his mouth. With his hands clasped around the arrow, he fell forward, driving the arrow deeper into his neck.

"H-E-L-P! H-E-L-P!"

Now it was Lenny's turn to cry out. This time Moose and the nurse came running down the hall. They burst into the room, nearly colliding with the startled security guard who had been stationed across the hall. The trio saw Brunner sprawled on the floor, Carlton standing over him holding his bow, and Lenny tied to the bed.

Lenny cried out, "For Christ's sake, untie me, I'm fucking bleeding to death!"

Moose hurried to the bed and struggled with the knots while the nurse grabbed a stack of gauze pads and pressed them into Lenny's abdominal wound. With one hand stanching the wound, she picked up the bedside phone and dialed the page operator. "Page the trauma team to room seven-ten *stat*. Yes, the trauma team. This is Miss Begum."

Hanging up the phone, the nurse reached for the IV pump controlling Lenny's intravenous infusion and pulled open the door. She freed the tubing and opened the roller clamp, sending a rapid bolus of fluid into his vein. "This will give you a little support until we can get some blood into you," she said.

Having freed Lenny's hands, Moose stood with Carlton and the guard watching Brunner twist in his death throes. Moose and Carlton were smiling wickedly; the guard was horrified.

A minute later Doctor Farr rushed into the room followed by the code team. Farr saw Brunner on the floor with the two arrows stuck in him, barely breathing. Lenny was panting and going into shock, blood from his belly spilling over the bed onto the floor. Recognizing Brunner from conversations he had with Briana, the surgeon did not hesitate for a second deciding which trauma victim to help.

"Shall I repair your wound *again,* Mister Moss?" said Farr, donning gloves as a resident hurriedly ripped open more packs of gauze. "Or do you want me to let you lie there exsanguinating while you search for another surgeon that you trust."

"For Christ's sake, patch me the fuck up!"

With a smile on his lips Farr pressed a thick wad of dressing firmly into Lenny's wound, eliciting a moan from the stricken man. The surgeon told his team they were taking the patient to the OR STAT. "It seems this wound needs to be debrided one more time."

"Uh, Doctor Farr," said one of the resident, "what about the guy on the floor?"

"Has he got a pulse?" Farr asked, seeing that Brunner had stopped writhing.

The resident pulled on a pair of gloves and felt for a pulse. "No, sir, he's pulseless."

"Good. You can make out the death certificate, *after* we finish debriding the live patient's wound in the OR."

In seconds the trauma team had Lenny's bed through the door and on the way to surgery. All the way down the hall, in the elevator ride, and going into the OR, Farr kept a satisfied smile on his face. It was a smile that Lenny had no reason to question.

FIFTY-SEVEN

Lenny looked up into a blinding white light. The light filled his field of vision; he couldn't see past it. He tried to close his eyes to block out the glare, but he found they wouldn't close. *Somebody was holding his eyes open!* He wondered if the killer was torturing him before performing the coup de grace. He reached his arm up and tried to pull the hand away.

"I see you are waking up," said a familiar voice. The bright light withdrew. As his eyes grew accustomed to the softer light in the room, Lenny saw Dr. Farr standing over his bed. He looked from side to side, saw the familiar crew of doctors accompanying the surgeon and the row of stretchers in the Recovery Room.

"Jesus Christ, did you open me up *again?*"

"Certainly I opened your wound, that Brunner character ripped out all your stitches." Farr had a bemused look on his face. "Actually, in a way, it's a good thing that he did. While I had you open I was able to remove the bullet, it had migrated to a site where I could safely extract it."

The memories slowly seeped back into his consciousness. Lenny remembered that Carlton had been in the room. Had let go a couple of arrows, even. He recalled Brunner on the floor gagging, with an arrow in his neck.

"I have this hazy memory of my friend Carlton being there. Did he kill the bastard?"

"That he did. I'm told the police are still weighing whether or not to charge him with manslaughter, but the general consensus seems to be that it was justifiable homicide. I'm no lawyer, of course, I'm just a simple surgeon."

Lenny reached down and felt his abdomen. There was no pain this time.

"I have a catheter in your spinal canal administering pain medicine. It is blocking the pain signals from the wound." Farr turned to go, but stopped, adding, "Of course, if you still wish to change physicians, I have no objection to turning your case over to a lesser practitioner."

Lenny reached out and grabbed his arm. "No, I'm okay with you as my doctor. But can you stay a second? I have something I need to ask you." When Farr gave him a skeptical look, Lenny added, "It's personal."

Farr told his team to go on to the next patient, he would meet them shortly. "What is on your mind?" he asked.

Taking a minute to consider how he was going to frame his question, Lenny said, "You know me and my friends were investigating Briana Nearing's murder. And you probably know that you were one of the suspects."

"The police questioned me about my relation with Bri. What about it?"

"The thing I want to know is, did she tell you she was pregnant?"

Farr hesitated as he remembered the woman he had loved and lost and the child that might have been his. Finally he looked into Lenny's eyes. "Yes, she told me. Briana came to me and asked if I would order her early lab tests. She wasn't experiencing the typical early pregnancy signs. Something was wrong, and it was frightening her."

"Did she tell you about the steroids that Brunner was putting in the lotions he was giving out at the gym?"

"No, I didn't know about that. If I had known I would have told the police straight away. I only knew she was so troubled about the pregnancy she was considering an abortion."

"Briana didn't want to keep the baby?"

"Oh no, she wanted the baby, but she was afraid it would be malformed. She definitely wanted to be a mother, and I was willing to support her in any way I could."

"I can understand that, given you have no children of your own."

Farr drew back his head, surprised that Lenny knew so much about him. "You're not just a simple custodian, are you, Mister Moss?"

"None of us are simple, doc. We all have talents and resources you can't spot just by looking at the uniform."

"Even me?" said Farr.

"Yes. Even you." Lenny saw a crack in Farr's crusty exterior. For a few seconds the arrogant surgeon looked disconsolate and beaten. As Lenny recalled his own hopes of being a father, and how those hopes would probably never come to be, he couldn't help but feel a touch of compassion for Farr.

As the surgeon turned to join his colleagues, Lenny said, "Hey, doc, what's the chance I can get out of bed and go to the fund raiser for Jimmy Jones. It's on Saturday. I should be a whole lot better by then, don't you think?"

"Saturday is tomorrow, Mister Moss."

"Really? Today is Friday? Damn, where did the week go?"

"You will not be well enough to travel. I'm truly sorry."

Lenny lay back in bed. Although he had been told *no* by a whole lot of supervisors and administrators and doctors and gone on to win his case, this time he was so exhausted, so weak and winded, he didn't see how he could turn Farr around. It was a huge disappointment, he'd put a lot of work into planning for the party, but there it was. They would hold the party without him.

He tried to take consolation in the thought that Moose could sneak some food and a couple of beers into the hospital after the affair and slip them to him. He might even get to taste one of Carlton's venison steaks, if the crazy bastard was out of jail by then.

FIFTY-EIGHT

As the sound system blasted a recording of Jimmy and his band, Patience held Lenny's arm to help him out of the wheelchair. He walked slowly and carefully toward Carlton and Moose, who were cooking deer steaks on the grill. The new stitches in his belly gave Lenny twinges of pain. Dr. Farr at first refused to give him permission to go off the ward and attend the wake for Jimmy Jones. "It's on campus!" Lenny protested, "in the medical school gym. I can be back in my room inside an hour, no sweat." Only when Patience promised to personally take him down in a wheelchair and act as chaperone did his surgeon relent.

He watched Carlton stick a long two-pronged fork into a venison steak and turn it over on the gas grill while Moose slathered on the barbecue sauce. "Man oh man, that sauce rocks!" said Carlton. "What you got in it?"

"Heh, heh. It's my own secret recipe. I call it my Kiss Your Mama Sauce, on account of it's so lip smackin' good, it makes you want to lock your lips with your woman." He tipped his brush into a saucepot and lay on more sauce.

"You can't have any steaks!" Patience told Lenny, seeing him sniff the fragrant aromas. "The doctor said you can't eat any fatty food."

"Deer meat is leaner than chicken!" Carlton said. "It's health food."

"See," said Lenny. "It's health food."

"All right, but don't go crazy," said Patience. "I have to help set up the tables."

Avoiding Lenny's eyes, Carlton focused his attention on the cooking. As blue smoke swirled around his face, he wished he could disappear in the mist and not have to face his friend.

"So. Carlton," said Lenny. "How does it feel to come out of hiding?"

"Feels good, Lenny. Feels real good. The cops gave me back my Mongolian bow. They didn't even charge me for killing Brunner. Can you believe it?"

"They was embarrassed, hunting you like a *dog* when the killer was running around loose," said Moose, stirring the sauce in the pot and spreading more on the steaks.

Seeing two open bottles of beer on the serving table by the grill, Lenny said, "You got another beer for me?"

Carlton reached into a cooler and handed Lenny a bottle of Yeungling dark beer. Lenny unscrewed the cap. "To Jimmy!" he said.

Carlton and Moose raised their bottles and tapped Lenny's bottle with their own. "He was a good man died too soon," Moose said.

"Our fucking HMO, it's for shit," said Lenny. "If we had Blue Cross he'd have had the transplant months ago."

"True that," said Carlton.

"We'll give the money we raise today for the family," said Moose.

"Yeah, his sister's taken charge of the funeral arrangements. The women always come through." Taking another swallow, Lenny saw that Carlton's eyes were teary, whether from the smoke blowing in his face or something else, he couldn't tell.

Seeing the awkward silence between the two men, Moose said he needed to get more sauce and left them alone by the grill. The meat sizzled and smoked. Carlton plucked a few steaks from the fire and set them on a platter, concentrating on the cooking. Finally he cleared his throat and said, "I'm real sorry I wasn't straight with you, bro'. I wanted to be, but . . ."

"You could have trusted me," said Lenny, "You *know* I can keep a secret. You were in the park that night to meet Briana Nearing, weren't you?"

"Yeah, that's why I had my bow. She was scared, so she asked me t' watch her back. She knew I was all into hunting in the park at night with the bow and all."

"So you were supposed to be her protector."

"Yeah. Supposed t' be. But I fucked up. I mean, I went to the spot at nine o'clock and waited in my van just like she asked me to. I waited till almost midnight, but Bri didn't show and she didn't answer her phone. I figured the guy she was supposed to meet canceled on her, so what the fuck, I had my gear with me, I figured I'd try for a deer, and if she drove up I'd hear her car. It's got a rusty exhaust pipe, you can hear it a mile away."

"I get that you decided to do a little hunting when she didn't show, but you could have told me you knew her. That would have put me a million miles ahead of the game."

"Yeah, you right." Carlton wiped his eyes with his sleeve and stepped out of the smoke. "The thing is, I was afraid you'd think I really *was* the one that killed her. I couldn't take that, Lenny. Not from you."

"Christ, Carlton, I knew from the get-go you were holding back. *That's* what made me suspicious." Watching his friend turn the steaks over and slather on more sauce, he said, "You broke into Farr's office and found the picture of him and Briana on the beach, and you checked the medical records in Recovery to prove she wasn't allowed to give out narcotics, but you didn't know she was ingesting steroids from the cream Brunner gave her at the gym."

"She never told me about that, swear t' god! If I'd have known Brunner was poisoning her with that shit when she was *pregnant,* I'd have shot him a long time ago."

"And gone to jail for real. Okay. You found what you thought were Brunner' footprints in the dirt behind his office window where he dropped to the ground."

"I figured he sneaked out of his office through the window. He got to the hospital and shot you in the parking lot, come back the same way."

"Unfortunately we'll never know for sure with him dead," said Lenny. "Not that I'm complaining! Brunner confessed to killing Briana when he was ripping open my gut, but he didn't say anything about shooting me."

Carlton moved the steaks from the grill to a platter. "You gotta admit, in the end everything turned out for the best."

"Oh, sure it did. I got beat up and shot and nearly died, and then the killer comes and rips my belly open with a knife, but it was all for the best."

"I guess I brought some heat down on you. Sorry, man. Won't happen again."

Even though Carlton had been the source of most of his problems, Lenny couldn't stop from feeling bad for his friend, He stuck his finger in the barbecue sauce and tasted it just as Patience came up to him with the wheelchair. "You need to sit down and rest!" she told him.

"Okay, let's find a spot." He settled back in the chair, held the bottle of beer between his knees and pushed the wheels. He had rolled a few yards through the crowd when he felt a steely hand grab him.

"Lenny, my main man, it's wonderful to see you out of bed. Wonderful!"

"Easy with the shoulder, Tony, I'm still awful sore."

"Ah, you're made of steel, nothing can hurt you." Tony released Lenny's shoulder and sniffed the smoke wafting toward them from the grill. "The sweetest smell on earth is the smell of red meat cooking on an open fire, eh my friend?"

"Carlton brought a good twenty pounds," said Lenny. "There's plenty for everyone."

Tony stood facing Lenny, his smiling face turning serious. "Hey, I want your opinion on an enterprise I'm considering. Your counsel is always dear to me."

Lenny groaned. "I don't know, Tony, I try to stay on the right side of the law, if at all possible."

"*If at all possible.* Classic Lenny Moss. Listen to this. You know how a lot of these poor folks still are losing their homes. The banks are foreclosing on them, taking the roof from over their heads, casting them out in the street . . ."

"Yeah . . ."

"I'm thinking about going into the home refinancing business."

"Tony, if you're going to take advantage of people already in trouble with their debt," said Lenny.

"No, no, I wouldn't be taking *advantage* of them, I'd be *helping* them! I'd offer a better deal than the banks! See, I pay off the mortgage, and they rent the house from me. I use the rent to cover my payments, and when they save up enough for another down payment, I sell the place back to them at market value, guaranteed. And the beautiful part is, *they never have to leave their home!*"

"Where do you get that kind of money, Tony? You're talking a lot of cash."

"I got a few investors with deep pockets looking to put their money someplace save."

"Yeah, well, fax me a prospectus and I'll have my accountant look it over," said Lenny. He hoped for a laugh from Tony over this remark but was surprised when the man seemed to take him seriously. "Tony, tell me one thing, will you?"

"What's that?"

"You mentioned awhile back a client that owed you money moved beyond your reach. Were you talking about Briana Nearing?"

Tony's smile was big and bright and pleased with himself. "You hit the nail on the head. The girl had a debt from way back when she was using. Best she could do was make the interest payments, bein' out of work for a stretch. You know. Rehab."

"That's what I thought."

"S'far as I know, she was clean and doin' good, making her payments on time, until she bit it."

Regis came up to them, saying, "Hey, I heard the doctor finally retrieved the bullet that nearly killed you, Lenny. Is that right?"

"It feels like he scooped out half my insides," said Lenny, touching his belly, "but, yeah, Doctor Farr said the bullet migrated to a place where he could grab hold of it."

"Ah," said Tony, "but did you hear that the bullet is *not* from the same gun that killed Briana Nearing?"

Lenny shook his head. "*How* do you know that? I don't know anything about the bullet!"

"It never hurts to have a friend on the force. The bullet that brought you down was fired from the same gun used in a drive by shooting at Pickett couple of months ago. The cops figure it was a drug war."

"So that means Brunner *didn't* shoot me!" said Lenny.

"Apparently not," said Tony. "Although I guess he could have shot into a crowd of teens outside the school just to put the cops off his trail; he was capable of anything."

Regis said, "Man, you got t' make your next case the shooter in the parking lot! I'll help you with it."

"No way! I am *through* with detecting. From this moment on, I'm taking the pledge. I'm sticking to mopping floors and writing grievances, and nothing more."

The two men held up bottles of beer and cried in unison, *"BULLSHIT!"* Lenny tried to protest, but they would have no part of it. "Here's to crime!" said Tony, clinking his bottle against Lenny's and Regis's. Lenny agreed, even though he wasn't sure what type of crime his loan sharking friend was celebrating.

A moment later Gloria, Jimmy's sister, approached Lenny and gave him a warm hug, holding on for a long minute. He could feel the sorrow in her trembling embrace.

Separating at last, she said, "Thank you, Lenny, for being such a good friend. You organized this wonderful affair. You—"

"I can't take the credit, Glory, we all worked on it. All of us."

"I know," she said, gently touching his cheek with her hand. "I'd like to ask you for one more favor, if that's okay."

"Of course. Name it."

"Will you say a few words about my brother?"

"I'd be honored." As Lenny pressed down on the armrests of the wheelchair, Moose reached over and helped lift him to a standing position. Regis turned on the microphone from the sound system and handed it to him, and the DJ turned the music down low.

Lenny looked out over the crowd. At Moose and Regis and Gary. At Patience and her two children. His children. He saw Birdie and Betty and Tyrell, Sandy and Celeste, and Carlton standing at the grill with smoke in his eyes, and he felt a mixture of great joy and great sorrow. Joy at the strength and loyalty and love of so many good people, and sadness that Jimmy Jones was no longer among them.

As the crowd grew silent, Lenny said, "You know, I think we can all take comfort that Jimmy's voice will be with us forever, because Jimmy has earned his true immortality. It's in his music, and his music is in us. Starting tonight, I'm going to play a Jimmy Jones song every day for the rest of his life."

Pointing to the DJ, he said, "Turn that music back up! Turn up Jimmy!"

Jimmy's smooth baritone voice filled the air, bathing them with his sensuous, luscious voice. People began to rise and sway with the music, holding their drinks with one hand and their partner with the other. The faces of the dancers were streaked with tears of sorrow and joy, knowing they were rich with Jimmy's memory and impoverished by his passing.